LOTTIE

CHERRY POPPING DADDIES
BOOK II

STELLA MOORE

Cover art by Wicked Smart Designs
Editing by Bossy B-Word Editing Services

PROLOGUE

A MYSTERY IS AFOOT

BRADEN

pplication Accepted.

Braden Elliott glared at the bright red letters scrawled across the top of the email he'd just opened. His application to the sex auction his club was supposedly running had just been accepted by the mystery person—or persons—who were using his club to legitimize their illegal activities.

How charitable of them.

Leaning back in his office chair, he sipped a glass of the exceptionally smooth whiskey he was taste testing for the bar. It, like the rest of his club, was extraordinary. The best of the best.

A secret online sex auction, especially one that

preyed on young virgins, did *not* meet those same requirements.

Not that the 'merchandise' wasn't top-notch. At least from what he could see, considering most of the people putting themselves up for auction had chosen photos with their faces cropped out, or they'd opted to wear a mask. But the full body pics were certainly impressive, and a nice mix of everything from toned and athletic to muscular to full and curvy.

Still, he ran a respectable business. And if money ever exchanged hands for 'services provided' in his club, he preferred not to know about it. The idea of Club BDE sponsoring this kind of activity sat in his stomach like a lead weight.

The sooner they could figure out who was actually behind the auction so they could get it shut down, the better.

Sheer curiosity moved him to click out of the virgin auction to the other areas of the website. As he'd seen when Damian had first shown him the site, there were plenty of his members auctioning off various other fantasies. Like Princess Raven—whose real name he knew to be Ivy—who was available for a whole list of fantasies, as long as her girlfriend was allowed to watch. Ivy and Cordelia had come to work for him years ago, and even before they'd officially become a couple, they'd been so attached at the hip they'd affectionately earned the nickname 'The Twins'. Delia enjoyed watching others torment her poor little subbie as much as she enjoyed doing the deed herself, so it didn't really surprise him to see Ivy's listing.

Some of the others, however, did. Men and women alike who he knew were in committed, monogamous relationships, offering themselves up for various fantasies he knew for a fact their partners would never engage in.

Not that he wasn't sympathetic to their plight. He had his own needs, his own desires he'd learned to ignore over the years. Even at the club, he never indulged his more intimate fantasies. Truthfully, he rarely played at all anymore. He couldn't remember the last time he'd had a willing subbie up on a cross with his welts crisscrossing down her body from a thorough flogging. Or bent over a bench with the lines from his cane neatly stacked down her bottom and thighs.

Longer, still, since he'd had a woman to warm his bed.

It wasn't even that he had particularly unusual or depraved needs. Running a BDSM club on a daily basis, he'd seen enough to know he was nowhere near as sadistic as some of his friends. But he'd grown tired of scene after scene with the subs who all but fell at his feet. He'd come to realize over the past few years that what he really wanted was someone to match him, to challenge him. Someone who could walk confidently on his arm and match wits with the wealthy, educated types he tended to surround himself with. A graceful, sophisticated lady in public.

And Daddy's filthy little whore in private.

Such a woman, he'd yet to find.

Shaking off the melancholy settling over him, he stood and drained the rest of his drink as he made his way over to the one-way glass that allowed him to keep an eagle eye on his club while keeping his own privacy intact. He scanned the restaurant area on the upper floor briefly before shifting his attention to the lower floor, where the real action was happening.

To his relief, he recognized everyone who was playing tonight. Ever since he'd found out about that damned auction, it hadn't set well with him whenever he'd spotted someone he didn't know, especially those coming in as guests of his existing members. Newbies who wanted an actual membership had to undergo a thorough screening and in-person vetting process, so he wasn't as concerned about them.

But those who were brought in on guest passes had a much more surface-level background check. Which had never been a problem before, back when he'd trusted his members. Now, however...

Turning away from the windows, he made his way back to his desk and pressed the button on his phone that connected directly to the security room. "Martin. I need a word with you in my office, please."

"Uh, sure thing, boss. Be right there."

Settling back at his desk, he scrolled through the other fantasies, making mental notes as he waited for his head of security.

"Come in," he called at Martin's tentative knock.

"You wanted to see me?"

Tall and thin, with thick-framed glasses and a head of dark hair that always seemed in desperate need of a comb, Martin Hall looked every bit the computer geek Braden knew him to be. "I did. I want to change the process for screening guests. Until further notice, every application must be reviewed and approved by me once it has gone through our usual process."

Behind his glasses, Martin's eyes went wide. "*Every* application, boss?"

"Did I stutter, Martin?"

"Ah, no. I just... that's a lot of extra work for you to take on and I know how busy you are." Color rushed to the other man's face, giving him the look of a ripened tomato and making him seem much younger than he was. "I can take on the extra review, if you want."

"I appreciate the offer, but no. Just between us, there's something going on in my club and I want to keep a closer eye on things."

"What kind of something?"

It wasn't in Braden's nature to share his problems. Growing up with identical twin older brothers who'd once been thick as thieves, he'd learned to rely on himself at a young age. And now that Damian and Desmond seemed to hate each other, though nobody could really tell him *why*, he was reluctant to add his own drama to the mix. If it hadn't been Damian himself who'd brought the auction to his attention in the first place, he wouldn't have involved either of them until he'd gotten the situation sorted.

But he'd hired Martin because he trusted him. And because he'd passed the most intense background checks—including being tailed for a month by a private investigator—Braden could buy. So if he was going to confide in anyone, it would be Martin.

"What I am about to tell you does not leave this office. Understood?"

"Of course, boss."

"Someone is running an illegal auction, and using the club to make it seem legit. I'm working on finding out who the man behind the curtain is, but in the meantime, I want to keep a closer eye on who our members are bringing in. Maybe if they know I'm watching, they'll stop fucking around in my club."

"An auction? What kind of auction?"

"Sexual fantasies." He would keep the virgin part to himself for now, because it still made his stomach churn to think about it. "Which wouldn't be an issue except for the part where they're being paid for said sexual fantasies."

"Holy shit." Shaking his head, Martin let out a low whistle. "Do you want me to do some digging? If you send me the site, I can probably track them down."

"I appreciate the offer, but the police are already looking into it."

"That's good." Martin's smile flashed, a rare show of confidence. "But I'm better."

The laughter knocked some of the tension from Braden's shoulders. "If they don't find something soon, I may take you up on that. In the meantime, send any guest applications through me, and just keep a general eye on things for me."

"Got it, boss."

"Dismissed. Oh," he said as Martin turned to go. "Do me a favor and find Ivy and Cordelia and send them to me. I believe they're working tonight."

"Sure thing."

Braden turned back to his computer as the door

shut behind Martin and clicked on Ivy's profile, studying the picture and the presented fantasies while he waited. It was, he was ashamed to admit, tempting to take them up on what they were offering, even if he had to pay for it. But they were committed to each other, and while he was certain he'd enjoy helping Cordelia torment her girl for an evening, it still wouldn't ease the pain of going home to a cold, empty bed.

As always, Cordelia only gave a cursory knock before bouncing into his office, her usual wide grin on her face. Blonde and curvy, with a bright and bubbly personality, she was every man's fantasy of the popular cheerleader. Right up until that man found himself on his knees begging for mercy. She was, without a doubt, one of the fiercest Dommes he'd ever come into contact with.

Behind her was Ivy, quiet and mysterious where Cordelia was loud and cheerful, though no less alluring for it. They were of a similar height, but where Delia was all soft curves, Ivy reminded him of the kind of elf you might find in a high fantasy. Slender and so pale she almost seemed ethereal.

More than one man had made the mistake of thinking quiet, reserved Ivy was the dominant part-ner, and Delia took great delight in making them pay for their assumptions.

Settling into one of his visitor's chairs, Delia pulled Ivy down into her lap, ignoring her girlfriend's brief struggle. A single look from her quelled Ivy's protests, and then Delia was all smiles again as she turned to Braden. "What's up, boss? Martin said you wanted to see us."

"I did." Gripping the top of his monitor, he turned the screen toward them, while he watched their faces for any sign of discomfort.

But there was none, though there was a hint of confusion in both of their expressions. It was, of course, Delia who spoke first. "Okay? What about it?"

"How did you find out about the auction?"

The confusion in Delia's expression intensified. "What do you mean? You told me about it."

Jaw clenched, he forced himself to take a deep breath through his nose before he said something he couldn't take back. "I certainly did not."

"Yes, you did," Delia insisted, her own temper flashing in her eyes. "You emailed me the information a few months ago, after we talked about me getting a raise. I thought it was kind of a dick move at the time, but after I saw the guaranteed bids, I realized it was a hell of a lot more money than you'd ever be able to pay me."

"Cordelia, I am telling you that I did not send you

that email. I just learned about this auction last week."

"And *I'm* telling you, the email came from your work account. That's the only reason I let Ivy sign up for it. You really think I'd risk my girl on some sketchy ass auction if it didn't come personally recommended by someone I trusted?"

Ivy snuggled closer to Delia, dark eyes wide in her pale face. "Mr. Elliott... if you're not the one running the auction, then who is?"

"I don't know." Turning the screen back to face him, Braden sent them both a determined glare. "But I'm damn sure going to find out."

POOR LITTLE NOT-SO-RICH GIRL

LOTTIE

Brunch with The Girls might have been Charlotte Duvall's favorite thing ever. On the surface, she knew what they looked like. A bunch of spoiled rich girls drinking too many mimosas and laughing too loudly at each other's jokes.

But these girls were her whole world. They'd been there for her when her mom had gotten sick, ordering food and pulling strings to help get her mom into the best facilities money could buy. And later, when even the best of the best treatments had failed, they'd stepped in, helping her plan every detail of the funeral her dad had been too devastated to help with.

They were her rocks, and she loved them with every fiber of her being.

"Oh my god, you slut!" Head thrown back, her perfectly platinum locks falling down her back, Eva Barker let out a laugh that had more than one head turning their way. "Tell us *everything*, Frankie."

Across the table, Frankie Legare smirked. Frankie's real name was Francesca, but only her family actually called her that. The masculine nick-name was at odds with her slender build and long, fiery-red hair. But the name infuriated her mother, and since Delphine Legare was single-handedly responsible for giving Frankie the eating disorder that had almost landed her in the hospital, it was an unspoken agreement amongst their friend group to do everything humanly possible to piss off Delphine.

"I already told you everything." But judging by the mischief dancing in Frankie's dark eyes, she was definitely keeping some of the juicier details to herself.

Eva narrowed her eyes. "Liar. You just want us to beg you for details."

It was Frankie's turn to laugh. "Guilty as charged. All right, fine, but you bitches have to promise not to laugh or be weird about it."

"Deal," they said in unison as they leaned in for the details.

"Okay, well." Frankie glanced around, as if she

were worried about being overheard, but it was all just part of the show. "I already told you we hooked up, and it was the hottest fucking night of my life."

"Yes, yes." Lottie waved a hand, impatient for her to get on with it. "Get to the good stuff."

"All right, all right. So this guy, he was really kind of bossy, right? But like in the hot way. Not in that douchebag kind of way like Alan."

A chorus of groans met the name Alan. He'd been Frankie's boyfriend for way too long, as far as Lottie was concerned. Controlling and degrading, he'd caused Frankie to relapse more than once during their relationship, and by the end she'd been on the verge of a return trip to the rehab center. The entire friend group had all been more than happy to help her give him the boot—up to and including physically moving his shit out of Frankie's apartment and onto the street—when she'd finally decided she'd had enough.

"I know," Frankie said with a pained smile. "But I swear, it was nothing like that. It was more like... ordering me to do things, like sexy things, and calling me a good girl when I did what he said."

"What if you didn't do what he told you to?" Lottie wasn't even sure what made her ask the question, but there was a weird pull of something she vaguely recognized as desire as she listened to

Frankie's description of her night with the older man who'd picked her up at the club Friday.

Leaning in even further, Frankie lowered her voice. "He spanked me. And not just like, a couple little love taps while he was fucking me. I mean, put me over his knee and spanked me *hard* until I finally agreed to do as I was told."

"No!" Portia Williams, the newest addition to their group after her parents had moved her from California to South Carolina her junior year, gasped, her impossibly blue eyes wide with shock in her cherub-like face. Impossibly blue, because she hid her natural hazel with contacts to add to that perfect fantasy of the curvy, blonde-haired, blue-eyed, virginal girl next door. Except, she wasn't actually a virgin any longer.

No, that honor was reserved for Lottie and Lottie alone. A fact her friends occasionally teased her about, but for the most part they didn't make her feel like an outsider when they were sharing their most recent exploits or comparing notes about everything from dick size to whether or not it was normal to come so hard you blacked out. The latter concern had, of course, been Frankie's. She was not only the most experienced of the group but by far the most adventurous.

"Yes," Frankie confirmed with a nod. "And you know what?"

Unable to help herself, Lottie asked, "What?"

"I liked it. Like, I really, really liked it. I've always liked a little pain with my pleasure, if you know what I mean, but there was something so deliciously primal about being spanked like a naughty little girl. And I also really liked the other thing he made me do."

Now it was Eva giving into her curiosity, even though Lottie knew for a fact she thought Frankie sometimes overexaggerated her sexual conquests. "What other thing?"

"He made me call him Daddy the whole time. And it was really fucking hot."

On either side of Lottie, her friends squealed in equal parts disbelief, disgust, and delight. "You really did that?" Portia asked, her nose wrinkling slightly.

Lifting her champagne flute to her lips, Lottie sipped, as much for the hit of alcohol as to hopefully hide the blush rising to her cheeks. Part of her wondered if she should be horrified by Frankie's exploits, as Portia clearly was.

The other part of her just wanted to hear more.

"Hey, the brunch table is a no-judgment zone," Frankie reminded Portia with a mock glare. "And yes, I absolutely did."

Propping her chin on her fist, Eva grinned. "I wonder what the world would think if they knew Dr. Francesca Legare was a kinky little bitch who got off on getting her ass spanked by a man she calls Daddy."

"I'm not a doctor yet." Frankie once again rolled her eyes. "I haven't even started med school yet."

"Please." Lottie waved a hand, swatting away her friend's protests. "We all know you're going to kick med school's ass and go on to be the best fucking neurosurgeon the world has ever seen."

"Neurosurgeon by day, kinky bitch by night." Giggling, Frankie lifted her mimosa in a toast. "Has a nice ring to it."

And that was yet again one of the other ways Lottie didn't quite fit in with her friends. While she'd made it through college without any real struggle, her business degree was much like her hymen. She had one, but she'd never really bothered to do anything with it.

Meanwhile, Frankie was off to med school in the fall, Eva was working on her MBA while also learning the ropes at her father's media empire, and even Portia—who had only ever talked about finding Mr. Right to sweep her off her feet and turn her into the perfect trophy wife—had turned into something of a human right's activist during her college years. After brunch, in fact, she was flying to DC for dinner with some powerful people in the hopes she could persuade them to vote for an upcoming bill on paid maternity and paternity leave in the states.

Her friends were as impressive as they were rich. And then there was Lottie, whose greatest achievement so far was the vintage Birkin bag she'd managed to find in a random little boutique in the south of France during her last trip overseas. The owner, bless him, hadn't realized what a rare find he had in his possession, and she'd snatched it up before he'd changed his mind and upped the price on her.

Of course, she'd felt so bad about 'cheating' him that she'd gone back and purchased a horribly overpriced watch which she'd given to her father for Christmas. Dad had loved the gift, and it had eased some of her guilt, so she'd considered it a win-win.

The memory brought her full circle to Frankie and her 'Daddy'. If Lottie had a Daddy, would he have spanked her for her dishonesty with the boutique owner? Maybe he would have marched her back to the shop, with her bottom still red and sore, and forced her to apologize.

Jesus. There had to be something wrong with her that the idea of not only being punished like a little girl, but publicly humiliated as well, nearly had her squirming in her seat.

"Lottie, are you all right, babe?" Frankie's

concerned voice jolted Lottie out of her fantasies. "You look a little flushed."

"Oh, ah... yes. I'm fine."

Eyes dancing with amusement, Eva wiggled her shoulders. "Did Frankie's kinky tales get you all hot and bothered?"

"Eva! Leave her alone." Ever the 'mom' of the group, Portia leaned over and patted Lottie's hand. "Ignore her, sweetheart. She's just cranky because she struck out two nights in a row this weekend."

"I am not! Okay, maybe a little," Eva agreed with a shrug. "But tell me I'm wrong. Either Lottie here has a fever, or something else has her temperature rising."

There was definitely a God somewhere looking out for her, because the waiter arrived with their check before Eva had a chance to grill her anymore. It was Lottie's turn to pay, so she had the excuse of searching her ill-gotten Birkin for her wallet while the other girls chattered on. And by the time the waiter returned for her card, Eva seemed to have forgotten she was supposed to be teasing Lottie.

"Excuse me, ma'am." In the discreet murmur waiters of his caliber had been well-trained to use, their waiter held the small tray with their check and Lottie's card back out to her. "There appears to be a problem with your card."

"A problem?" Frowning, Lottie picked up the card

and double checked the expiration date just in case she'd forgotten to swap it out for a new one.

But no. It didn't expire until September of the following year. Weird.

"Could you try it again?"

"I ran it three times, ma'am. Do you have another card, perhaps?"

All too aware of her friends' curious stares, Lottie opened her wallet and pulled out another card. "I'm so sorry about that. Try this one."

"Everything okay?" Portia asked when the waiter had disappeared again.

Shrugging, Lottie reached for her mimosa to drink the last of it. "Yeah, just a problem with the card, I guess."

"Your dad probably got a new one without telling you." Frankie's smile was more sympathetic than pitying, but Lottie could feel her face growing hotter all the same. "They're always moving money around on those things to get a better interest rate or whatever."

"That's probably it." Or a problem with the system. God knew it wouldn't be the first time a glitch with the WiFi or a shop's computers kept a transaction from going through. It was an annoyance, but one that usually worked itself out relatively quickly.

The waiter returned, his polite smile looking a bit

more strained around the edges. "I'm very sorry, ma'am. There appears to be a problem with this card as well."

"Are you sure it's not your system?" Lottie asked, doing her best not to let her annoyance with the situation color her tone as she took the card from the tray and reached back into her purse. "There must be some kind of computer glitch."

"I can assure you it's not."

"Well, there must be something going on," Lottie insisted, irritation sharpening her tone.

"You know what, I'll get it." Pulling her wallet from her bag, Frankie waved away Lottie's protests. "It's fine, babe. You can get it next time."

"It must be their system. There's literally no other reason for two separate cards to have the same problem."

But when the waiter returned with Frankie's card and a slip for her to sign, a knot formed in Lottie's stomach. What the hell was going on?

Her unease must have shown on her face, because Eva squeezed her hand and leaned over, dropping her voice low so that nobody else could hear. "It's probably just some weird accounting error. Ask your dad about it when you get home. I'm sure there's nothing really wrong."

An accounting error. That had to be it.

Right?

IT DEFINITELY WASN'T AN ERROR. OR IF IT WAS, HER father had somehow missed it for what looked like several months.

Sitting at the desk in his office, she clicked on yet another account, tears blurring her vision at yet another giant PAST DUE notice flashing across the screen.

Maybe he'd just forgotten to pay them. The past two years had been rough on both of them, but while she'd at least somewhat moved on from her mother's death, her father hadn't. He almost never left the house anymore, and she couldn't remember the last time any of his friends had come by. The constant stream of visitors they'd had while mom had been sick had dried up almost as soon as the funeral had ended.

Mr. Elliott, their next-door neighbor and her dad's best friend, was the one exception to that rule. He came by at least once a week to check on Dad, and he'd even managed to talk him into dinner out once or twice.

It was entirely plausible that her father was simply so mired in his own grief that he'd completely lost track of his bills. She'd just check the bank accounts, find a way to get everything caught up, and then keep a closer eye on things until he was better.

Easy.

But that last little bit of hope went up in flames when she logged into her father's bank accounts. While they weren't flat broke, there also wasn't nearly enough to cover the credit card bills. And she didn't know enough about the mortgage, or the utilities, or any of the dozens of other charges she saw listed on his main account to know how much she could risk paying to help get things back under control.

There was a series of charges that caught her attention, however. Because they were for such exact amounts. One hundred, five hundred, five thousand. Over and over again, more times than she could count. When she clicked on one of the charges, she saw a website listed in the description, and her fingers trembled as she typed the site into a separate window.

And her heart sank when a woman in a barely-there glittery shirt popped up, smiling and holding a pile of betting chips.

Gambling. Her dad, the most responsible man she'd ever known, had gambled away what looked to be a good portion of their wealth. She wasn't sure she could even stomach totaling up the charges, but she tried.

She had to stop when she hit the six-figure mark, which didn't take her nearly as long as she might have hoped.

Feeling numb, she clicked the red X at the top of the screen to close out the internet windows. Just as she was about to log off, a voice called her name, making her jump in her seat.

"Charlotte? What are you doing in your father's office?"

Mr. Elliott, the sharp edges of his gorgeous face set into stern lines that made her stomach jump with nerves, stepped into the room. Part of her wanted to tell him exactly why she was there, to throw herself in his arms. Arms that had held her and comforted her when she'd sat by her dying mother's bed and again when she'd watched them put her mother in the ground. Maybe he wouldn't be able to help, but at least then she would have someone to confide in. Someone who might actually be able to give her some direction.

But she couldn't be sure Mr. Elliott knew the truth about her dad's situation. And if he didn't, then she couldn't risk embarrassing her dad that way. If she'd learned anything these past few years, it was that when push came to shove, all they had was each other. So as much as she ached to have *someone* to share her newly discovered burden with, she would just have to be an adult and find a way out of this mess herself.

With that decision made, she sat back in the chair, and gave him her best 'spoiled little rich girl' smirk, the one she knew drove him crazy when he felt her dad was letting her get away with too much. "It's my house. I can be wherever I want. What are *you* doing here?"

"Looking for your father. We were supposed to meet for lunch an hour ago, but he never showed. Have you seen him?"

"I'm not my father's keeper, Mr. Elliott." She wasn't even sure why she was being so antagonistic toward him, other than she was having a really bad fucking day and it made her feel a little better to poke at him. If there had been one constant in her life, it had been the way Mr. Elliott reacted when she was being a brat.

A muscle in his jaw jumped, and even though that was exactly the reaction she'd been expecting, today her heart beat a little faster and her stomach twisted with an emotion she couldn't quite name. It wasn't fear, not really. Mr. Elliott had never given her a reason to fear him.

But it was close, kind of like the 'fear' she felt

whenever Frankie managed to talk her into watching a scary movie. Like she knew *something* was about to happen, she just wasn't sure *what*.

Odd.

"Well, perhaps you can come help me locate him. I'm fairly certain you have no business snooping around in his office, anyway."

The accusation stung, but she forced a smile to cover the insult. "Of course. I'm sure he's around here somewhere."

As discreetly as she could, she locked the computer before rising to her feet and following him out of the office. Mr. Elliott pulled the door shut behind her, and she couldn't help but feel like it was deliberate, to remind her she didn't belong there.

And just as deliberately, he put his hand at the small of her back and nudged her toward the main living area. Electricity shot through her at that simple touch, and she sucked in a sharp breath before she thought to hide her reaction.

Where the hell had *that* come from? Years of parental touches and embraces, and she'd never once felt that zing from Mr. Elliott before now.

"Are you all right?" he asked, snapping her attention away from her odd reaction.

"I'm fine." If her tone was a little sharp, it was just because she was so off- balance from everything that had happened today. And not at all because she'd just realized she was feeling something very similar to what she'd felt during Frankie's story about getting spanked by her 'Daddy'. "We should check the den. He might be having a whiskey."

"A whiskey?" Beside her, Mr. Elliott frowned. "It's not even one in the afternoon."

"You'll have to take that up with him. I'm not my—"

"Father's keeper. Yes, you said as much."

The disapproval in his tone told her he didn't approve of her stance. But she didn't have the luxury of caring what he thought about her just then.

Her very sudden and very confusing feelings for Mr. Elliott aside, Lottie had more important things to worry about. Like the fact that her father had dug himself into a hole the size of the Grand Canyon. And it was up to her to figure out how to drag him back out.

2

EVERY PROBLEM HAS A SOLUTION

BRADEN

He should move his hand. But the way Lottie had reacted, that too-sharp little intake of breath had apparently frozen him in place, unable to remove his hand from her back. If anything, he was tempted to dip lower and cup the full, generous curves of her—

Jesus Christ, Braden. That is your best friend's daughter. A little girl who used to play with your daughter, for fuck's sake. Get a goddamn grip.

With what felt like a Herculean effort, he pulled his hand away and deliberately stuck it in his pocket just as she swung open the doors to the opulent room her father favored when he was in the need of solitude.

Braden had spent a lot of time in this den since Natasha's passing, making sure his friend didn't descend too deep into those pits of loneliness and despair.

And sure enough, Emmett Duvall was exactly where his daughter had said he would be. Slouched in one of the overstuffed leather armchairs, an almost-empty glass of whiskey in his hand and a despondent expression on his face that made Braden's chest ache. Ever since they'd gotten the news of Nat's illness, Braden had watched Emmett become more and more a shell of his former self. Once she'd passed, Emmett had pretty much stopped existing all together.

Plastering a smile on his face and praying it didn't look as brittle and fake as it felt, he stepped around Lottie and strode into the room. "I see you started without me."

Emmett looked up, the bleariness in his eyes telling Braden that it wasn't his first glass of whiskey. And, unless he was able to coax his friend out of the den for a bit, Braden doubted it would be his last.

"Braden! I didn't know you were coming over." His words were slurred slightly, but not as much as they should have been under the circumstances. In fact, they were almost *too* well-enunciated, as if he were trying to hide how drunk he actually was.

Nice try, old friend.

"Well, we were supposed to meet for lunch. But I'm nothing if not adaptable." Settling into the chair beside Emmett's, Braden plucked the glass from his hand and drained the rest of it without bothering to return it to its rightful owner. If he didn't actually see the glass, odds were Emmett would completely forget he'd been drinking in the first place.

From the corner of his eye, he saw Lottie still in the doorway, her expression drawn and worried. Poor girl. She'd really been through more than her fair share of pain and heartache.

Turning his head, he sent her a reassuring smile. "It was nice seeing you again, Charlotte."

She jumped, just enough for him to notice because he'd been watching her. The worry on her face smoothed away, replaced by the polite-bordering-on-bored smile so many socialites were trained to use in uncomfortable situations. "You too, Mr. Elliott. I'll just be… around."

"Charlotte," Braden called when she went to close the door behind her. He waited for her to poke her head back in before cocking an eyebrow and pinning her with what his employees called his 'Daddy Glare'. "No snooping."

Red colored her cheeks, but instead of nodding or dropping her head like the subs at his club would have, she raised one of her own eyebrows in return. "Goodbye, Mr. Elliott."

He physically had to dig his fingers into the arm of his chair to keep himself seated. It had been ages since his palm had actually itched to connect with a bratty little girl's bottom the way it did just then.

Of course his dormant sex drive would choose the most inopportune moment possible to come roaring back to life.

Apparently oblivious to his closest friend's completely improper thoughts about his daughter, Emmett grinned. "So, Braden. How are things at the club?"

Right. The club. The BDSM club he owned, packed wall-to-wall with willing subbies who would gladly offer themselves up for a night of kinky debauchery if he so much as looked in their direction.

Subbies who were much more appropriate targets for his desires than pretty little Charlotte Duvall.

"Things are good. You should come by tomorrow, let me buy you lunch."

Just like the last hundred—or more, Braden had given up counting—times he'd made the offer, Emmett shook his head. "No. I'm not ready for that."

Grief had its own timeline. Braden knew that, logically, but there was still a part of him that wanted to shake his friend, to tell him to snap out of it. To remind him that he had a daughter who needed him, and at forty-six, he still had so much life left to live.

But that wasn't his place. So he didn't force the issue the way he so badly wanted to. Instead, he settled in for an afternoon of listening to the same stories of Nat and Emmett's life together he'd heard a million times.

And tried not to think of all the filthy, perverted things he wanted to do to their daughter.

LOTTIE

With her cheeks burning from Mr. Elliott's scolding, Lottie hurried upstairs to her bedroom.

She needed money. Logically, that meant she needed to go to work. But she wasn't under any delusions that she could find a job that would pay anything near what she needed to pay off her father's debts.

And even if she could start putting a small dent in the credit card payments, it would all be for nothing if she couldn't stop her father's gambling problem and keep him from hemorrhaging money.

Mr. Elliott could fix it. Unless he was also hiding a

mountain of debt, he could probably bail them out and never even feel the pinch. The part of her that still loved the fairy tales where the prince swooped in to save the princess from a lifetime of hardship wanted so badly to run back downstairs and throw herself on his mercy. If anyone could get through to her father and make sure he got the help he needed, it would be Mr. Elliott.

But she'd already promised herself she wouldn't tell him. Losing their fortune was enough of a blow, and if she could help her father keep his pride, then she was willing to do whatever it took to do so.

Flopping down onto her pretty four-poster bed, she plucked at the ruffles on her perfectly white duvet cover as she stared at the ceiling and ran through her options.

Which took her all of about thirty seconds, since she didn't really *have* any options. Groaning, she forced herself to pull her phone from her pocket and make the phone call she'd been dreading.

Frankie wasn't just the smartest, or the richest member of their friend group. She was also the one with the biggest heart. So even though she wasn't entirely convinced she was doing the right thing, Lottie hit the button to dial the one person in the world she thought might be able to help.

"Hey, Lottie baby. Figure out what's going on with your accounts?"

Lottie opened her mouth to explain what she'd found. And promptly burst into tears.

"Oh, honey. I'm on my way. Do you want me to bring the girls?"

"No! J-just y-you," Lottie managed to choke out between gulping sobs.

"All right. I'll be there as soon as I can."

Finally giving into the despair that had been brewing inside her since she'd opened the first credit card bill, Lottie rolled onto her stomach and wept. She sobbed until the tears ran dry and she felt like a sponge someone had wrung out and tossed to the side. If she'd cried that hard since her mom's funeral, she couldn't remember.

Oddly enough, though, she felt better for it. Sniffling back a few straggling tears, she rolled off her bed and made her way over to her en suite bathroom. Jesus, she looked a mess, with her mascara all smudged around her red, puffy eyes.

By the time Frankie burst into her bedroom a few minutes later, Lottie was looking and feeling much more presentable. She'd managed to wash her face and reapply a light coat of makeup without her eyes watering and ruining it all over again. There was nothing to be done about the redness or the puffiness, but she figured Frankie already knew she'd been crying so there was little point in trying to hide it completely.

"You poor thing." True sympathy, not the fake kind so often employed by the women in their circles, echoed in Frankie's voice as she rushed across the room to wrap Lottie up in a tight hug. "Tell Mama Frankie all about it."

And so she did. She told Frankie everything, about the overdue bills, the bank account, the gambling. All of it.

"I just don't know what to *do*. I mean, I could get a job, obviously. I don't mind working. But I'd need to be making six figures at least to even begin paying down those cards, and even with that it would still take forever."

"And in the meantime, your dad would still be there, gambling away what little money you have left." Anger burned hot and fierce in Frankie's eyes. "I can't believe he did this to you!"

"I can't be mad at him. You haven't seen him, Frankie. He's so lost without mom."

"Well, *I* damn well can be mad at him. And there's nothing you can do to stop me. So there."

Sniffling back a fresh wave of tears, Lottie leaned on Frankie's shoulder. "Thanks."

"No problem, honey." Frankie cleared her throat,

and when she spoke she sounded uncharacteristically hesitant. "I, ah, may have a solution for you."

"Really?" Bolting upright, Lottie grabbed her friend's arm. "You better not be fucking with me, Francesca."

"I would never. Well, not about something as serious as this." Worry replaced the anger in her gaze, and for once the confident, self-assured Frankie looked unsure of herself. "Just fair warning that it's a bit... unconventional."

"And I'm a bit desperate. What's the deal?"

"Okay, so, you remember how I said that guy from the other night took me to a club?"

"Yeah. The sex club."

Frankie rolled her eyes. "I didn't see anybody actually having sex. But yes, the kink club. Well, it took *forever* for them to process my guest pass, and when my... fuck it, I'll just call him Daddy. When Daddy asked what was taking so long, the girl at the front desk told us there was a new process. Apparently, the owner of the club has started reviewing all of the guest passes at the club before anyone can get in."

Impatience nearly had her shaking Frankie to get the information out of her. "Okay. What does that have to do with me?"

"Patience, grasshopper. Anyway, Daddy asked

why, and the girl said she didn't know. But another girl, who had apparently been eavesdropping, came over and told us she'd heard a rumor about some auction happening at the club."

"Auction? What kind of auction?" But even as she asked the question, part of her knew the answer. What other kind of auction would a kink club be hosting?

"A sex auction," Frankie said, confirming Lottie's thoughts. "Nobody could really give us any details, but the girl who was eavesdropping said one of her friends was getting like fifty grand a pop to provide her 'services' as a Domme."

"Good for her. But why the hell are you telling me this? I don't know anything about that stuff."

"Would you just be patient? Anyway, the girl at the front desk piped up and said she'd heard about the auction too, and—here's where you come in—she said how she wished she hadn't had her cherry popped already, because some girl got paid like four hundred thousand for hers."

For a long moment, all Lottie could do was stare at her friend. "Someone paid almost *half a million dollars* to take some random girl's virginity?"

"That's what they said. Obviously, I don't know if it's true, but I figured it might be worth a shot."

"I don't know, Frankie. Doesn't that seem kind of... crass? Letting someone buy my virginity?"

"Maybe." Frankie shrugged, far too nonchalant for the topic of conversation as far as Lottie as concerned. "But it's not like you've been saving yourself for marriage or anything. So would you rather give it up for free, or get some use out of an otherwise useless social construct?"

"True..." The only reason she was still a virgin was because she couldn't stand the immaturity of boys her own age, and the older men they occasionally ran into at the clubs creeped her out. It was her own pickiness that had kept her virginity intact, so it wasn't like she would be giving anything up, really, if she auctioned it off.

That didn't mean a part of her didn't grieve the thought of giving it up to a complete stranger instead of someone she loved, or at least someone she'd known more than thirty seconds.

Apparently sensing her hesitation, Frankie reached out and squeezed Lottie's hand. "Look, how about this. Daddy's taking me to the club again tomorrow night. I'll ask around, see if I can get you the information for the auction. You don't actually have to sign up, but it can't hurt to have it as an option, right?"

"Maybe." Lottie sighed and rubbed at her

temples. "I mean yes. Yes, get me as much information as you can, and I'll think about it. In the meantime, I guess I should start applying for jobs."

"Do you want me to talk to my dad? He always wanted me to come work for him, and you're basically part of the family. I'm sure he'd be happy to take you on."

"Really? That would be amazing." Throwing her arms around Frankie's neck, Lottie squeezed. "I love you so much."

"I love you, too." Frankie returned the hug, and for the first time since she'd learned about her crumbling fortune, Lottie felt like she could breathe again. "Don't worry, honey. One way or another, we'll get you out of this mess. I promise."

3

INTERROGATIONS AND REVELATIONS

BRADEN

Sitting at the bar on the lower level of the club, Braden let his gaze wander over the couples in the pit as he nursed the single glass of scotch he allowed himself when he was on the floor.

And tried to stop imagining a certain bratty little brunette in any number of compromising scenarios.

The club was relatively quiet, which wasn't unusual for a Monday night. Really only the hardcore players came out during the week, unless they had a specific event planned. Vivian had been trying to get him to do more theme nights for a while now, and the more time he spent on the floor, the more he was forced to admit she might be right.

He'd just about decided to make his way up to the restaurant level to check on things when Shane, one of the club submissives, came hurrying up, a worried expression on his face. "Mr. Elliott, we have a problem."

It wasn't like Shane to cut to the chase so quickly without a pun or teasing remark. Alarm bells ringing in his head, Braden straightened on his stool. "What's wrong?"

Glancing around, Shane jiggled the ever-present bag of candy corn in his hand. "Okay, well, you know how you've been keeping an eye on the new guests because of that auction thing?"

Braden narrowed his eyes at the nervous subbie. "Yes. How do *you* know about that, is the question."

The look Shane sent him clearly said he thought Braden was being obtuse. "Please, everyone knows. Anyway, there's a girl here, asking questions. Specifically about the virgin auction. Thought you might like to know."

His annoyance at club gossip running amok fading temporarily, Braden lifted his head to scan the club. "Who?"

"The pretty redhead with Mr. Prescott. She's not even being discreet about it."

"Thank you for letting me know. Would you tell

Mr. Prescott I'd like to see him and his guest in my office immediately, please?"

"Sure thing, Mr. Elliott." With a mock salute, Shane turned to head toward the pit.

"And Shane." He waited for the other man to turn back. "You can let your fellow submissives and the employees know that anyone caught talking about this auction in any capacity, especially with our clients and their guests, will be answering to me."

Eyes wide, Shane nodded before hurrying off toward the platform where Holden Prescott was busy attaching his guest to a St. Andrew's cross. Satisfied Shane would deliver his message, Braden drained the last few drops of his drink and slid from his stool to head back upstairs.

He'd only just gotten seated behind his desk when someone knocked on the door of his office. "Come in."

Holden entered, clearly annoyed despite his attempts to look unperturbed. Beside him stood a willowy redhead who, unlike her Daddy, was doing absolutely nothing to hide her aggravation with the situation.

Something about her seemed familiar, but he couldn't quite place it.

"You rang?" Holden drawled, one eyebrow raised

in deference to his obvious irritation at being summoned.

"Apologies for interrupting your scene, my friend. I needed a word with your guest, and I didn't think you'd be amenable to her being interrogated alone."

"Interrogated?" Fury snapped in the redhead's eyes and echoed in her voice. "What the hell is your problem, Mr. Elliott?"

Okay, obviously she knew him, even if he didn't fully recognize her. Who the hell *was* she?

Before he could ask, Holden glared down at her. "Francesca. Quiet."

The puzzle finally snapped into place. "Francesca. Frankie. Frankie Legare?" One of Lottie's friends, who he'd seen around while Lottie was growing up, and then on a far more consistent basis when Natasha had been sick.

"Yes," Frankie snapped, crossing her arms and tilting her chin with an open defiance that had Holden growling at her. "Now, what the hell do you mean 'interrogation'?"

"*Francesca*, mind your manners." Holden's scolding tone earned him a glare from his guest that would have had Braden chuckling under different circumstances. It was well known within their circles that Holden did not tolerate brats, though he tended to attract them. The man was, to put it bluntly, gigantic, and nearly every sub who came through Club BDE's doors dreamt of being manhandled by Holden Prescott.

"*My* manners? I'm not the one going around threatening to 'interrogate' people!"

"To answer your question," Braden interrupted, mostly due to his own impatience but partially out of pity for Francesca who obviously had no idea what kind of grave she was digging for herself, "I own this club. And I just have a few questions, then you can be on your way."

"Fine." Tossing her long ponytail over her shoulder, Francesca shot him a haughty glare that was so reminiscent of the looks Charlotte had given him the day before that he nearly had to adjust himself under the desk. "What do you want to know?"

"Where did you hear about the virgin auction?"

"I don't see how that's any of your business."

Glaring down at her disapprovingly, Holden lifted his hand to rest it on the nape of her neck. Apparently, Francesca wasn't entirely unaffected by him, because she immediately stiffened, her eyes going wide in her suddenly pale face.

"Little girl, unless you want to answer Mr. Elliott's questions with a red-hot bottom, I suggest you tone down the attitude. Now."

"But Daddy—"

"One."

Francesca pouted, but wisely didn't argue further. "I heard about it from some of your employees," she finally answered.

"Who?"

"I don't know. It was the first night Daddy brought me here, when you were reviewing my application. The girl at the front desk said she didn't know why it was taking so long, and then some other girl came along and said it was because of the auction the club was running and then the front desk girl said she'd heard about it and how some girl got like, an insane amount of money for letting someone pop her cherry."

"The girl at the front desk—short hair, buzzed on one side, currently some shade of blue I believe?"

"Yes, that's her."

"Thank you. One last question. Why were you asking around about the virgin auction?"

"For a friend." Tilting her chin up again, Francesca glared down her nose at him. "And you can threaten me all you want, but that's private information and I'm not telling you anything else."

"Fair enough. You may go." Now he did let some of his amusement with her brattiness show. "I believe your Daddy will be impressing on you the importance of proper manners when addressing other Dominants while you are within the walls of my club. Do I have that right, Holden?"

"Absolutely. Come, Francesca. I think it's time you learned there's more than one way to punish a naughty bottom."

"But Daddy, I wasn't even that rude!"

"I beg to differ, little girl."

Francesca's protests cut off as the door shut behind them. Leaning back in his office chair, Braden considered his options.

Obviously, he'd already lost control of the gossip train in his club. Which meant he'd need to have a meeting with his employees and explain the reality of the situation, before they got any more of his members embroiled in this... unpleasantness. He probably should have done so as soon as he'd learned about the auction and his club's involvement, but he'd naïvely hoped he could keep it under wraps until they'd managed to ferret out the person running the auction and shut it down.

There were a few things he could do in the meantime, however. Picking up his phone, he sent off a couple of texts and waited for the next knock on his door.

When it came, he grinned up at Mistress Rogue and Master James as they stepped into his office at his invitation. Rogue, with her hourglass figure on display in the corsets she loved to sport when playing at the club and her dark hair pulled back in a high, tight ponytail. And James, only a few inches taller than Rogue in her thigh-high boots, his hair slicked back and curiosity dancing in his dark eyes. They would have made a striking couple if they hadn't both been Dominants with absolutely zero interest in switching positions.

"Perfect," Braden said as James closed the door behind them. "Two birds with one stone, as they say."

One eyebrow raising over her favored cat-eye glasses, Mistress Rogue smirked. "To what do we owe the pleasure?"

"There's a bit of an ongoing issue here at the club, and I need a favor from you two." He gave them a rundown of the nitty-gritty, how the club had been used to 'legitimize' the auction and how he was working on finding out who was actually behind the whole thing. "My brother has some contacts looking into it as quietly as possible. Martin is passing new guest passes onto me for review."

"What do you need from us?" Master James, one of the club's original members and Dungeon Masters, crossed his arms, fury dancing in his dark eyes. "Whatever it is, you know we've got your back."

"I'm glad to hear you say that. I have an employee in need of a reminder not to gossip with our clientele.

Would you mind taking care of that for me once Vivian's shift is over?"

Unsurprisingly, James's eyes lit up at the request. It was no secret he harbored a crush on the cute girl with the ever-changing hair at the front desk. "I'd be happy to."

"I thought so." With that handled, Braden shifted his attention to Mistress Rogue, who was watching him with an eagerness only a true sadist anticipating punishing a naughty little subbie could exhibit. He almost hated to disappoint her. "As for you, Rogue, Shane was a *very* good boy tonight. He came to me immediately to let me know one of our guests was asking around about the virgin auction. I believe he deserves a reward."

Mistress Rogue sighed, but he didn't miss the way her lips twitched. "Fine. I'll go find my candy corn strap-on. It's his favorite."

"Thank you. I appreciate you both. And if you feel like putting the fear of God into the other submissives and my employees with regards to club gossip, I won't be upset."

That seemed to cheer up Mistress Rogue, enough that she was practically skipping on her way out of his office.

Trusting that all was handled for now, Braden forced himself to forget all about sketchy auctions and focus on actual club business for once. He was halfway through his quarterly reports when he realized he'd gone a whole hour without thinking about pretty little Charlotte Duvall. Good. Maybe his sudden obsession with her was just an odd blip after all, and he was already over her.

Liar.

❦

LOTTIE

"Did you get the information?" Lottie all but pounced on Frankie when she walked through Lottie's front door Wednesday morning.

"Yes." Unusually sullen, Frankie pulled a card from her purse and held it out to Lottie. "And you owe me *so* big."

"What? Why? What happened?"

Glancing around, Frankie grabbed her arm and pulled her toward the stairs. "Let's go up to your room."

Though she was dying of curiosity, Lottie forced herself to wait until they made it up to her bedroom with the door shut behind them before asking again. "Okay, what the heck happened?"

"Apparently, the owner of the club didn't like me

asking around about the auction." Frankie flopped down onto Lottie's bed with an annoyed huff. "He had Daddy bring me up to his office so he could grill me about it and tell me to stop asking questions."

"Oh." Nerves bubbled up in Lottie's stomach as she glanced down at the card in her hand. "Do you think that means it's a bad idea?"

"Nah. He probably just doesn't want word getting out, you know? I don't think this whole thing is exactly legal."

"That's true. Is that why I owe you? That doesn't sound so bad."

"No. You owe me because Daddy didn't like my attitude while I was being interrogated. That was two days ago, and my butt still hurts."

"Really?" Fascinated, and slightly ashamed of it, Lottie lowered herself onto the bed beside Frankie. "What did he do?"

Propping herself up on her elbows, Frankie raised an eyebrow. "You sure you want to know?"

"Yes." Heat rose to her cheeks at her own rushed response, and Lottie shrugged, hoping it would cover her eagerness. "I mean, if the guys paying money for girls in this auction are members of the club, I feel like I should know more about what I'm getting myself into, right?"

"True... All right." Sitting up fully, Frankie crossed

her legs under her, excitement dancing in her eyes, despite her earlier sulking. "Well, for starters, he took me down to what they call 'the pit.' It's like, the main area of the club where people play and other people can watch. That's the bottom floor, and the top floor is a restaurant that looks down into the pit. Dinner and a show, I guess."

"So, people watch you... you know?"

"Yes. That's part of the excitement, at least for me." Frankie hesitated before lowering her voice, as if they weren't completely alone in the room. "If you tell the other girls this, I will never ever forgive you. Got it?"

"Got it."

"It's kinda hot, knowing that everyone is watching you. Wanting you. Especially when I'm in trouble. I get really fucking turned on knowing that everyone knows I was a bad girl and Daddy has to punish me."

Need, hot and shocking, flashed through Lottie at her friend's words. "That sounds..."

"I know, I know, I'm a weirdo." Rolling her eyes, Frankie waved a hand in the air, batting away Lottie's nonexistent judgments. "I wish I could explain it, but I can't. So anyway, the other night, Daddy strapped me to this thing called a St. Andrew's cross, which is like this big metal X that the restraints hook onto. And he lectured me really loudly about being respectful to other Doms in the club, blah blah blah. Then he spanked me again, the hardest he's ever spanked me before."

"Oh, Frankie. I'm sorry."

"It's fine. That was the easy part. It was the part that came after that, when he… you're sure you want to hear this?"

"Yes. And no. But yes, I think I need to."

"Okay, well, after he spanked me, he took out my plug—oh, I should have mentioned he's been making me wear a butt plug to help 'train me'—he took out my plug and then he took this huge dildo and he, ah, put it where the plug used to be."

"He *what*?"

"Yeah. And the whole time he's lecturing me about how naughty girls don't get Daddy's cock in their bottoms. They have to earn that privilege. And I swear to god, Lottie, I almost came just from him telling me how naughty I was, while he was fucking my ass with a fake dick."

Speechless, Lottie stared at her friend for several long moments before she found her voice again. "Then what?"

"Then, he left the dildo inside of me while he put me on my knees and made me suck him off as an 'apology'. But you know what the worst part was?"

She couldn't imagine anything could be worse than what Frankie had just described. "What?"

"The big jerk didn't let me come all night. And he sent me home with instructions not to get myself off until he gave me permission. I'm *dying*, Lottie. I feel like I could spontaneously combust at any second."

"That was the worst part? Not... all the rest?"

"No. Well, I mean, that part sucked, and I did actually start to feel bad about being so rude to Mr. Elliott. But—"

"Wait." Lottie's heart slammed against her ribcage. "Did you say Mr. Elliott?"

"Yeah, your hot as fuck next-door neighbor? He owns the club. Didn't I say that already?"

"No, you did not say that already!" Groaning loudly, Lottie fell back on her bed as the knowledge that her dad's best friend owned the club where she was supposed to sell her virginity sank in. "I'm so fucking screwed."

4

LADYBUG, LADYBUG

LOTTIE

"**W**hy are you screwed?" Frankie asked, confusion coloring her tone.

"I can't sell my virginity through my next-door neighbor's kinky auction! It's too weird! I've known him almost my whole life. His daughter and I were like, best friends until her mom moved her to the other side of the country."

"It's not that weird." Frankie paused. "Okay, it's a little weird. But I mean, it's not like you're selling it *to* your dad's best friend."

"But he'll know! You said he reviews all the guest passes! He'll never let me past the front door."

"You don't know that." When Lottie glared at her, Frankie just shrugged. "You don't. I mean, any guy who runs a kink club and a website where people auction off their virginity has to be pretty open-minded, right? And honestly, if it's his club, then you'll probably be safer there than just about anywhere else."

"That's true…" The idea of having Mr. Elliott looking out for her did make her feel a little warm and fuzzy inside. "If I get there and the guy turns out to be totally skeevy, I'm sure Mr. Elliott would let me out of the deal."

"Totally." Frankie grinned. "Just bat those pretty blue eyes at him and turn on the crocodile tears, and he'll be a goner."

"I don't know about that. He can be kind of a hardass sometimes."

"Please. From what I've heard, almost all the Doms at the club are Daddies. There's no way he'll turn away a sweet little girl in need."

She wasn't quite convinced Frankie knew what she was talking about, at least when it came to Mr. Elliott, but she also couldn't see him forcing her to go through with the auction if she truly didn't want to. He might have been a hardass, but he wasn't an asshole.

"All right. I'm going to do it."

"You're going to need sexy pictures." Practically buzzing with excitement, Frankie jumped off the bed and raced to Lottie's closet. She disappeared for a minute before reemerging with her arms full of lace and silk. "Let's get you ready for the auction block, babygirl."

⁂

BRADEN

Countdown to Opening Bid: Thirty minutes

Scowling at his computer, Braden scrolled through the virgin category for what felt like the millionth time in the past forty-eight hours. It felt a little like watching a train wreck and being unable to look away.

There was a new entry on the page. Another woman, offering herself up like some sacrificial lamb for a ridiculous amount of money.

On the surface, she didn't seem that different from the other auctionees. Early twenties, minimal personal data in her bio, and a short list of kinks she was willing to try. Her face was blurred out, so he had no clue what she actually looked like, but her body was uncomfortably stunning. Maybe it was just the lingerie she'd chosen to highlight her curves, or the artful way she was draped over a rather expensive-looking couch, but he couldn't stop staring at her pictures.

Couldn't stop imagining her draped in a very different position, so he could spank her ass red for such a stupid fucking stunt.

None of the other entrants had garnered such a strong reaction from him, and he couldn't for the life of him figure out why 'Ladybug' did. There was just something about her, something almost familiar, something he couldn't quite put his finger on...

Annoyed with himself for obsessing over her and the auction in general, he forced himself to minimize the site, since he couldn't quite bring himself to close it completely. Part of that was simple curiosity. He was, despite himself, dying to know exactly how much a virgin was worth these days.

He managed to lose himself in the day-to-day minutiae of running a business until nearly ten, when he took a break to do his rounds on the floors. There were no new guests tonight, which he was grateful for, but he found himself wondering how many new requests would come through in the following days.

That thought made him pause. If the auction followed any kind of set pattern, perhaps he could go back through the club records and match the auction days with any new guest passes. There had to be some way to track down the source of the auction, and the only way he could think to do that was by backtracking through the people involved.

Unless he wanted to get Martin involved, which he wasn't quite ready to do just yet. He wasn't even sure why he was being so stubborn on that front when Martin could probably have the culprit locked down and the website out of business in under an hour. But knowing that someone was using his name, his club, to lend even an ounce of legitimacy to their bullshit auction made it personal. And he was self-aware enough to know he was going to continue being a stubborn ass about figuring it all out on his own, unless he was left with no choice but to call in reinforcements.

It was bad enough his brothers were already involved. But that couldn't be helped, so he'd just have to tolerate them continuing to butt their noses into club business.

Oh, and look who just walked in, with the new love of his life on his arm? Damian, one of the twin banes of existence, with pretty little Emily beaming beside him as they made their own tour of the pit. Despite the grin on her face, Emily was walking a bit stiffly, which sent Braden's mind tumbling down a rabbit hole of wondering what his brother had done to her before they'd come to the club.

It probably should have made him feel like a dirty

old man, considering Emily was twenty years his junior, and his niece's best friend. But there were plenty of submissives Emily's age in the club who would—and had—thrown themselves at his feet if he gave them half a chance.

The fact that he couldn't remember the last time he wanted any of them, regardless of their age, kneeling for him, wasn't something he really wanted to think too much about.

"Damian. Emily. What a pleasant surprise."

And it was a surprise, seeing as how his brothers almost never came by the club, despite being silent partners in the business. They'd taken the 'silent' part far more literally than he'd ever intended, but it suited him just fine.

Emily's smile widened and she sent him an enthusiastic wave. "Hi, Braden!"

Beside her, Damian raised a gray brow in a gesture that managed to be both amused and slightly disapproving. "I figured you'd be upstairs."

Watching the auction. The words were there, even if he didn't say them. "I was, but I didn't see much point in just sitting around. Did you have a room booked for tonight?" He knew they didn't, as he'd also taken to reviewing all room requests as well as the guest passes, but he enjoyed putting his brother on the spot.

Not that Damian seemed bothered by the inquiry. "Nope. Just figured we'd come by and check on things."

"He means check on you," Emily said with a roll of her eyes. "We were worried because a little birdie said you've practically been sleeping here. What?" she added, eyes wide with innocence when Damian glared at her. "It's the truth!"

Equal parts amused and delighted by her, Braden leaned in to brush a kiss over her cheek. "Thank you for worrying about me, sweetheart. And whenever you decide to dump Mr. Grumpypants over here, you know where to find me."

As he'd hoped, Emily's cheeks turned red and Damian's hold on her waist tightened, eliciting a small squeak of surprise from her as he pulled her closer. "You have a club full of willing submissives, Braden. Go find your own."

Again, the image of Ladybug, draped suggestively over her fancy furniture, her face obscured by a mask, flitted through his mind.

Goddammit Braden, get it together. Forcing a smile, he gave his brother and Emily a small nod. "I think I will. Have fun, you crazy kids."

With his brother occupied, Braden made his way out to the lobby, where Shane was perched at the front desk. Compared to his usual club wear, he looked almost professional in a well-fitted corset and equally well-fitting dress slacks. "Hey, Daddy B. All quiet on the western front?"

"For now." Stopping in front of the desk, Braden crossed his arms and stared down at his brattiest member. "Shane. Did you tattle on me to my brother?"

Shane cleared his throat and busied himself with straightening the front desk. "I don't know what you mean."

Uncrossing his arms, Braden leaned down to brace his hands on the sleek dark wood. "Shane. Look at me."

Bottom lip puffed out in a pout any brat could be proud of, Shane reluctantly lifted his gaze to Braden's. "Sir?"

"I appreciate your concern," Braden said, letting his tone gentle a smidge. "And because I know your heart is in the right place, I will not be calling Mistress Rogue in so you and she can have a very public chat about keeping your nose out of other people's business. I can't guarantee I will be feeling so magnanimous should it happen again. Understood?"

Shane gulped audibly, his eyes going wide. "Yes, Sir."

"Good." Straightening, Braden plucked a candy corn from the bag on the desk and popped it into his mouth. Almost immediately, he regretted the decision. "Jesus. How can you eat these things? They taste like wax."

"Delicious wax," Shane returned with a grin, the sting of his chastisement already fading. "You should try the Thanksgiving mix. It's awful, but I love it anyway."

"I know the feeling."

At Braden's pointed remark, Shane threw his head back and laughed. "Touché, Daddy B. Touché."

Satisfied that his mini dressing-down would keep Shane in line for at least a couple of days, Braden headed back up to his office. He'd gone and done his duty by the club, now it was his chance to indulge his curiosity.

Seated at his desk once more, he opened the window with the virgin auction and nearly choked on air when he saw the bids. Not a single one of the women up for sale had a bid lower than a quarter of a million.

Ladybug, however, was beating them all at nearly four hundred grand. Knowing that others wanted her as badly as he did… Braden's finger hovered over the button of his mouse as a primal urge welled up inside of him.

He had the money. That wasn't the problem. Thanks to the club and several lucrative investments over the years, he could afford to bid on every single girl and still have enough money to pay his ex-wife's alimony and their daughter's tuition to the ridiculously expensive, and also ridiculously elite college she was currently attending.

And if he didn't buy Ladybug, someone would. Maybe he couldn't save them all, but he could save one. Save her, and then live out his fantasy of punishing her naughty little bottom until he was certain she'd never, ever do something so incredibly reckless again. He wouldn't even take her virginity in exchange.

Not unless she begged like a good girl, first.

In the end, though, his principles won out. He had no right to punish a complete stranger for risks she took with her own life. So even though it killed him a little inside, he pulled his hand away from the mouse.

And spent the rest of the evening watching as Ladybug's price climbed higher and higher.

5

TEMPTATION COMES IN
MANY FORMS

LOTTIE

Four hundred and twenty-seven thousand dollars.

Holy fuck.

Somebody wanted to have sex with her so badly, despite not even seeing her face, that they were willing to pay almost half a million dollars for the honor.

Granted, she was only getting just a smidge over three hundred grand, thanks to the twenty-five percent fee Mr. Elliott was taking for himself.

Well, that was assuming he was doing it all on his own. She couldn't remember him ever mentioning anything about computers, but she didn't really know him well enough to know if he was smart enough to put something like this together on his own. But even if he was splitting the profits evenly with a partner, he was still getting a hefty payout.

It seemed a little unfair, since he wasn't the one letting some slimy asshole with more money than sense put his dick inside him.

Ugh. If she kept thinking about it like that, she was going to end up talking herself out of it. And even if she could find another way to make some money, she couldn't really afford the ten-thousand-dollar penalty for backing out at the last minute.

Which was depressing in and of itself. There'd been a time she wouldn't have thought twice about spending ten grand on a single shopping trip. Now, it seemed like an irresponsible amount of money to spend on anything.

She wasn't even sure the three hundred thousand would be enough to pay off her father's debt, but surely it would be enough to stop them from hemorrhaging until she could get a game plan together. And Mr. Legare may still come through with a job, so things weren't entirely hopeless.

Now all she had to do was meet up with a complete stranger and let him take her virginity.

No problem.

Big problem.

Grabbing her phone, she hit the button to call

Frankie. "I can't do this," she blurted out when her friend answered.

"Do you need me to come over?"

Gratitude and love swelled in Lottie's chest. "Yes. Maybe. No." Dragging in a deep breath, Lottie closed her eyes and held it. Frankie would be there, no matter how things went, and she could do anything with her best friend by her side. "I'm just being a big baby."

"It's okay to be nervous your first time." Frankie paused, her amusement clear through the phone. "So... how much did you get?"

"Just over three hundred thousand, after the auction takes their cut."

"Hot damn, girl. Too bad you need the money for your dad. We could go on a hell of a vacation."

"Is it bad that part of me wants to do that? Or just like, take the money and go get an apartment in the city and go to work for your dad and just let my father deal with his shit himself?"

"Nobody would blame you if you did exactly that."

"I would blame me," Lottie said with a sigh. "I can't just leave him, Frankie. I'm all he has."

"I know, honey. Which is why you're going to suck it up and let this guy pop your cherry. And who knows, if he's a Dom from the club, he might even make it good for you."

"Yeah right." Rolling her eyes, Lottie snorted. "Guys who are that good in bed don't have to pay for it."

"Fair point. Have you heard from him yet?"

"Let me check." Heart pounding against her ribs, Lottie opened her email. And promptly had to swallow back the rising bile. "Fuck. He wants to meet, like, tomorrow."

Frankie let out a low whistle. "Well, I guess that makes sense. If you'd spent that much money on something, you'd want to get your hands on it as soon as possible."

"Way to make me feel like a piece of merchandise, Frankie."

"Sorry. But you know what I mean."

"I do." And as tempting as it was to keep putting the guy off, she figured it was a bit like ripping off a band aid. Best to just do it and get it over with.

Especially since she could only put him off for two weeks before she forfeited her payment and got hit with that ten-thousand-dollar fee.

Dammit.

Scanning the rest of the email, Lottie blew out a relieved breath. "Okay. He wants to meet at the club first. He says there's a restaurant on the top floor where we can have a drink and get to know each other a bit first. So as long as Mr. Elliott doesn't try to kick me out, that should be a good place to meet, right?"

"Definitely. And I seriously doubt he's going to kick you out."

"All right. I'm going to email Master O back, then."

She typed out a quick response, agreeing to meet him at nine the next evening, and added in a little bit of fluff about how excited she was to meet him even though what she was feeling felt more like dread than excitement. And, before she completely lost her nerve, hit send.

"I did it. Holy shit, I did it."

"Breathe, Lottie, breathe."

"I am. At least, I think I am. But I can't believe I'm actually doing this."

"Still don't want me to come over?"

"I'm okay. I'm going to go downstairs and pour myself a glass of wine, and then figure out what the fuck I'm supposed to wear to get my cherry popped."

"Something white and innocent-looking. Might as well play up the fantasy."

"I hate how much sense that makes. Ugh. I'll talk to you later."

"Give me a call if you change your mind and want

me to come over. We can get drunk and see if we can find him on social media."

Snorting out a laugh, Lottie shook her head. "I love you."

"Love you too, babe. You better call me afterward and give me all the dirty deets!"

"Duh."

Feeling somewhat steadier, Lottie ended the call and hopped off her bed, deliberately ignoring her laptop. If 'Master O' needed anything else from her, he could wait until she'd had a glass of wine. Or three.

She was in the kitchen pouring the first glass of the Bordeaux she favored—and, for the first time in her life, wondering how much each glass actually cost—when her dad walked in. His smile brightened when he spotted her, a rare sight that normally would have thrilled her, and she hated herself a little for the anger that bubbled in her gut.

Forcing that anger back down, she forced a smile of her own. "Hi, Daddy."

Ew. After learning that Frankie called men Daddy while they fucked her, the word just felt wrong.

"Hi, pumpkin. Bit early for a drink, isn't it?"

"What's the saying? It's five o'clock somewhere, right?" Lifting the glass, she toasted him with it before draining half the liquid in a single swallow. The alcohol burned in her stomach, or maybe that was just her fury at being lectured about drinking by a raging fucking alcoholic.

"I suppose that's true," he returned with a chuckle.

The silence that fell between them felt more strained than usual. Could he feel it? Could he tell something was wrong?

If he could, he did a damn good job of hiding it.

Tears formed a lump in her throat. There'd been a time her parents would have been tuned into every nuance of her moods and behavior. Her mom, especially, but even her dad had always been able to tell when something was bothering her.

She hadn't realized how much she'd taken that for granted, having someone who knew her moods inside and out like that, until it was gone. And, standing there in her spacious kitchen with her too-early glass of wine, and her father smiling serenely at her like her entire world wasn't crumbling down around her, she couldn't help but feel as though she'd lost both her parents when her mother had died.

Maybe if she could bail him out of this hole he'd gotten himself into, he would get better. Even as the thought popped into her mind, she recognized the desperation in it. But her heart stubbornly clung to that hope.

Because if she went through with the auction, and

he gambled it all away again, she wasn't sure she could ever forgive him.

"How are things with the businesses?" The question popped out of her, seemingly of its own volition.

If she hadn't been aware of their troubles, she probably would have missed the way his smile tightened just a bit at the edges, the way his eyes dimmed slightly at the question. "Everything's good. Why do you ask?"

"I dunno." Shrugging as nonchalantly as she could manage while her emotions boiled and raged inside her, she lifted her wine again. "I've got that fancy degree hanging in my room, not really doing anything. Maybe I should, you know, start to get more involved."

"We can certainly talk about it."

Dad-speak for *"I don't want to hurt your feelings by telling you 'no' outright, so I'll just dance around making an actual decision until you get bored and move onto something else"*.

"Just a thought. But if you'd rather keep funding my pampered-princess lifestyle, I'm certainly not going to complain about it."

His smile turned teasing. "Is that your way of telling me you're planning another girls' trip soon?"

"Actually, Frankie wants to do something big for Memorial Day, since she's going to be so busy the next... well, the rest of her life, I guess, with the whole 'becoming a hotshot surgeon' thing. We might go down to the Maldives."

It wasn't entirely a lie. Frankie did want to do something spectacular for Memorial weekend, but she was actually planning a trip up to her dad's cabin. But Lottie wanted to watch her dad's face as she presented him with the much more extravagant, and wildly more expensive option.

But he barely even flinched. "I'm sure you girls will have a lovely time."

For a moment, she could only stare at him. Had she completely misinterpreted how dire their situation was?

Or, more likely, was he just lying to her fucking face? Again.

"Yeah. Sure." Grabbing her nearly empty glass and the rest of the bottle, she rounded the wide island and prayed he wouldn't notice the tears swimming her eyes as she paused to press a kiss to his cheek. "Love you, Dad."

"Love you, too, pumpkin."

With her heart breaking in her chest, she made her way up to her room where she planned to spend the next twenty-four hours as drunk as possible so she didn't have to think about what a fucking mess her life had become.

BRADEN

Finger hovering over the Duvall's doorbell, Braden briefly wondered again why he was here for the second time in less than a week. While he'd made it a point to check in with Emmett as often as possible since Natasha had died, he hadn't visited more than a couple of times a month since those first few weeks after the funeral.

But he'd been on his way out the door to head to the club, and he'd found himself drawn to their front door by some invisible force he couldn't name.

Well. The force had a name. He just wasn't quite ready to admit that the reason he was ringing the doorbell to his closest friend's home was just to get a peek at his daughter.

It took three rings for the door to swing open. But instead of Abigail, the housekeeper who had been running the Duvall home and answering their door for longer than Braden could remember, it was Charlotte who yanked the door open, a lopsided smile plastered across her face.

"Another visit so soon? To what do we owe the pleasure, Mr. Elliott?"

The slight slurring of her words was enough to

dampen the thrill of pleasure he'd gotten from seeing her. Narrowing his eyes, he stepped over the threshold, grabbing her arm to steady her when she stumbled back. "Are you drunk?"

"Not that it's any of your business, but yes. And if you'd be so kind as to let go of me, I'd like to go get another bottle of wine so I can stay that way."

"No."

Even wasted, she managed to raise an eyebrow in that haughty, spoiled-princess way that made his palm itch. "I don't remember asking for permission."

She hadn't. And he had no right to deny her, or to give orders. But fuck if he wasn't still tempted to drag her into the parlor so he could wear his hand out on her gorgeous ass for being a defiant brat. "You've obviously had more than enough, and it's not even four in the afternoon, Charlotte."

Instead of jerking out of his grasp or scowling at him as he'd expected, a slow, sultry smile curved her lips and she leaned in. "Have I been a naughty girl, Daddy?"

Heat flashed through him at the sound of his title on her lips. Before he could stop himself, he'd hauled her against him, her lips a hair's breadth from his own. "You've been very naughty, little girl."

"Yeah?" He didn't think he was imagining the flush on her cheeks or the way her pupils widened at his words, but he also couldn't be sure it wasn't just the alcohol. "What are you gonna do about it?"

Spank your ass and then put you to bed, so you wake up thinking of me and remembering how naughty you were.

That was what he wanted to do. More than he could remember wanting anything in a very long time. But it was beyond wrong to want those things with her, so he pushed her away, gently but firmly. "Go take a nap, Charlotte. Sleep off the alcohol."

Now she did jerk away, her bottom lip puffed out in a pout that nearly had him hauling her back to him so he could kiss it away. "Fuck you. You're not my Daddy."

"It's a good thing for you I'm not, or else you'd be going down for that nap with the taste of soap on your tongue."

Her eyes widened at the threat, and she stumbled backward before scurrying off to the kitchen. Probably in search of another bottle of wine.

Ignoring every instinct he had, he stalked past the kitchen to go track down his friend. And to see if he knew why the fuck his daughter was absolutely blitzed in the middle of the afternoon.

6

MEETING MASTER O

LOTTIE

The alcohol had done its job. She couldn't remember much of anything from the last twenty-four hours, other than a hazy memory of Mr. Elliott coming to the door and looking very stern about her drinking. But then, Mr. Elliott often looked stern about one thing or another. She'd had a fleeting worry that perhaps he was angry because he'd found out about her putting herself in the auction, but if that had been the case, she had no doubt he would have raised holy hell with her father. And since neither of them had approached her about it, she figured it was safe to assume he hadn't discovered who 'Ladybug' actually was.

Overall, she was left feeling mostly numb about

everything, thanks to the alcohol and whatever self-preservation mechanism her brain had engaged to keep her from actually thinking about what the evening would entail. Numb enough that she was able to get ready for her... date? Appointment? Whatever the fuck you called it when you met a strange guy in a club and handed over your virginity in exchange for an obscene amount of cash, she was no longer feeling anxious about it. In fact, she wasn't feeling anything really, though some distant little voice in the back of her head was telling her she should be worried about the fact that she wasn't worried.

Whatever. Worst-case scenario, she could talk through the whole mess in therapy after she got her dad's debts back under control. Every poor little rich girl had a therapist on tap to help them through all of life's little inconveniences, and Lottie's would have an absolute field day with this whenever she went back.

Imagining her therapist's expression when she explained the whole sordid ordeal kept Lottie occupied and amused the entire car ride to the club. The auction had sent a car over, and while it wasn't as nice as the service her dad used, it wasn't shabby, either.

The club was a lot nicer than she'd expected it to be, too. Well, she honestly wasn't sure what she *had* been expecting, seeing as how she'd never actually been to a sex club before. But while the outside was rather unassuming with its plain dark brick exterior, the interior was stunning. Every surface was either gleaming wood or padded leather, and the whole place was lit with dark red lighting that managed to be sexy and mysterious rather than cheesy. Overall, the entire atmosphere whispered of wealth and privilege, which she supposed made sense considering one of the club's members had shelled out nearly half a million dollars for her virginity.

Across the expansive lobby, a woman with rainbow-colored hair smiled at her from behind a sleek desk as Lottie approached. "Hi! You look a little lost. Are you here with someone?"

"I'm supposed to be meeting someone." Lottie had never considered herself the type of person to get easily embarrassed, but heat rushed to her cheeks and she had to swallow several times before she could get the words out. "I'm, ah, here with… Master O?"

The woman's eyes went wide. "Are you sure that's the right name?"

Before Lottie could second-guess herself, a deep rumbling voice answered. "She's sure."

Turning around, Lottie felt her own eyes go wide as her gaze traveled up, taking in the impeccably fitted three-piece suit and the broad chest it covered, until finally she landed on his face. His gorgeous, sculpted face with its perfectly cropped beard that held just a hint of gray. There was a dangerous edge to his expression, despite the indulgent smile he granted her as he looked down into her eyes.

"Hello, little one. You look lovely." His gaze shifted to the woman at the desk behind Lottie. "I trust my table is ready?"

"Um, well, I'm sure it is, Master Killian, but I can't let you up there without vetting your guest."

Shit. After finding her three sheets to the wind in the middle of the afternoon the day before, she wouldn't put it past Mr. Elliott to deny her entrance into the club just to teach her a lesson. It seemed like the petty kind of move he would pull, especially since the one thing she really *could* remember about his visit was how annoyed he'd seemed with her behavior.

"I've already been approved," she blurted out, causing the woman behind the desk to narrow her eyes skeptically while Master O raised a disbelieving brow.

"I know the owner, Mr. Elliott," she continued in a rush of words. "He's my neighbor, and my dad's best friend. When Master O asked me to meet him here, I went to Mr. Elliott and he said to tell you I was cleared to go in."

"That's not really how this works…" the woman

behind the desk said, her tone and expression still openly doubtful.

"We won't go into the pit until we speak with Braden," Master O assured her with a flash of teeth. "But we will be going up to the restaurant so we may get to know each other better."

With that, Master O slid his arm around Lottie's waist and guided her toward the stairs. "That was very naughty, little one," he murmured in her ear as they made the climb.

"What?" She was aware her voice was a little breathless, and she was even more aware of the way her stomach tightened not altogether unpleasantly at his words.

"You lied to poor Vivian. Knowing her boss as well as I do, she will likely pay a hefty price for your dishonesty."

Guilt twisted Lottie's stomach into a knot. "You don't think Mr. Elliott will fire her, do you?"

They paused at the top of the stairs and Master O looked down at her, his expression full of amusement and something that looked almost like delight, but scarier. "You really have no clue what you've walked into, do you, little one?"

"Not really, no." Might as well be honest at this point, especially since he seemed to have some kind of sixth sense that told him when she was lying.

"That's what I thought. Come, let's have a drink."

⚜

BRADEN

Rising from his desk chair, Braden stretched, wincing a little at the pull in his lower back. Getting old was for the birds.

He made a mental note to schedule a massage as he made his way down to the lobby. "Evening, Vivian. Quiet night?"

The flash of guilt across her face did not bode well. Whether it didn't bode well for him or for her ass still remained to be seen. "Mostly, yeah."

"Mostly?"

"Um, well, Master O is upstairs. With a new girl."

"That's hardly surprising." Killian O'Rourke rarely visited the club with the same woman. "But I don't remember seeing a guest pass request."

"I didn't process a guest pass."

Eyes narrowing, Braden pinned her with a hard glare. "And why not?"

Vivian shrank back. "She said you'd already approved her. And I know that's not really proper protocol, but Master O said they wouldn't go into the pit before they talked to you, and no offense Master Braden, but he kinda scares me more than you do.”

“We’ll see how you feel about that by the time I deal with your punishment for allowing an unvetted guest into my club, Vivian.” Vibrating with fury, Braden turned on his heel and stalked up the stairs to Killian’s usual table.

But just as he was approaching, the brunette tucked in beside Killian tossed her head back, her bold laughter ringing out at something he’d said, and Braden froze. Anger, need, and jealousy all welled up inside of him, overwhelming him to the point he could only stand and stare for a long moment.

Charlotte.

Charlotte was here, in his club. And she was sitting next to one of the most dangerous men in South Carolina, completely oblivious to who she was tucked so cozily against.

She was never going to sit comfortably again.

Charlotte glanced up just as he approached, her face draining of color for a moment before she jerked her chin upward, defiance etched into her expression.

“Charlotte. Killian. I’d like a word with both of you in my office. Now.”

Unsurprisingly, Charlotte leaned into Killian, her expression turning smug as she lifted her martini glass and sipped at the bright pink concoction. "This is a *private* conversation, Mr. Elliott."

Bracing his hands on the table, Braden leaned in, excitement licking along his nerves as her eyes widened with a hint of fear. "You are in my club, little girl, so let's get something straight right now. My club, my rules. And seeing as how you are already in a world of trouble for lying to my receptionist, I suggest you don't make things any worse for yourself than they need to be. Now, would you like to discuss your misbehavior in the privacy of my office, or would you prefer to be strapped to a bench in the middle of the pit so the entire club can watch Master Killian and I teach you the lesson you so obviously need?"

Just like the day before, her pupils widened with every word and by the time he was finished, her breath was coming in short little pants past her parted lips. And now, he couldn't even blame it on the alcohol. No, her reaction was purely that of a naughty little girl who had been caught red-handed by a very angry Daddy.

He couldn't remember ever being so fucking hard in his entire life.

"Come, little one. Let's not make a scene." Killian's grin flashed, full of all the same filthy thoughts currently running through Braden's mind. "At least, not yet."

"Fine." Still clutching her drink, Charlotte slid from the booth. "But I'm taking my cosmo."

"Good." Braden smiled, deliberately putting a bit of wicked anticipation into the gesture. "It will give me a color to match when I paddle your ass in a moment."

He took great pleasure in watching her falter on those impossibly high heels that made her legs look a million miles long, even as he reached out to steady her. And if he didn't release her immediately, it was just because he wanted to be sure she didn't fall. Nothing more.

Killian followed behind them all the way up to Braden's office, and he swore he could feel the amusement rolling off the other man in waves. The smirk on Killian's face was confirmation as he brushed past Braden and settled himself on one of the leather couches and patted the spot beside him. "Come sit with me, little one."

Braden opened his mouth to tell her otherwise before clamping it shut. Regardless of how he felt about her lying her way into the club, the fact of the matter was, she wasn't his submissive.

That knowledge didn't help to curb the swell of possessive jealousy that rose up in him when she flounced across the room and snuggled up under Killian's arm with a smirk of her own.

"Before we get into the nitty-gritty of your lack of honesty,"—he pinned Charlotte with a glare before shifting his focus to Killian—"and your lack of respect for the club rules, I have a few questions."

"Ask away," Killian said with a lazy wave of his hand.

"First off, how the hell did you two even meet?" If Emmett had gotten himself in with the Irish mob, he and Braden would be having some words. And most of them would probably make a sailor blush.

"As if you don't know," Charlotte answered with a derisive snort.

"Me? How the fuck should I know?"

The pair on the couch shared a look before Killian turned his piercing gaze back to Braden, all trace of amusement suddenly gone from his expression. "The auction. I had assumed you were kept apprised of each transaction."

Images flashed through Braden's mind, of a gorgeous body draped over expensive-looking furniture and his stomach churned with the mixture of emotions flooding his system. But that couldn't have been her. That girl had claimed to be a virgin. "Charlotte. Tell me you did not put yourself up for auction."

"I thought I wasn't supposed to tell any more lies." Her voice was syrupy sweet as she batted her eyes up at him and it took every ounce of self-restraint he had not to haul her up and bend her over right then and there.

Luckily, Killian had obviously caught onto the fact that things were not as they seemed, and he frowned at her with all the ferocity of a disapproving Daddy. Charlotte shrank in on herself, as if she could somehow make herself small enough to escape his wrath.

"A sharp tongue will get you nowhere, little one. Answer Master Braden's questions politely, or you'll be answering them with a striped bottom."

Charlotte's mouth fell open at the threat. "You can't spank me!"

"Quite to the contrary. The contract you signed allows me to do whatever I wish with you for the evening, within your limits, which includes spanking that naughty little backside of yours. Unless I hear the word 'red' from your pretty lips, you will do as you are told, or you will be punished by either myself or Master Braden. Have I made myself quite clear?"

"Sure. Whatever."

Killian's lips twitched with amusement. It was well known he had a soft spot for bratty submissives. "Thank you. Braden, continue."

"Answer the question, Charlotte. Did you put yourself in a sex auction?"

"Yes."

"What was the fantasy?" He didn't need to know for any other reason than he *wanted* to know. What kind of fantasies was a girl like Charlotte Duvall looking to fulfill?

And how well did they align with the ones he'd been having about her lately?

Looking distinctly more uncomfortable now, Charlotte squirmed in her seat. "I don't understand. Don't you run the auction? Shouldn't you know all of this already?"

"Humor me."

"Ugh. Fine." She rolled her eyes, but a pink blush was already creeping into her cheeks. "It was the virgin auction, if you really must know."

He'd known. Somehow, he felt like he'd known the moment he'd seen the photos. He just hadn't wanted to admit it. "So you lied. Again."

"No!" Indignant fury vibrated in her voice. "I did *not* lie!"

There was a sincerity in her tone that nearly convinced him. "Fine. Say you aren't lying, then. What the hell possessed you to sell your virginity to a man you'd never met?"

"I thought it was your auction! I thought it was

safe!"

Warmth blossomed in his chest at the knowledge she felt safe with him, because of him, before he realized it was probably because she saw him as a non-threatening sort of father figure. After all, he'd known her almost her entire life, and he'd never given her a reason to be afraid of him.

Perhaps he should have, and they wouldn't be in this fucking mess.

"But why?" he pressed, even as she glared daggers at him. "It's not like you need the money."

"None of your business."

Temper replaced the warm glow and he just barely managed not to snarl. "You've made it my business by coming to my club and using our relationship to get yourself in the door."

"Oh my god, why are you making a federal case out of this? I needed money; I found a way to make money. What's your problem?"

"What do you need money for, Charlotte? Did Emmett finally get tired of you leeching off him, so you decided selling yourself to the highest bidder was easier than getting a real job?"

As soon as the words left his mouth, he regretted them.

Tears sparkled in her eyes as she glared up at him. "Fuck you." Her voice trembled, nearly cracking, and he could see the betrayal she must be feeling written all over her face.

Fuck.

"Charlotte." Killian's tone managed to be both scolding and soothing at the same time. "Despite being an utter cad, Master Braden is still the owner of this club and as such deserves your respect. Apologize."

"No, I'm the one who owes Charlotte an apology," Braden said, running a hand through his hair as his stomach rolled with regret. He'd been more than a cad; he'd been a true fucking asshole. "This auction business has me out of sorts, but I shouldn't have taken it out on you. I'm sorry, Lottie-bug."

As he'd hoped, the childhood nickname seemed to ease the tension in her shoulders, though she was still looking up at him with those wounded eyes that made him want to gather her up in his arms and cuddle her until the hurt feelings faded. "Sorry I swore at you."

"Apology accepted."

"Now that we've cleared the air," Killian said dryly, pulling the attention back to himself. "What the hell is going on, Braden?"

7

MAKING A TRADE

LOTTIE

When had Mr. Elliott turned into such an asshole? She'd had a feeling he wouldn't be happy about her lying to the front-desk girl, but she hadn't expected him to literally accuse her of leeching off her dad. Tears burned in her throat as the scene played over and over in her mind. It wasn't *fair*, especially when the only reason she was doing any of this was to help her dad.

Not that she was going to tell him any of that, especially after what he'd just said to her. The sting still hadn't faded, and being scolded like a naughty little girl by Master O hadn't helped. The childhood nickname Mr. Elliott had pulled out of nowhere had mollified her a bit, but she was still feeling hurt and sulky as the men talked about the auction.

"I don't fucking know," Mr. Elliott said, frustration clear in his voice. "I just learned about the auction a few weeks ago, and that whoever is running it has been using my club to try and make it seem more legitimate."

"If I'd known that, I certainly would not have utilized the site." Master O's tone was tight and controlled, like he was holding back a fierce temper. A little shiver of fear went up her spine, and suddenly she wished she wasn't sitting so close to him. "Why haven't you told the members?"

"For starters, I was hoping to get it shut down before the next round." Sighing, Mr. Elliott ran a hand through his dark hair again, leaving it adorably mussed and she felt a tug of sympathy at how distraught he appeared, which she immediately squashed. Just because a man with a chiseled jawline and stunning blue eyes looked sad didn't mean he got a pass for being a complete dick. "And pride, I suppose. I didn't want the members thinking I can't control my club."

"Well, that's ridiculous," Master O said with a snort of derision. "We would all understand it's beyond your control. At the very least, you should have come to me. I have the resources to get the site shut down quickly and cleanly."

"And leave myself indebted to the mob? No, thank you."

The mob? A shocked squeak escaped before Lottie could stop it, and both men turned to look at her, Mr. Elliott with an "I told you so" sort of smirk and Master O with a lopsided smile that somehow felt playful and threatening at the same time.

"Don't worry yourself, little one. I'm no danger to pretty little girls like you."

It was Lottie's turn to snort disbelievingly. "I've seen *Goodfellas* enough times to know that's not true."

"Hollywood loves to glamorize us and demonize us with the same broad brush. But I promise, you would be safe with me."

"Absolutely not." Anger snapping in the icy blue of his eyes, Mr. Elliott shook his head. "She's not going anywhere with you, Killian."

"Of course she is. I paid for her, after all."

The reminder that she'd been bought and paid for left Lottie feeling a little sick to her stomach. And, judging by the expression on Mr. Elliott's face, he didn't appreciate it either. "Why is that, exactly? It's not like you have a shortage of women at your beck and call."

Master O lifted a shoulder in a nonchalant shrug.

"I haven't had a virgin in a while. I thought it might be a nice change of pace."

"A four-hundred-thousand-dollar change of pace?" Lottie asked, raising an eyebrow in disbelief, and hoping the men couldn't tell that her stomach was churning. She felt as though she might puke all over Master O's custom suit. It was one thing to put herself up for auction, it was quite another to listen to them talk about her as though she were a piece of meat.

"It's just money," Master O said with another shrug. "You can't take it with you, after all."

"It doesn't matter how much you spent; she's not going through with it."

Lottie took a sip of her cosmo, praying it would help calm her nerves. "Yes, I am."

"Like hell you are."

"I signed a contract, and despite your low opinion of me, Mr. Elliott, I am a woman of my word."

"You're a fucking child."

"I'm twenty-two. An adult by every metric."

"I don't care how old you are. I am not letting this happen."

"There is a contract." Master O's tone gave away nothing of what he was feeling, and somehow still managed to have the hair on Lottie's neck standing up. "And I believe there's a hefty fee for breaking it."

"I'll pay the goddamn fee, and you can get your money back."

Shit, shit, shit. "Excuse me." Lottie raised her hand and waved it between them. "What about me? I still need the money."

Mr. Elliott's eyes narrowed, and she instinctively shrank back against Master O, which felt a bit like escaping a lion only to run into a tiger's cage. "Why do you need the money, Charlotte?"

"That's none of your business."

"Then you obviously don't need it that badly. I'll pay the fee and get you out of this mess you've gotten yourself into."

"Counterpoint," Master O said before she could respond. "You wish to find the person who is actually responsible for the auction, correct?"

"Yes, but—"

"Let me finish. The most likely scenario is that someone in the club, possibly even an employee is running the auction. Agreed?"

"Yes," Mr. Elliott agreed with obvious annoyance.

"Then there's a chance that person saw you approach us this evening. Which is not in and of itself unusual. But if I cancel the contract, it's going to alert them that something is wrong. Which you do not want."

"And why is that?"

"Because then you risk them moving the entire operation, making it more difficult to locate them. As I said, I have the resources to ferret this person out for you. And right now, I have a money trail to follow. If they catch wind of your investigation, however, and shut everything down..."

"We lose the one good lead we have," Mr. Elliott said with a sigh.

"Exactly."

"So what exactly do you propose? Because allowing Charlotte to go through with the contract isn't an option."

"You pay me what I paid for the lovely Charlotte, and we call it even. I will put my best men on the trail of your auctioneer and send you whatever information we are able to find."

"In exchange for...?"

Master O grinned, and Lottie was hit with the sudden realization that the tiger was even more lethal than she'd given him credit for. "A favor. The next time I bring a girl to your club, you approve her membership, no questions asked."

"No. I can't do that. I won't risk the other members by skipping the vetting process."

"I'm not asking you to. I am simply asking you to not interfere, regardless of how you may feel about the woman I choose."

A muscle jumped in Mr. Elliott's jaw, as if he were holding himself back from saying something he might regret. "As long as she is of legal age and can pass the background checks and vetting process, I won't interfere again."

"Excellent. It's settled, then. You'll pay me the four hundred thousand and change, and I'll mark the transaction as complete. Charlotte will get her money and you'll have your auctioneer in hand by the end of the week."

Relief flooded Lottie's system and she drained her glass before pushing to her feet. "Sounds like you boys have it all figured out. It was a pleasure doing business with you."

"Not so fast, little girl." Mr. Elliott snagged her arm as she tried to walk past him. Dark eyes locked with hers, and her stomach jumped at the determination in his gaze. "You have a contract to fulfill."

BRADEN

Watching Charlotte's pupils go wide with that little hint of fear in the ever-changing gray of her eyes sent a thrill through him he hadn't felt in a long while. "You want me to... with you?" Her voice rose to a squeak at the end of her question.

"Absolutely not. But you have a debt to pay off, and tonight you're going to start paying it off by going over my knee for a long lesson about putting yourself in unnecessary danger."

"Don't forget the lying," Killian added cheerfully.

"Ah, yes. I think a few minutes in the corner with a bar of soap in your mouth will cure any desire you have to lie to your new co-workers in the future."

"My co-workers?"

"Yes. You'll be working here, at the club's starting wage of eighteen dollars an hour, until your debt has been paid off."

"Ugh." Her lip pulled up in a sneer. "I'd rather just let you fuck me."

"Oh, little girl." Pulling her close, he gave into the urges that had been riding him ever since he'd seen those pictures of her on the auctions site and gripped her face in his hand, forcing her head back. "You say that because you think it would be the easy way out. But I am not an easy man, Charlotte. If I demanded that you fulfilled the original terms of your contract, you would not be allowed out of my bed until I'd left my mark on every inch of your body. I would hurt you, not just because you've been a very naughty girl, but because I enjoy hurting pretty little things like you."

Her breath hitched and every instinct he had was spurring him on, telling him to take and conquer. "You wouldn't," she whispered.

"I absolutely would, little girl. You may have known me nearly all your life, but I can promise you know nothing about the man I truly am."

"Christ, Braden. Ease up a bit there. You're even starting to scare me."

Killian's flippant remark jerked Braden out of the desire-induced fog that had seemed to invade his brain and back to the present. Releasing his hold on Charlotte, Braden stepped back and adjusted his suit jacket so his hands had something to do that he wouldn't regret in the morning. "Right. Well, if we want this to look legitimate, Killian can't leave alone. I suggest the three of us leave together, give whoever is running this bullshit show the impression we'll be spending the night together. We'll split off around the corner, Killian can go home, and I'll take Charlotte back to my house to deal with her... discipline."

"Ah, a shame." Killian grinned and placed a hand over his heart. "I had hoped to enjoy the show. You know, for my troubles and all."

With any other sub, Braden would have jumped at

the chance to add a dash of humiliation to a punishment by inviting an audience.

But not Charlotte. She was *his* even if it was only for this one night. And he didn't intend to share.

8

FAILED NEGOTIATIONS

LOTTIE

She still wasn't sure how this had all spiraled so completely out of her control so fast. One minute she was sitting down for a drink with a gorgeous hunk of a man who she would have happily let punch her v-card, the next she was in Mr. Elliott's car on the way to his house so he could put her over his knee and spank her like a child who'd been caught misbehaving.

And the worst part of all of it wasn't even the burning humiliation or the looming threat of a painful punishment on the horizon. It was the thrum of desire low in her belly as she tried to imagine exactly what the rest of her evening would entail.

It was all Frankie's fault. She was the one who had

filled Lottie's head with all those ideas of how hot it was when her Daddy punished her, and now Lottie's libido was just confused.

That didn't stop her clit from throbbing painfully when Mr. Elliott pulled his sleek sports car into the garage and told her to stay put in that no-nonsense tone he'd been using with her all evening. A little voice in her head told her this was her chance to make a run for it. She'd run track in high school and if she left her shoes in the car she could make it to her house well before he was able to catch up with her.

But if she did that, she'd have to come clean to her father. Or risk Mr. Elliott doing so. And while she didn't regret the choice she'd made, no matter how badly everything had turned out in the end, she didn't want her father ever knowing what she'd done.

So when the door opened and Mr. Elliott held out a hand to help her out of the car, she drew on every ounce of courage she had and lifted her gaze to his. "I'll only go through with this on one condition."

"Do you really think you're in a position to be negotiating, little girl?"

Ignoring him, she tilted her chin up without breaking eye contact. *First rule of negotiation: never let the other person smell fear, even when you're fucking terri-*

fied. Especially when you're fucking terrified. "I don't want my father to know about any of this. Ever."

"Worried he'll cut you off?" Mr. Elliott winced. "I'm sorry, I didn't mean for that to come off the way it did. I just meant—"

"It's fine." It wasn't, because obviously he still saw her as a spoiled little girl who couldn't survive without Daddy's money. Which, to be fair, she was. "But, no. I just don't want him to worry about me. You've seen him. He's... fragile."

Surprisingly, Mr. Elliott's expression softened, making him look almost sympathetic. "Alright. This is just between us, then."

"Thank you." Placing her hand in his, she allowed him to help her out of the car. But instead of releasing her once she was on her feet, he pulled her into him, much like he'd done in his office.

"You played your hand too early, Lottie-bug," he murmured in her ear. "I would never want your father knowing about what I have planned for you tonight."

Oh, she was so fucked. "Let's just get this over with."

"So eager to get that pretty little bottom turned red. Come on, then. We'll take care of this in my office."

"Pink," she said primly as he led her into the house, still holding her hand in his.

"What?"

"You said my cosmopolitan would give you a color to match. Cosmos are pink, not red."

Pausing in front of his kitchen island, he turned to her. And, in yet another surprising move, threw his head back and laughed, the first genuine laugh she could remember hearing from him in what felt like forever. "You're right. I'll be sure to aim for a nice, bright pink instead."

"Thank you."

"Oh, believe me, it will be entirely my pleasure."

And there went her traitorous pussy again, making her weak in the knees just when she was feeling steady again. The bitch.

She tried not to think about how good it felt to have her hand firmly clasped in his, though she was pretty certain he was only holding it to keep her from bolting.

He finally released her when they reached his office, which was refreshingly modern, especially compared to the rich 'old-money' feeling of the club. The couch he pointed her toward was more comfortable than it looked, and she tried not to think about how it might feel beneath her as he pounded her into the cushions.

Jesus, girl, get a fucking grip.

Taking a seat in the middle of the couch, she

tossed her hair over her shoulder and lifted her gaze to his, refusing to be cowed despite the hammering of her heart against her ribcage. Mr. Elliott stood in front of her, arms crossed, and damn him if she didn't feel exactly like a naughty little girl about to get a lecture from her disappointed Daddy.

"All right, Charlotte. I'm going to give you one last chance to come clean. Why do you need that much money so badly you were willing to put yourself in harm's way to get it?"

Apparently he brought out the bratty little girl in her, because she immediately rolled her eyes at his question. "I didn't think it was dangerous, first of all, because I thought you were running it. And second of all, it's still none of your damn business why I wanted the money."

"Even if you thought I was running the auction, you should have known better than to sell yourself to a complete stranger."

"A stranger I assumed *you* had vetted and approved!"

Mr. Elliott raised an eyebrow. "And you really think that makes a difference?"

"Uh, duh."

"Watch the attitude, little girl." Sighing heavily, Mr. Elliott rubbed a hand over his face. "Fortunately for you, I can understand your logic. So I will make you a deal."

"What kind of deal?"

"You are still getting your mouth washed out for lying to my receptionist. But if you tell me why you wanted the money, you can forgo the spanking."

Fuck, that was a tempting offer. Though not as tempting as she wanted it to be. Because there was a not-insignificant part of her that desperately wanted to know what the fuss was all about. From the little bit she'd been able to see at the club, Frankie wasn't the only one who enjoyed being punished by her 'Daddy'. And Lottie's own libido was practically jumping up and down, screaming for him to do it.

The fear of the unknown and the potential pain paled in comparison to the burning need to *know*.

So even though she was positive she was going to regret it, she tilted her chin just a little higher. "I already told you, that's none of your fucking business, Mr. Elliott."

Maybe it was her imagination, but she could have sworn his eyes lit with anticipation at her response. "Have it your way, little girl."

BRADEN

He tried to tell himself he wasn't happy she refused the out he'd given her. But while his ex-wife may have begged to differ, he'd never been a very good liar.

Excitement raced along his nerves, but he forced himself to slow down. "Here's what's going to happen. We're going to go to the bathroom, where you will stand with a bar of soap in your mouth for a full minute to help wash all of those nasty lies. Then we'll come back in here, so I can give you the spanking you deserve for putting yourself in danger with that stupid auction. Do you know what a safeword is?"

"Yeah."

"Your safeword is 'red'. You can use it to stop anything that is more than you can handle, whether that's physically or emotionally."

The little brat raised her hand, like she was in school.

"Yes, Charlotte?"

"How am I supposed to say 'red' with soap in my mouth?"

"That's a very good question. Thank you for asking." He tried not to notice the way her eyes lit up at his praise. And he failed miserably. "If you can't speak, you can snap your fingers. Does all of that make sense?"

"I guess."

"Charlotte, as disappointed as I am in your behavior, I'm not proceeding with your punishment until you have fully consented. Say 'Yes, Sir' if you understand what I've told you and you consent to the punishment I've laid out for you."

"I wasn't aware I had an actual choice in the matter."

"You always have a choice, Charlotte."

"So what happens if I say no? Will you call Master O and have him cancel the transaction?"

"I could." But holding that over her head felt a little too much like blackmail for his tastes. "But no. If you decide to walk out of here without going through with your punishment, then that's that. You'll still be coming to work for me, to pay off your debt, but I won't hold it against you if you don't consent to being disciplined."

For several tense seconds, they simply stared at each other until she finally sighed. "Fuck. Fine. Yes, Sir. I understand. And consent."

"Good girl." Straightening, he held out his hand to her. "Let's go get all those lies washed out of your mouth, and then you can have your spanking."

Nose wrinkling with distaste, Lottie pouted up at him. "Couldn't you just spank me for all of it?"

"I believe the punishment should fit the crime.

When your mouth gets you in trouble, your mouth pays the price."

Of course, if she'd been *his*, her mouth would be paying the price in an entirely different manner. But if he let himself think about that too hard, he was going to end up doing something he'd regret for the rest of his life. His very short life, if Emmett ever got wind of what was happening here tonight.

"It wasn't even a very big lie," she grumbled under her breath as she pushed to her feet, completely ignoring his hand.

"Maybe not to you." Opening the door to the bathroom just off his office, he nudged her inside and flipped on the light. "But I take my members' safety very seriously. And I can't protect them if I let just anyone through the door."

As he knelt to pull a small bar of hotel soap from the cabinet below the sink, she huffed out an annoyed breath. "But I'm not just anyone. Would you have even needed to run a background check? Really, I was just saving us all some time."

He paused in the middle of unwrapping the bar to shoot her a hard glare. "You can keep looking for a loophole, Charlotte, but I promise you won't find one with me."

"That's not what I'm... fine," she admitted with a

roll of her eyes when he raised an eyebrow at her. "But it's still true!"

"Regardless of how well we know each other, I still put all of my members through the same vetting process. So, no, you weren't saving anyone time. And not only have you gotten yourself in trouble, Vivian has an appointment with Master James once her shift is over tomorrow." Inspiration struck, and he just managed to smirk. "I'm tempted to make you watch her punishment to help you remember not to involve other people in your lies going forward."

"What? But that's not fair! She didn't do anything wrong!"

That much was partially true. He couldn't fault Vivian for not wanting to stand up to a literal mob boss, or to someone who claimed to be close personal friends with her own boss. Which he planned to discuss with her before her scene, so she wouldn't be carrying any unnecessary guilt with her.

Luckily for him, Vivian was a hardcore masochist, and a fantastic actress. If he asked her to put on a show for Charlotte, she would gladly do so, and she would enjoy every second of Master James' attentions.

"Vivian knows what her duties are," he said, deliberately keeping his voice stern so he could watch the indignant fury spark in Charlotte's eyes. "And your lie encouraged her to circumvent those duties. You need to learn that your actions have consequences, Charlotte, and sometimes those consequences hurt other people."

Flipping the tap on, he ran the bar under the water until it was good and slick, then held it up to her mouth. "Open." When her mouth pressed into a thin line, he let his expression harden and put a good bit of steel behind his next words. "Open, Charlotte. You won't enjoy what happens if I have to make you."

"Right, because I'm going to like this so—"

He took advantage of her mouthing off to shove the bar of soap between her teeth. She immediately tried to spit it out, but he wrapped her hair around his fist, holding her head in place and the soap in her mouth.

"Settle down." The words were a whip crack of authority, designed to bring even the naughtiest subbies to heel.

It didn't work.

Fury turned the pale gray of her eyes to storm clouds as she fought against his hold for all she was worth. And as he was wrestling her into submission, a blinding pain, fiercer than anything he'd ever experienced, shot straight through from his groin through every nerve ending in his body.

"Jesus Christ!" Dropping the soap and her hair, he

grabbed his crotch, manfully fighting back the urge to whimper.

The little brat had kneed him in the balls.

It took him several deep breaths to realize she was scooping water into her mouth and spitting into the sink. When he finally had the pain under control, he straightened, wrapping her ponytail around his hand again to pull her up so that her head was tilted back, her smug gaze meeting his.

"You are going to pay for that, little girl."

9

I'M NOT YOUR DADDY

LOTTIE

Maybe a knee to the crotch wasn't the best choice of action when a man held the fate of your ass in his hands, but she hadn't even meant to do it. She'd just wanted to get away from that godawful soap, and the self-defense courses Portia had insisted they all take back in high school had kicked and the next thing she knew he was bent in half, groaning in pain.

Now she was staring up into furious blue eyes, seriously rethinking all of the life choices which had led her to this moment and simultaneously doing her best not to let him see how worried she was about the fate of her ass. "You really think you didn't deserve—"

"Quiet." He didn't snap at her, like he had when he'd told her to settle down after he'd shoved the soap in her mouth. This order was delivered in a deadly quiet tone, and her stomach clenched at the sound of it.

She was in so much fucking trouble.

"Good girl," he said in that same low, softly lethal tone when she didn't respond. "You will not speak again until I ask you a direct question, or otherwise give you permission to speak. If you say one word out of turn, I will put you on your knees and show you how I really punish mouthy, disobedient little subbies. Say 'Yes, Sir' if you understand."

"Yes, Sir," she whispered, her words constricted by the fear tightening her throat.

"Good girl. Now, I am going to take you into my office, and you are going to bend over the edge of my desk so I can turn that naughty little bottom of yours *cosmopolitan pink* before I take my ruler to your ass and teach you a lesson about what happens to bratty little girls who knee people in the balls during a well-earned punishment."

It wasn't funny. Logically, rationally, she knew it wasn't the least bit funny, especially with that icy fury still burning in his eyes.

But god help her if a tiny little giggle didn't escape before she managed to press her lips together.

"We'll see how funny you think it is when I'm through with you, little girl. Come on."

He used her hair to guide her back into the office, which forced her to scurry a bit to keep up with him if she didn't want him to pull on it. And beside the pain, there was the fact she paid an obscene amount of money for her hair to look as good as it did on a regular basis, and she didn't want his Neanderthal hands fucking it up.

She did, at least, have enough self-preservation not to tell *him* that.

When they stopped in front of his desk, he nudged her head down toward the sleek wood. "Bend at the waist, forearms and elbows on the desk, feet shoulder-width apart."

Figuring it was better not to poke the bear any more than she already had, she moved into position, the hair he'd just released falling down on either side of her like a curtain.

Something hard pressed against her right ankle, and it took her a moment to realize it was his foot, telling her to spread her legs wider. By the time she was positioned to his liking, she felt more on display and vulnerable than she'd ever felt in her life.

And then he pulled the hem of her dress up over her hips, and she wished for a Lottie-sized hole to open up and swallow her whole so she could escape the humiliation of knowing her father's best friend was staring right at her bare ass.

Of all the nights to wear a fucking thong.

"Such a pretty canvas," he murmured, so softly she almost didn't hear him. "I can't wait to see it painted pink." Resting one hand on her back, he raised his voice. "Stay in position, or it's an extra count of five with the ruler. Say 'Yes, Sir' if you understand."

"Yes, Sir," she managed to squeak out past the dryness threatening to close her throat entirely. A tremor racked her body as the full weight of her situation settled on her. Not only was she bent over his desk, with her ass completely on display, she was about to get her first-ever spanking.

Would it hurt? *Of course it's going to fucking hurt, dumbass.* Which left her wondering exactly *how much* it was going to hurt. What if she couldn't take it? What if, despite her bravado, she chickened out after the first swat because she was actually a big wimp?

"Good girl." Mr. Elliott's praise snapped her out of her anxiety spiral and back to the present.

She only had a moment to wonder about the strange warmth that pooled in her belly at his praise before his hand connected sharply with her bare ass. Motherfucker, that hurt so much more than she'd expected! What the hell did Frankie like about this?

Some part of her brain was screaming at her to fight him off and flee, but she didn't move a muscle, even when an equally hard swat landed on her other cheek. There was no guarantee she'd make it past the front door before he caught her, and she wasn't about to add anything more to what seemed like an already unbearable punishment.

And you deserve this.

Well, that little voice could shut right the hell up. Tolerating a spanking wasn't the same thing as accepting it. The only reason she was still here was to feed her own curiosity and to avoid making things worse. It had nothing to do with feeling as though she'd actually earned this punishment, or that she actually wanted it.

Liar.

Seriously. Fuck that little voice, whoever it belonged to.

Six solid swats landed before Mr. Elliott spoke again. "I don't know what possessed you to try and sell yourself to a random stranger online, but you will not do so again. I don't care how safe you think it is. Am I making myself clear, little girl?"

"Yes, Sir." The words were forced out through gritted teeth as her ass grew hotter and hotter with each swat, but she managed to say them all the same.

"There is absolutely nothing in this world more

important than your safety, Charlotte. Whatever it is you're wanting to buy, it is not worth you risking yourself to get it."

Tears pricked at her eyes, and once again she wished for that hole in the ground. Did he really think so little of her that he assumed she'd be willing to sell her virginity for spending money?

The truth burned on her tongue, and for a moment she was tempted to tell him everything. If for no other reason than to prove she wasn't the shallow, spoiled little rich girl he obviously thought she was.

But she still had enough pride left to keep that to herself. If he wanted to think so poorly of her, then fine. Let him. She had nothing to prove to him, or anybody else.

It seemed like forever he went on, peppering her bottom with sharp little slaps, occasionally interspersed with short lectures on being more careful, keeping herself safe, blah blah blah. By the time he stopped to ask if she'd learned her lesson, she very nearly sagged against the desk in relief.

"Yes, Sir. I'll be more careful." Hopefully she sounded more sincere than she felt.

She must have, because he patted her bottom lightly, and his tone was filled with warmth when he gave her another, "Good girl".

When she tried to stand up, however, the hand on her back pressed her back down into position. "We're not quite finished, Charlotte. That spanking was just for putting yourself in danger. You still have to answer for your behavior in the bathroom."

Oh, fuck. She'd completely forgotten about kneeing him in the groin. "Please, Sir. I've learned my lesson. I'll be a good girl forever." The plea in her voice was only somewhat fake. Even if she wasn't feeling very remorseful, she also didn't want any more spankings, especially with a ruler, which sounded a hell of a lot meaner than just his hand.

Then he ran his hand over her scorched skin, and her clit throbbed at his touch, making her wonder if maybe Frankie wasn't as crazy as she'd thought after all. "Naughty little girls always say the sweetest things when they're in the middle of getting their bottoms properly spanked," he said with a low chuckle. "Ten with the ruler, and then you're free to go, Charlotte."

She watched as he made his way around the desk. If she was going to escape, this was her best chance. But it was as though she'd been glued into place by some invisible force, and she could only stand there and watch as he pulled a long wooden ruler from the top drawer, running his hand over the pale wood almost lovingly.

Looking up from the ruler, his piercing gaze met

hers and he smiled, his teeth flashing in a way that made her stomach tighten and her pussy clench. "Ten, to remind you not to fight me the next time I decide you need that beautiful ass of yours reddened."

Next time?

She left the question unasked as he made his way back to stand beside her and tapped the ruler against her already aching bottom. "Count them out for me, Charlotte. One, Sir, two, Sir, etcetera."

"Yes, Sir."

The first swat from the ruler took her breath away, and the tears she'd managed to fight back filled her eyes once again. "One, Sir."

A second swat, just below the first, had her sucking in a sharp breath as the pain radiated across her skin. "Two, Sir."

At the third, she went up onto her toes with a squeal of pain. Goddammit, that hurt. "Etcetera, Sir."

"What?"

Surprise echoed through his tone, giving her the strength to draw in a deep breath and look over her shoulder at him with a smirk. "That's how you said to count. One, two, etcetera."

"Does this seem like a good time to get sarcastic with me, little girl?"

"I wasn't being sarcastic. I was following instructions. Sir."

The ruler snapped across the tops of her thighs, twice, making her cry out at the extra sting. "Just so we're clear, those didn't count. And neither did the 'etcetera' stroke. Starting again, at number three. Count correctly, or you will find sitting down comfortably to be very difficult tomorrow."

Worth it. "Yes, Sir."

Maybe it was her imagination, but sassing him seemed to make it easier to take the next few swats. It wasn't until they reached number six that her eyes welled with tears again. By number eight, her voice was thick with them, and by ten, those tears had slipped down her cheeks to splatter against the dark wood of his desk.

"All done, Lottie-bug," he said, his tone far more gentle than she would have expected. "Come here."

Despite knowing he was the one who had just put her through the most painful, humiliating ordeal of her life, she instinctively turned to him for comfort. Sniffling pitifully, she allowed herself to be wrapped up in his arms, her tears soaking into his shirt.

"That's a good girl," he murmured, rocking her gently from side to side. "Are you going to keep yourself safe from now on?"

"I'll try, Sir."

His chest rumbled with laughter. "I suppose that's

the best I could ask for. At least while you're working for me, I can keep an eye on you."

Pulling away slightly, she pouted up at him. "You're really going to make me work for you?"

"Yes. Unless you'd like to tell me the truth about why you signed yourself up for the auction."

Once again, the urge to tell him, to lay all of her worries and burdens at his feet, welled up inside her. And maybe it was the pain, maybe it was being cuddled by him after he'd so thoroughly punished her, but she found the words very nearly spilling out of her mouth. So she did the only thing she could think of to stop them.

She kissed him.

It was a move of pure desperation, and she thought for sure he would shove her away in disgust. But he didn't. For a moment, he simply froze, as if he wasn't sure exactly what was happening.

Only a moment, though, before he was kissing her back. And not just kissing her. *Devouring* her. Consuming her. As his arms tightened around her, she forgot all about the fact that she was supposed to be distracting him from his determination to learn her secrets, and she surrendered in a way she hadn't quite managed during her spanking. For one brief, shining moment, the world fell away. She was just a woman, being kissed breathless by a man.

"Fuck!" The word exploded out of him as he yanked away, his eyes filled with what looked far too much like regret for her comfort. "Lottie, I'm so sorry. I should never have… I'm so sorry."

"You didn't," she reminded him, putting her pride on the line to close the distance between them. "I did. And I want to do it again. I want to do more." Putting on what she hoped was a seductive smile, she tilted her head back and leaned into him. "Take me to bed… Daddy."

She knew before he spoke again it was the wrong thing to say. As soon as the word left her lips, the shutters slammed down over his eyes, closing him off from her. Wrapping his hands around her upper arms, he gently but firmly pushed her away. "You need to go. I'm not your Daddy, Charlotte, and you will not use that title without permission ever again. Am I making myself perfectly clear?"

Hurt and humiliation turned her face into an inferno. "Yes, Sir," she said stiffly.

Turning on her heel, she grabbed her purse from where she'd dropped it on the couch and hurried for the front door.

She didn't let the tears come until she was safely tucked away in her bedroom, where nobody could hear her shame.

10

REGRETS

BRADEN

*F*uck.

That wounded look in Charlotte's eyes was going to haunt him in his sleep, he just knew it.

But what else was he supposed to do? Taking her to bed as she'd requested was off the table.

Why?

Because she was his best friend's daughter, for fuck's sake.

So? It worked out for Damian. Why shouldn't you get a chance at what he has?

Annoyed with that little whisper of doubt in the back of his mind, Braden tossed the ruler he'd just used on Charlotte's perfectly round ass back into the desk drawer and slammed it shut. He stalked upstairs to his bedroom, not for the first time taking note of how big and empty the house seemed these days.

There'd been a time he'd dreamt of filling it with children. It was the whole reason he'd bought such a stupidly large house in the first place, even though Damian and Desmond had both rolled their eyes at him.

Well. Perhaps not the *whole* reason. He was self-aware enough to admit he enjoyed the status of the gated community with its spacious lots and towering mansions. But he had wanted a large family, too, and that had certainly factored into his purchase.

Then one thing had led to another, and the next thing he'd known Laura was gone, and she'd taken Aria with her.

He'd assumed he'd remarry again, at some point, so he kept the house. After all, he owned a kink club. He had no shortage of beautiful, submissive women in his life.

And yet, here he was, fifteen years after Laura had walked out of his life, and still all alone in this huge, empty, fucking house. Having completely inappropriate thoughts about the girl next door, who was less than five years older than his own daughter.

There was something seriously fucking wrong with him.

Not that it seemed to matter to his cock, which was still straining painfully against the zipper of his dress slacks.

Standing at the window that overlooked his side lawn and, from a distance, the Duvall house, he squeezed the bulge in his pants to give himself a bit of relief. But it wasn't nearly enough. Not when he could still taste Charlotte on his lips, could still feel the heat of her well-punished ass against his hand. The same hand he now used to free his aching cock from the confines of his slacks.

Guilt swirled with arousal in a shameful, intoxicating cocktail as he let the memory of Charlotte, bent over his desk with her bottom turning redder and redder under his ruler, play over in his mind. It was, without a doubt, the hottest fucking scene he'd been a part of in years, even if he hadn't meant for it to be the least bit erotic. He'd meant to teach her a lesson, nothing more.

Liar.

In an embarrassingly short amount of time, his cock swelled in his hand, and white jets of his cum splattered across the window. Breaths ragged, he leaned his forehead against the cool glass and closed his eyes.

He was the worst kind of asshole. Not just

because he'd so readily taken advantage of his best friend's daughter.

But because he couldn't wait to do it again.

LOTTIE

> Report to my office this evening at
> seven o'clock sharp. You'll be given
> a uniform and assigned a trainer
> after our discussion.

Glaring at her phone through puffy, tired eyes, Lottie just barely resisted the urge to throw it at the wall. He had some fucking nerve, ordering her around like that after he'd humiliated her and kicked her out of his home the night before. She was tempted to just ignore him. Master O had marked their transaction complete, and the money should be in her account any day now. Braden Elliott could go to hell, as far as she was concerned.

Just as she was giving serious consideration to the 'throw the phone against the wall so she wouldn't have to read his stupid message again' plan, Frankie's face popped up on the screen.

Shit. She hadn't even thought about what she was going to tell Frankie. But then, if anyone would know a way out of her current predicament, it would be Francesca Legare. Blowing out a breath, Lottie hit the button to answer the call. "Hey."

"Uh oh. Was he really that bad?" Sympathy wound its way around Frankie's words. "Do we need to call in reinforcements?"

Reinforcements meant calling the other girls in their group, and Lottie still wasn't quite ready to let them in on the truth of her situation. "No. Nothing like that. We never actually got to... you know."

"Really? What happened? Do you still get the money?"

"Yes, it's complicated, and yes." Groaning loudly, Lottie flopped onto her bed and stared up at the ceiling. "I met the guy who bought my you-know-what at the club. And he was fucking gorgeous. But I'm pretty sure he's in the mob or something."

"Holy shit. This is already a hell of a story. Go on."

"Well. He took me up to the bar area so we could have a drink, get to know each other. And then Mr. Elliott showed up."

"Going by the tone of your voice, I'm guessing that didn't exactly go well."

"Not in the least." The story came out, in halting stops and starts at first, but by the time she got to the part where Mr. Elliott had dragged her to his house for a spanking, she was practically word-vomiting in Frankie's ear.

"And then he stuck that fucking soap in my mouth and it was so gross I just sorta reacted and I kneed him in the balls and—"

"Wait! Wait, wait, wait. You kneed a Dom in the balls while you were in the middle of a punishment?"

Lottie let out a watery laugh and swiped at the tears she'd barely noticed streaming down her cheeks. "Out of this entire story, that's the part you find the most outrageous?"

"Umm, yes. I've met Braden Elliott. You are one brave, brave girl."

"Brave or stupid?"

There was a long pause, followed by Frankie's loud laugh. "I'm not entirely sure. Either way, I'm in awe of you. So what happened after you kneed him?"

"He took me back out to his office and spanked me. Hard. And then he used a ruler on me."

"Wood?"

"I think so. It looked like wood."

"Ouch. Poor Lottie."

"Definitely ouch. But after my spanking, he hugged me, and that was kinda nice, but then he started asking me about why I needed the money again and I kinda panicked and I might have sort of... kissed him."

"That's hot." Frankie's imitation of Paris Hilton's famous catchphrase was dead on. "Tell me he at least got you off, even if you didn't fuck."

"No. That was the worst part. One minute he was kissing me back and it was fucking amazing, the next he was practically patting me on the head and telling me to run along home. It was *humiliating*."

"Oh, honey. I'm sorry."

"It's fine. I don't even know what I was thinking. It's not like I'm attracted to him, everything was all scrambled up in my brain."

"Uh huh."

Lottie rolled her eyes. "I am not attracted to my father's best friend, Francesca."

"Sure. You just agreed to let him punish you in a very intimate way and kissed him. Totally no attraction there at all."

"I didn't really have a choice with the spanking, and the kiss was obviously a mistake."

"Lottie, babe, rule number one of BDSM, the submissive always has a choice. Even allowing those choices to be taken away is a choice. You could have put a stop to it at any second. I'm assuming he gave you a safeword."

He had, and he'd also demanded her explicit consent to punish her. "Yes, but—"

"But, what? But you were too curious to back out

and now you're trying to act like you didn't actually want him to punish you because you're embarrassed by how it ended?"

"I hate you a little right now, I just want you to know that."

"Would it help if I pointed out that he's obviously attracted to you, too?"

"What?" Lottie let out a derisive snort. "No, he's not."

"Of course he is. If he wasn't, he would have just called your dad to come and pick you up at the club. He sure as hell wouldn't have taken you back to his home to spank you. And he definitely wouldn't have kissed you back."

Staring up at her ceiling, Lottie replayed the night before in her mind. "I called him Daddy. He told me never to call him that again without permission."

"See?" Frankie's tone was triumphant. "If he wasn't attracted to you, he would have just told you never to call him that again. The 'without permission' part means he's open to it."

"Then why the hell didn't he take me to bed? Why kick me out?"

"Umm... duh? You're his *best friend's daughter*. Any man with half a conscience would be fighting that attraction tooth and nail right now. So, props to him, honestly, for trying to do the right thing."

It made sense, in a very convoluted, messy kind of way. Just the thought of a man as gorgeous and powerful as Mr. Elliott being attracted to her made her feel gorgeous and powerful in her own right.

For years, she'd been holding back on getting her cherry popped because nobody had ever met her standards. But Mr. Elliott checked all her boxes. He was hot, successful, charming when he wanted to be, and he cared for her. The latter was, and always had been, the real sticking point for her.

So why shouldn't she give him what he'd paid for?

Sitting up in bed, Lottie crossed the room to her closet and scanned the contents. "Hey, Frankie?"

"Yeah?"

"Wanna come over and help me pick out an outfit for my first day at my new job?"

She could practically hear Frankie's grin through the phone. "I would love to."

11

PUSHING HIS BUTTONS—
AND HERS

BRADEN

She was late.

And not just a little late. By quarter 'til eight, he was pacing his office as he contemplated calling her again to see where she was. Not that she'd answered any of his other calls, the little brat. If she'd been anyone else, he would have happily texted her and told her not to bother coming in. But part of him wondered if that wasn't secretly what she wanted. After all, he was the one who would be out nearly half a million dollars if she didn't come to work for him.

Needless to say, by the time his office door opened, and she sauntered in wearing a white dress that hugged every curve of her body, somehow both reminding him violently of the innocence she still had intact and making him want things he had no business wanting, he wasn't in the best of moods. "You're late."

"Fashionably late," she shot back with a sassy smirk, cocking her hip to the side in a way that brought his attention to her impossibly long legs and the high, white heels that would undoubtedly be killing her feet by the end of her shift.

Dragging his eyes away from her legs, he forced his gaze back up to her face, and the dramatic makeup she'd chosen for the night that made her look much older than she was. Old enough that he could almost make himself believe he wouldn't be risking the most important friendship in his life if he actually did allow her to fulfill her contract the way she'd originally intended.

Almost. But not quite. "There is no such thing as fashionably late for work, Charlotte. Spanking or lines?"

Her eyes went round in her face, but he didn't miss the spark of excitement in the pale gray. "What?"

"Your punishment for being tardy. Would you prefer a spanking or writing 'I will not be late' two hundred times?"

Disciplining an employee this way was ethically

murky at best. He was fairly certain it was downright illegal. But the thought of getting pretty little Charlotte Duvall over his knee again was just too tempting to pass up.

Her tongue darted out, wetting her lips, and he just barely resisted the urge to groan. "Spanking, please."

If there was a stairway to heaven, he was taking the express elevator to hell. "Very well. Come here."

Taking her hand, he guided her over to the long black couch at the opposite end of his office, where he sat and pulled her down over his lap. His cock twitched painfully as he pushed the hem of her dress up over her hips to reveal the perfect pale globes of her ass. There wasn't a mark on her from the night before, and he wondered if she was still sore at all.

Obviously not, if she was testing him so soon.

Cupping one cheek in his hand, he squeezed, his cock twitching at the feel of her soft skin in his palm. "You will be on time from now on. If you are running late, you will text me as soon as you are able to. The next time I have to punish you for this, you will receive one swat of the paddle for every minute you are late. Am I understood, little girl?"

"Yes, Sir."

She didn't sound the least bit apologetic, but he figured he could change that quickly enough. Wrapping one arm around her waist, he lifted his free hand and brought it down on her ass with a *smack* that echoed around his office.

God, he loved that first swat. The way the skin turned white under his hand before he pulled it away to watch as that first pink handprint appeared. He gave himself a moment to admire it before really getting to work.

It didn't take long for her tone to change. Her bottom was barely pink when she began squirming over his lap. "Okay, okay, I'm sorry! I won't be late again!"

"I'm very glad to hear that." But he'd been punishing naughty little girls like her for long enough to know that they would say anything to stop a punishment well before they were actually remorseful. So he kept spanking, ignoring her cries and pleas as he reddened her beautiful bottom.

Charlotte's begging filled the air, and by the time he shifted the focus of his swats to her sit-spots, his cock was so hard he worried that a stray touch from her might set him off.

By the time he capped the spanking off with six extra-hard swats, she was sniffling pitifully over his knee. Another woman, another time, he would have slipped his hand between her thighs to test how wet she was. Even without doing so, he could smell her arousal in the air, and his hand drifted lower, lower.

Another sorrowful sniffle from her managed to snap him out of his trance before he did something they'd both regret. "Come here, Lottie-bug. It's all over."

She scrambled to sit up, wrapping herself around him as he rocked her gently, rubbing his hand in circles over her back. Fucking hell, he'd missed this. Aftercare was one of his favorite parts of a scene, and it had been far too long since he'd allowed himself to indulge. Normally, he negotiated to have someone else care for a submissive he scened with, but not only had he not set that up prior to punishing Charlotte, the idea of letting anyone else hold her, comfort her, made him want to rage.

"Are you going to be late again?" he asked softly.

Another of those pitiful little sniffles that simultaneously made him want to snuggle her closer and put her on her knees so he could look down into those tearful blue eyes as she swallowed his cock. "No, Sir."

"Good girl."

To his surprise, she snuggled closer. "I probably shouldn't like that so much."

"Shouldn't like what? Being called a good girl?"

"Yes. It's not very feminist of me. And I'd slap the

fuck out of anybody else who said that to me, but when you say it... I feel all... tingly."

She squirmed, grinding her crotch against his leg so he was left with no doubt as to where exactly she was feeling *tingly*. Where the hell had this come from? "Charlotte..."

"I'm sorry. It's just, I've never felt like this with anyone before." There was an unmistakable plea in her voice, so different from the defiant and cocky woman she'd been the night before it was hard to believe it was the same person snuggled on his lap.

And god, he wanted to give her what she was so clearly asking for. If he'd ever wanted anything more in his entire life, he couldn't remember. Moving of its own accord, his hand drifted down to her hip, stroking the soft, bare skin. Charlotte whimpered, grinding herself against his leg again, and he closed his eyes against the wave of guilt crashing over him.

"Sir, please. I need... please."

Never in his life had he failed to give a submissive what they needed after a scene. He enjoyed making a naughty girl wait for her pleasure, but this wasn't the same. If she'd been his babygirl, he would have happily teased her, drawing out her punishment until she was a whining, whimpering mess. And while part of him longed to do exactly that, Charlotte wasn't his. Keeping on her edge the rest of the evening would just distract her from her work, and it wouldn't be fair to her.

Better to give her a quick orgasm so she could focus on her training. Even as he made the decision, a part of him recognized it as the weak rationalization it was for him to finally get his hands on her. But God help him, he couldn't find the strength to care.

"Do you want me to make you come, Charlotte?"

"Yes, Sir. Please." Her response was as immediate as it was eager, which helped to ease some of the guilt gnawing at his stomach.

"Back over my knee then, little one."

"No! I don't want another spanking!"

It was adorable that she thought he wouldn't simply flip her over if he felt she needed her bottom warmed again. "You're not getting another spanking, Charlotte. I'm going to help you feel better."

"Oh." Perfect white teeth nibbled at her bottom lip, making her look impossibly young and adding more weight to the lead ball of guilt in his gut. "You promise you're not going to spank me again?"

"Just trust me, little one."

Everything about her seemed to light up from within. "I do."

"Then get back over my knee, before I decide you do need another spanking for not doing as you're told."

That got her moving. With a shocked little squeak, she hurried to drape herself back across his lap, her pink bottom propped up over one thigh.

This is just a scene. It doesn't mean anything. "Can I pull your pretty panties down, Charlotte?"

"Yes, Sir."

She helpfully raised her hips so he could peel the barely-there thong down and off her long legs. When she was completely bared to him, he indulged himself for just a moment, stroking his hand over the warm flesh of her well-spanked ass. Lower and lower until the tips of his fingers brushed against her equally bare pussy.

Her bare, absolutely *soaked* pussy.

He was so fucked.

Gritting his teeth against his own painful arousal, he slid a finger inside her. And although he knew enough about human anatomy to know her virginity didn't actually make her any tighter, it certainly seemed as though she was impossibly tight around his finger as he slowly pumped it in and out of her pussy, a pale mimicry of the act he truly wished to be committing with her.

"Oh!" Charlotte's startled gasp had his lips curving up in a smile as she lifted her hips again, this time to press herself more firmly against his hand. "That feels... amazing."

"Has nobody ever touched you here before, Charlotte?" He had no right to ask, but once again his blasted curiosity was getting the better of him.

"Not like this, Sir," she admitted in a breathless whisper.

"Has any man ever made you come, little one?"

"No, Sir. Never."

"Then I'll happily be your first." *And your only*.

Shaking off the swell of possessive need, he focused on pleasuring her, the way she should have experienced long before she'd ended up over his knee. With every stroke of his finger, he discovered something new about her. What she liked, what she didn't. What made her sigh with pleasure, and what made her cry out with need.

"That's a good girl," he crooned when her pussy tightened even further around his finger. "Are you going to come for me, Charlotte?"

"Y-yes, Sir!"

"Come, little one. Let me feel that sweet virgin pussy squeezing my fingers."

"Oh, god. Oh, god. Mr. Elliott!"

Bucking over his lap, she came with a loud cry, her pussy spasming around his fingers just as he'd demanded. "Good girl," he rasped out, his voice tight with desire as he continued stroking her, drawing every ounce of pleasure from her body until she collapsed over his lap, sweat beading on her brow and a dreamy smile curving her lips.

It would be so easy to flip her over and slide right into that hot, soaking wet pussy. And damn him if he wasn't tempted.

But his ears were still ringing with the sound of her calling his name as she'd come. Not Daddy, or even Braden. Mr. Elliott. Because she wasn't just some submissive he'd planned a scene for. She was as off-limits as they came, and he would do well to remember it.

Still, she deserved the attention he would give any submissive after a scene, and so he helped her back up onto his lap. "Come here, little one."

With a happy hum, she snuggled into his chest. "I should probably offer to suck your dick or something but I'm feeling too good to move just yet. Give me a few minutes and I might be up to it."

"Have you ever sucked a cock?"

"No. A couple of guys in high school tried to sweet talk me into it but I very firmly declined." Grinning more widely now, she tilted her head back. "I'd do it for you, though. If you taught me how."

Temptation incarnate. That's what she was. "Perhaps another time. For now"—he made a show of lifting his wrist to check his watch before pinning her with a stern glare—"you're more than an hour late for your shift. I'll call Delia and have her meet you up here. And I should warn you, she has strict orders to report any misbehavior directly to me. So unless you'd like to be sent home with an even sorer bottom than you have now, I suggest you do as she tells you."

Annoyance flashed across her features, wiping away her smile. It surprised him how sad he was to see it go. "I'm not a total fuck-up, you know."

"I never said you were. But you seem to enjoy pushing buttons, and I want there to be no misunderstandings between us." Gripping her chin, he matched her defiant glare. "Any disobedience, back talk, or general bad behavior will end up with either my hand or any number of implements turning that naughty bottom of yours bright red. Am I perfectly understood, Charlotte?"

"Yeah. Yes, Sir," she corrected herself with an eye roll when he raised a brow.

"Good girl. There's a bathroom just off the office for you to freshen up while I call for Delia. Go."

Huffing loudly, she shoved up from his lap and stalked toward the bathroom. When the door shut behind her, Braden forced himself to stand and walk to his desk to make the call.

Charlotte took her time in the bathroom, which suited him just fine. It meant he didn't have to deal with the temptation of her pouty mouth while he waited for Delia to knock on his door.

The knock came just as Charlotte was stepping out of the bathroom. He opened the door and Delia bounced in, all bright smiles and blonde curls as usual. "Hi! You must be Charlotte! I'm Delia. I hope you don't mind me saying so but holy *fuck* you are gorgeous. Let me see you smile."

Charlotte sent him a smug look before flashing a bright smile for Delia, who squealed happily in response. "Oh, our customers are going to love you. Come on, I can't wait for you to meet the rest of the staff!"

"Thank you, Delia. Would you make sure she eats something and drinks a bottle of water before her shift?"

The request clearly went over Charlotte's head, but Delia paused in the doorway to raise an eyebrow. "Of course. Anything else I should know?"

"Let me know if she gives you any trouble. Otherwise, that should be all."

The glare Charlotte sent his way would have been lethal for a lesser man. As it was, he was half tempted to check and see if she'd drawn blood. "You do realize I'm still standing right here and I haven't been suddenly struck deaf, right?"

Laughing maniacally, Delia looped her arm

through Charlotte's. "We are going to be the *best* of friends, Char. Can I call you Char?"

"My friends call me Lottie."

"That's adorable. Come on, Lottie. We'll get you fed and hydrated, and I'll tell you all the good club gossip."

Silently wondering if he'd just signed his own death warrant, Braden watched the door close behind them, cutting off Lottie's laughter at something Delia had said. Feeling as if he'd just run a fucking marathon, he made his way back to the couch, dropping down onto the cushions with a sigh. A flash of white caught his attention and he reached over to pick up the thong he'd peeled from Charlotte's body before finger-fucking her to a screaming orgasm over his lap.

No longer able to deny himself, he freed his cock from his pants and wrapped the soft material around his throbbing length. Dropping his head back against the couch, he closed his eyes and let the scene from earlier play out in his mind until his cum filed the gusset of her pretty silk panties. Only this time, when Charlotte came, it wasn't 'Mr. Elliott' she screamed.

In his fantasies, she cried out for her Daddy as she creamed all over his hand.

12

DESPERATE MEASURES

LOTTIE

Everything *hurt*. Her feet, her arms, her head. The only thing, ironically enough, that didn't ache by the time she stumbled into her house at almost two a.m. was her butt. Which just made her even poutier as she forced herself to shower and dry her hair before finally falling into bed.

Rolling onto her back, she picked up her phone from where she'd tossed it onto her nightstand and typed out a text to Frankie.

Operation Daddy Next Door is a go!

Despite the late hour, it was less than thirty seconds before the reply came through.

Oh?? Tell me EVERYTHING you ho.

You called it. He totally spanked me for being late. And then he made me come harder than I've ever come in my life. It was AWESOME.

Told you! Daddies can't resist an opportunity to teach a naughty girl a lesson. You gonna be late tomorrow too?

Idk, he said he'd use a paddle if I was late again so I may have to think of another way to get him to spank me. Maybe if I'm not too naughty he'll let me suck his cock this time.

Wait. Did he turn down a blowjob? Dude's got it bad.

Really? I sorta thought maybe he just didn't want one from me.

I've yet to meet a man who would turn down a blowie from a willing woman. Except in smutty books where he's making himself wait because she "matters" and he doesn't want to fuck it up.

Maybe. Trying not to get my hopes
up too high here.

Trust me. Braden Elliott wants to
pop all your cherries, Lottie-baby. He
just has to play the tortured hero a
bit first.

Clutching that knowledge close to her chest, Lottie drifted off to sleep, her dreams full of Mr. Elliott towering over her while she got her very first taste of a man's cock.

⌘

It was a solid week before she had a chance to make her dreams a reality. Not only was she hesitant to show up late again thanks to Mr. Elliott's promise to paddle her the next time it happened, she couldn't even seem to get herself in trouble at work no matter how hard she tried.

Delia was too nice, Lottie decided. Even when Lottie deliberately messed things up, Delia would give her the verbal equivalent of a pat on the head, show her the right way to do whatever it was she'd messed up, and send her on her way with a wink and a smile. Lottie almost felt guilty for continually fucking up on purpose.

Almost.

The one bright spot in her life was the money that had been deposited into her personal account. When it showed up Wednesday morning, Lottie took herself out for a mini shopping spree and lunch with Frankie to celebrate. But for once in her life, she actually paid attention to exactly how much she was spending in each store, and she resisted the urge to splurge on her favorite lunch spot, opting instead for a less expensive but no less delicious bistro in downtown Charleston.

Other than that one shopping trip, however, she was careful not to spend any of the money until she figured out a way to pay down her father's debts. For one thing, she had no idea where to even start. When she'd been able to sneak back into his office, she'd realized with a sinking stomach that what she'd made from the auction was only enough to pay off a couple of their credit cards, or to pay their mortgage for a couple of years. Which should have been enough considering her parents had bought this house before she'd been born, but she'd uncovered some paperwork from where he'd apparently borrowed against the house. Probably to continue funding his fucking gambling habit.

Paying the mortgage seemed more pressing, but what had even been the point of selling her virginity if they were just going to be in the same position two years from now? But then again, if she paid off the credit cards and he just ran them up again with his gambling addiction, they could potentially be in an even worse situation.

Needless to say, she was already feeling down and defeated when Portia called, inviting her to a girls' weekend at her family's house in the Hamptons. Three days on the beach, with nothing more stressful than what drink to order next sounded positively heavenly.

She could use some of the auction money for the trip. If she was careful, it wouldn't even put that big of a dent in her account since they'd be traveling on Portia's jet. And she had today and tomorrow off anyway, so she'd just have to fake being sick for a couple extra days, and make sure her friends didn't tag her in any of their social media posts.

But she'd made a promise to Mr. Elliott, and even though she'd much rather be packing for a trip to the Hamptons, she was determined to show him she wasn't just the spoiled little rich girl he seemed determined to paint her as.

"Sorry, babe. I can't make it this time. Rain check?"

"Please, please, please, Lottie? If you don't come I'll have to listen to Eva and Frankie talk about their latest sexual exploits all weekend. They don't talk about that stuff nearly as much when you're around."

The thought of prim and proper Portia sulking her way through an entire weekend of sexual depravity actually made it a little easier to do the right thing. "I really wish I could, but I've already got plans."

"What kind of plans?" Portia's tone turned suspicious. "Like, plans with a man?"

"Yes." It wasn't *entirely* a lie, and Lottie damn well wasn't going to tell Portia the full truth. "We're spending the weekend together at his place."

"That sounds serious. Where did you meet this man?"

Lottie couldn't help but smile at her friend's concern. "He's a family friend. I've known him forever."

"All right." But her tone clearly said she still had doubts. "Just don't do anything Frankie would do."

"I won't."

Another little white lie. Because as soon as the words left Portia's mouth, an idea began to form in Lottie's mind.

Francesca Legare would never sit around, pining after a man. If he didn't respond to her advances, she'd find a way to make him come to her. And Lottie had seen that exact scenario play out enough times to know exactly what Frankie would do.

BRADEN

Thank god Charlotte was scheduled off for the next two days. Watching her prance around his club, clad in increasingly skimpy outfits while his members openly ogled her was starting to wear on him. One more night and he was bound to drag her down to the pit so he could fuck her in front of God and everyone.

And if it meant throwing his weight around a bit to give her two nights in a row off, well, what was the point in being the owner of a club if you couldn't use your position to get your way from time to time?

For the first time in a week, he felt like he could breathe again in his own club. As long as he ignored the little itch between his shoulder blades at the thought of her being out of his sight for an entire evening.

"Good evening, gentlemen." Stopping by a large corner booth where Elias Turner, commonly known as 'Ice' to his millions of fans around the world, was sharing a drink with another of the club's long-time patrons, Braden flashed them both a welcoming smile.

They were a bit of an odd pair, Ice with his long, slightly unkempt hair and the beard he'd been growing out since he'd randomly shown up in South Carolina months ago. And Beckett Stone, clean-cut and still clad in the suit he'd probably been wearing since the crack of dawn. Beckett wasn't just the owner of Club BDE's favorite investment firm, he was hands down the strictest, most controlling Dom Braden had ever met. Compared to Ice's laidback rockstar demeanor, they couldn't have been more opposite if they'd tried. But from what Braden had seen, they'd become fast friends once Ice had shown up at the club. "I trust you're all enjoying yourselves?"

It was a tongue-in-cheek reference to the club submissive currently kneeling between them, her back serving as a table for their whiskey glasses. Judging by the look of pure bliss on her face, she was enjoying herself just as much, if not more, than they were.

Beckett held up his whiskey with a smirk. "As always." His grin widened. "Though we would certainly be enjoying ourselves more if we'd been able to get our hands on your new girl tonight before she'd gotten snatched up."

"New girl?" Braden's heart tripped in his chest as he tried to think of another 'new girl' besides…

"Lottie, I think her name is? Tall, dark hair, legs for fucking days." Now it was Ice who smiled, though it lacked the same wicked gleam as Beckett's. Despite his near-constant presence in the club, Braden hadn't ever actually seen him play with anyone.

"You must be mistaken." But even to his own ears, the words sounded hollow. "Lottie is an employee, not a member. She isn't available for scenes."

Beckett's brow raised, amusement clearly stamped across his face. "You should probably let Killian know that, then."

At Beckett's nod toward the pit, Braden spun around and leaned over the railing. Sure enough, there was Charlotte, naked as the day she was born, bound to a St. Andrew's cross. Killian stood beside her, stroking a hand down her spine as they shared what was clearly a private, intimate conversation.

He should let her have her fun. Killian was an excellent Dom, even if Braden didn't trust him as far as he could throw him outside the club. And Braden had absolutely no claim on Charlotte's person.

But even as his mind checked off all the reasons he had no business interrupting their scene, his feet were already moving, heading down the curved staircase to the pit, where Killian was putting on a show for their audience by 'warming up' with his favorite flogger, swinging it in complex circles as the crowd watched in awe.

Helpless, Braden watched, too far away to stop him as Killian stepped up behind the cross and took aim at Charlotte's pale, unmarked skin. Braden reached the platform just as Killian raised the flogger.

"*Red!*"

Everything around them screeched to a halt, and dozens of shocked stares turned toward him. But Braden ignored all of them as he climbed the stairs onto the platform, placing himself between Killian and Charlotte.

"What are you doing?" Charlotte demanded in a low, furious hiss.

"Hush. I'll deal with you in a moment, little girl." Fury churning in his gut, Braden lifted his gaze to Killian's face.

Which looked, Braden realized with a start, completely unsurprised by this turn of events. If anything, he looked downright... amused. And more than a little triumphant.

It's a fucking setup.

"Is there a reason you interrupted my fully consensual, negotiated scene?" Killian asked, deliberately raising his voice so the audience could clearly hear his words.

Goddammit. He was stuck. Even if he stepped down, the juiciest piece of gossip in his club would be everyone wondering why he'd tried to stop a scene that hadn't broken a single club rule.

Worse, perhaps, was the knowledge that if he backed down now, he'd have to watch Charlotte submit to another man. He'd be forced to sit back and watch as someone who wasn't him drew those breathless cries of pain and pleasure from his lips. And, depending on what they'd negotiated, he'd have to watch as she came apart at another man's touch.

The thought of watching all of that unfold, with Killian of all people, had him seeing red. Which basically left him with two options. One, fire Charlotte and ban her from the club, which was admittedly an appealing prospect other than the fact that he didn't actually have a *reason* to ban her from the club. And, if he did that, he couldn't keep an eye on her. At least if she was at the club, she was playing safely. If he kicked her out, there was no telling where she might go to satisfy her curiosity.

Then there was the second option: Claim her as his own. Teach her. Corrupt her. Mold her into his own, perfect little subbie.

Maybe his conscience was conflicted. But his heart already knew the answer.

"She's mine."

He ignored the shocked whispers from the crowd as Killian cocked an eyebrow. "Is that so? She isn't wearing a collar."

"I'll be rectifying that as soon as humanly possible, I can assure you."

"Lottie darling." Again, Killian raised his voice for their audience's benefit. "Is this true? Is Braden your Daddy?"

A long, tense silence followed Killian's question. So long, in fact, Braden was just about ready to say damn the consequences and unhook her from that blasted cross when Lottie's voice rang out, loud and clear.

"Yes. Yes, he's my Daddy."

13

I OWN YOU, CHARLOTTE DUVALL

LOTTIE

Success.

God, she loved it when a plan came together. And while Killian had played his part perfectly, Mr. Elliott had stolen the show. She had a feeling she'd be getting herself off to the way he'd growled, "She's mine" for a long, long time.

"Ah, well, my apologies. I'll leave you to it, then. I'm sure you have much to discuss with your naughty girl."

Alarm bells rang in Lottie's mind and she yanked helplessly at the chains connecting her wrists to the metal cross Killian had attached them to for their plan. He wasn't supposed to be encouraging Mr.

Elliott to punish her! That wasn't the plan! "Killian! Wait!"

"Quiet," Mr. Elliott said, his voice taking on a commanding quality she hadn't heard before. "The only words I want to hear out of your mouth right now are an apology to Master Killian for involving him in your disobedience."

It wasn't technically 'disobedience' since she hadn't been his submissive when she'd asked Master K to help her with her plan. But in order to point that out, she'd have to admit she lied in front of an entire crowd of people. And she had a feeling that confessing her lie would only earn her a worse punishment than the one she was probably about to get.

"I'm sorry, Master Killian. I should have been honest with you about my relationship with Mr. Elliott."

"Thank you for the pretty apology, Lottie darling. And I'm sure your Daddy will happily impress on you the importance of honesty and communication, especially within a dynamic like yours. Good luck."

"You double-crossed me!" she whispered when he leaned in to brush a kiss across her cheek.

"Aye, I did. But only because I think you're a lovely girl, and this could have ended very poorly for you if you'd chosen anyone other than me for your little scheme. You deserve the very sore bottom you're about to get, little girl."

"You're mean."

"And you're a brat. Have fun, love. Braden, she's all yours."

The shiver that raced up her spine as Mr. Elliott took Killian's spot beside her was more fear than excitement, but still it made her pussy clench with need. A hand rested on her bottom, and she very nearly whimpered as the seriousness of her situation began to set in.

"Now… what to do with my naughty little Lottie-bug, hmm? Should I leave you chained up while I play with that sweet pussy of yours until you're begging me to let you come? Perhaps I should send for my play bag so I can pick up where Master Killian left off and flog you until every inch of your skin is nice and pink before I fuck that pretty ass of yours. Or, since you insist on acting like a child at every turn, maybe I should take you to the nursery for a bit and let you be a naughty little baby until you get it out of your system."

"I am not acting like a child," she snapped, yanking once more at her chains.

"No?" Wrapping her ponytail around his hand, he pulled her head back, and she felt that same rush of fear and desire as before. "Breaking rules on purpose just to see what my reaction would be, pulling an elaborate prank just so you could get your way... None of that sounds childish to you?"

Guilt wrapped around her torso and squeezed. "That's not... You're making it sound worse than it was."

"Am I? Or are you so used to having everything you could possibly want handed to you on a silver platter that you couldn't stomach being denied one thing, even if it was for your own good?"

"I think I should be able to decide what's for my own good."

"That ship has long since sailed, little one. You wanted a Daddy, and now you've got one. I own you, Charlotte Duvall, and you're about to learn *exactly* what that means."

It wasn't until that very moment that she began to question her plan to lose her virginity to a man like Braden Elliott. Even when he'd spanked her that first time, she'd felt safe with him. Cared for. Cherished in a way she hadn't felt in a very long time.

Now... well, now she was wondering what the fuck she'd gotten herself into.

"Mr. Elliott, I—"

"Daddy."

Desire and fear stole her breath. "Wh-what?"

"It's Daddy to you now, little girl. I want to hear you say it."

What had come so easily before now seemed to stick in her throat. The hand holding her ponytail tugged, sending little pinpricks of pain through her skull. "Say it, Charlotte, or you'll lose any chance you have of being allowed to come tonight."

"Daddy!" The word burst out of her, spurred on by the threat of having her pleasure denied.

"Good girl. Since you're already chained up so prettily, I think we'll go ahead and handle your punishment now."

"No!"

"Excuse me?"

There was something dark and dangerous in his tone, letting her know immediately she'd made a mistake. "I-I just mean, can we go to your office? Please, Daddy?"

"No, I don't think so. You had no problem putting me on the spot in front of my entire club, so you can accept the consequences of your actions publicly as well." He turned toward a stunning brunette who had stopped to watch the show, her eyes wide in her pale, delicate face. "Ivy, would you mind terribly running up to my office to grab my play bag for me? It's the black duffel under my desk."

"Yes, Sir."

The brunette hurried off, and Lottie turned her head toward Mr. Elliott—Daddy—letting her bottom lip tremble and her eyes fill with moisture. "Daddy, please. I'm really sorry. I just didn't know how else to get your attention."

"Oh, Lottie-bug. You've had my attention from the moment I saw you at that table with Killian O'Rourke the first night you came to my club. What you *wanted*, was to force my hand, and you succeeded."

Well, she couldn't deny that. "What"—she paused to swallow past the dryness in her throat—"What are you going to do to me?"

"I'm going to do exactly what I said I would do that first night, little one. I'm going to hurt you. Because you were a very naughty girl, and more importantly... simply because I want to."

There was absolutely zero logical reason why those words should make her clit throb and her pussy clench with need. But she couldn't deny that her body had exactly that reaction, even if it still baffled her.

Daddy turned away again as the brunette approached with a black bag that was almost as large as she was. Despite the size, she didn't seem to be struggling, and Lottie vaguely wondered what kind of workout plan she was on.

She didn't have long to wonder about it before Daddy took the bag and thanked her, then placed it on the podium directly in Lottie's line of sight. Bound as she was, she was helpless to do anything more than simply watch as he removed item after item from his bag of tricks. A flogger, which she recognized thanks to Killian's brief tutorial before they'd come down to the pit. Something in a plastic container that looked like a 3D rendering of the spades on playing cards and a bottle of clear liquid. And a silver ring with two strips of leather attached.

It was the ring he held in his hand as he rose to his feet and approached the cross again. "Open."

"What's that?"

Daddy cocked an eyebrow, but didn't scold her for questioning him, which she appreciated. "It's a device to keep naughty little girls from telling lies, while also keeping their mouths open for anything their Daddy wants to use it for. Open, Charlotte. I won't tell you a third time without consequences."

Unwilling to test him considering how much trouble she was obviously in already, Lottie forced her lips apart. The steel ring settled just behind her teeth, forcing her mouth to stay open as he fixed the leather bands around her head.

"Perfect," he said in a low rumbling tone she

didn't recognize. "I can't wait to see how that pretty mouth of yours looks wrapped around my cock."

Another wave of need hit her, and she was fairly certain if she hadn't been attached to the cross it would have driven her to her knees.

"Now for your next accessory, little one."

Fear added a layer to the desire coiling in her belly as she watched him return to the pile of things near his bag and pick up the spade looking thing and the bottle of liquid. He ripped open the plastic covering the spade thing and held it up for her to see. "Do you know what this is, Charlotte?"

Considering he'd deliberately put something in her mouth to keep her from talking, it seemed like an asshole move to start asking questions now. She glared at him to let him know exactly what she thought of his question, then shook her head.

"It's a plug. Any guesses on which hole it's meant to fill?"

Another glare, another shake of her head.

"Well, it isn't your mouth, I can assure you. So what do you think? Ass or pussy?"

Hearing polite, well-spoken Mr. Elliott use such crass language had heat rushing to Lottie's cheeks. She shrugged, unwilling to try and guess, especially with her mouth full of metal.

"Ah, well, I suppose it will be a surprise, then."

It didn't stay a secret for long. Moving to stand behind her again, he cupped one cheek in his hand and pulled, exposing her bottom hole to the crowd on the floor. Humiliation flooded her, heating her entire body and making her stomach roll.

How much could they see? Getting naked in front of a crowd hadn't seemed like such a big deal when Master Killian had suggested it, but this was so much more. This was allowing an entire group of people to see parts of her she'd kept hidden her entire adult life.

And yet, even as the humiliation grew hotter, so did her rising need. The knowledge that she was on full display, that everyone knew she'd been naughty and now she was being punished by her Daddy made her pussy ache more than anything she'd ever experienced. Certainly more than the few ham-fisted groping sessions she'd experienced at the hand of boys her own age.

If this was what Frankie had felt with her own Daddy, no wonder she'd been going back for more.

Something cold hit her exposed hole, making her squeal. What the hell was that?

It was wet along with being cold, whatever it was. Lube, maybe, which made sense if he was planning to shove something up her ass.

Jesus, what a night.

Closing her eyes, she tried to block out the now-silent crowd as he pressed a finger into her, breaching that most private place. It didn't escape her notice that she was letting a man finger-fuck her ass before she'd even popped her cherry.

But then, she'd never been one to do things the traditional way.

"Such a tight little asshole," Daddy murmured in her ear. "I can't wait to feel it squeezing my cock when I fuck you here."

Another wave of that humiliation-tinged pleasure crashed over her at his words. And having her mouth held open yet unable to actually respond to his filthy suggestions only made it worse somehow. He'd taken her snark from her, and she was only just now realizing how much she'd relied on it to shield her from uncomfortable situations.

In and out his finger moved, and she couldn't help but wonder what it would feel like to have his cock there instead. There would be pain, that seemed inevitable, but would there be pleasure as well? With a man like Braden Elliott, it seemed like pretty even odds one way or the other.

Then his finger disappeared, replaced by something harder and far less forgiving. She whined through the gag as the plug pushed into her, forcing her hole wider than it seemed possible.

"Relax, little one. Bear down like you're trying to push it out. I promise it will make things easier on you."

Dragging in air through her nose, she forced herself to relax and follow his instructions. And, to her knee-weakening relief, it actually worked. There was still a pinch of pain, especially when the widest part of the plug breached her hole, but then it slid into place and she audibly sighed with relief as it nestled inside her.

"What a pretty picture you make, Charlotte. I have a feeling you'll look even more beautiful once I've painted your skin pink."

Oh, fuck.

14

ORGASMS AND ULTIMATUMS

BRADEN

She was everything he'd ever dreamed of in a submissive. Just defiant enough to pose a challenge, but she trembled so beautifully when she was caught.

Stepping away from the cross, Braden gave the flogger a few testing swings, refamiliarizing himself with the weight of it. He hadn't used this particular one in a while, and though he had every intention of ensuring she was thoroughly punished for her stunt with Killian, he didn't want to truly harm her.

When he felt comfortable with the implement again, he moved forward, letting the falls land softly on her back. And had the pleasure of watching the tension visibly drain from Charlotte's shoulders. No doubt she was thinking this wasn't as bad as she'd expected, that she'd be able to handle this without a problem.

Ah, to be young and naïve again.

He let her believe it for a bit, barely striking her skin with the leather. Until she relaxed fully against the cross with a dreamy little sigh.

Shifting his stance, he lifted the flogger up over his left shoulder and brought it down across her bottom with enough force to drive her up to her toes and pull a scream of pain from her throat. He repeated the punishment from the opposite side, then stepped back to admire the deep, angrily pink welts forming on her skin.

Charlotte's shoulders rose and fell with each ragged breath as she struggled to comprehend the change. While she grappled with the unexpected pain, he went back to the lighter strokes, across her shoulders, over the larger welts on her bottom, all the way down her thighs and up again.

When she was relaxed again, though not quite as relaxed as before, he delivered two more punishing blows to her backside. Charlotte cried out again, this time turning her head to glare at him over his shoulder.

Perfection.

Over and over he repeated the dance, torturing

her with soft, almost teasing blows, luring her into a false sense of safety before delivering another punishment. By the time he was satisfied, she was practically glowing pink from his attentions.

Switching the flogger to his left hand, he approached the cross, cupping her welted bottom in his hand. "Look at me, Charlotte."

She turned her head, the tears shimmering on her lashes doing nothing to hide the stubbornness in her gaze. Digging his fingertips into her bottom, he forced himself not to grin when she rose back onto her toes with a garbled sound of distress.

"You belong to me now, Charlotte. And if you ever try to force, trick, or otherwise manipulate me into doing your bidding, you will find out exactly how lenient I've been with you tonight. Nod if you understand what I'm saying."

It was fascinating, watching the struggle play out over her face. Even with her body on fire, she had to fight to actively submit.

God, he was going to have so much fun with her.

After several long seconds, she finally nodded, though with obvious hesitancy.

"Good girl. Let's get you down from that cross so you can apologize properly."

Suspicion filled her gaze, and rightfully so. Delighted by her, Braden unhooked her from the cross and guided her to her knees. Despite her natural elegance, kneeling gracefully was a learned skill, and one she obviously needed some practice in. The rush of endorphins and emotions from her flogging likely weren't helping her feel any steadier, either, which he took into account as he helped her to kneel in the middle of the podium.

When she was positioned where he wanted, knees spread and her arms held behind her back so her breasts pushed out, practically begging for his attention, he unhooked the gag from around her head and carefully removed the ring from her mouth. Charlotte sighed with relief, opening and closing her jaw to work out the soreness from having her mouth held open for so long.

"Eyes on me, little one."

Gray eyes still wet with tears met his and Braden reached for the buckle on his belt. Her gaze flicked to his hands before returning to his face, and he rewarded her with a smile. "Good girl. Keep your eyes on me unless I tell you otherwise. Say 'Yes, Daddy' if you understand."

"Yes, Daddy." Her voice was rough, her throat likely dry from having her mouth held open during her flogging. But there was a huskiness to it that had his cock throbbing as he pulled it free.

"From now on, when you receive a punishment, this is how you will apologize. Open."

To his surprise, her lips parted immediately, and her gaze turned hungry as he pushed the tip of his cock into her waiting mouth. Her tongue slid around the sensitive underside and he groaned at the pleasure that flooded his system. It had been far too long since he'd had his dick in a willing woman's mouth.

What she lacked in expertise, she more than made up for in enthusiasm. He let her explore for a while, enjoying the feel of her mouth and tongue as she licked and sucked. Whenever she found something that got a reaction from him, she immediately repeated it, experimenting with different ways to get the same response.

"Enough playtime," he growled when the pleasure bordered on pain. "Suck."

Grabbing hold of her hair, he thrust forward into her mouth. Not quite deep enough to hit her throat, but enough to remind her who was really in charge.

A message she received clearly, judging by the way her eyes went wide as he fucked her mouth with short, shallow thrusts. It took a moment, but she quickly matched his rhythm, bobbing and sucking for all she was worth.

"Fuck, Charlotte. Just like that. Keep it up and Daddy will let you swallow his cum as a reward."

Almost greedily now, she worked her mouth over his cock, even taking him deep enough to make her gag a few times. One day, soon, he'd hold her still while she took him down her throat, but he forced himself to hold back this first time.

"That's my good girl," he praised, his voice rough with burgeoning desire. "Just a little more and you can have all of Daddy's cum down your pretty little throat."

It did indeed only take a little while longer for his cock to swell in her mouth. Now he did hold her in place, his cock buried deep in her mouth, and her nose practically pressed against his groin as he emptied himself down her throat as promised. And like any good little girl, she swallowed every last drop.

Spent, he pulled free, and to his continued surprise she licked him clean until he forced her to stop.

"That's enough, little one. You did such a good job." Using his hold on her hair to tilt her head back, he smiled down at her. "Daddy's very proud of you, Charlotte."

Her grin lit her face, an expression of pure joy, and in that instant, he knew he was damned. Because no matter how wrong it was, no matter what it might cost him in the end, he was never letting Charlotte Duvall go.

LOTTIE

Pride swelled in her chest at her Daddy's words. No matter what else happened between them, she'd always have this moment to hold close to her heart.

Daddy's very proud of you.

His words still rang in her ears as he helped her to her feet. "Where are your clothes, little one?"

"My clothes?" The question got tangled in the haze fogging her brain, and for a moment she could only stare at him. "Oh! My dress. Umm."

She'd stripped down on the podium when Master Killian had first led her up there, but after that... Glancing around, she struggled to think through what had happened in those first few minutes before Mr. Elliott had taken over.

A flash of glittering white caught her eye and she pointed. "Over there."

Mr. Elliott crossed the podium and scooped up her dress and heels, but he didn't stop to hand it to her. Instead, he gathered all of his things and dropped them back into his play bag before looping an arm around her waist. "Can you walk, or do you need me to carry you?"

Oh. Oh, that made her swoon a bit. Probably all

the feminism leaving her body in a rush at the thought of a big, strong man carrying her off into the sunset. "I think I can walk."

"That doesn't sound very convincing, little one."

The sound of his play bag hitting the floor met her ears a moment before he scooped her up into his arms. Pain flashed through her as his shirt rubbed against the welts his flogger had left behind, and she wiggled in his hold.

"Stop moving." A disapproving glare accompanied the order, and damn if her pussy didn't spasm at the sight of it.

Forcing herself to stop wiggling, she huffed. "I can't help it. Your shirt is hurting me."

To her surprise, he didn't scold her again, but instead brushed a kiss over her cheek. "I'm sorry, Lottie-bug, but I don't want to drop you. It's just a bit longer, and then I've got a nice soft blanket for you in my office."

Considering they were approaching the solid metal steps that led up to his office, she didn't really want to be dropped, either. "Oh. Um, okay. Thanks."

The look he sent her was more amused than disapproving this time. "You don't have to thank me for taking care of you, little one. It's my job as your Daddy to make sure you're taken care of on all fronts. Which means not dropping you on your pretty head."

Now that was something she could get used to. Being coddled and pampered was definitely more her style than being flogged and face-fucked in front of a crowd. Not that she hadn't enjoyed the latter, and if it got her more of the former, she was all for it.

By the time they reached the top of the stairs, Mr. Elliott was breathing a lot more heavily and beads of sweat had popped out on his brow. Reaching up, she brushed some hair away from his face, then paused and narrowed her eyes as she lifted the dark locks up from the roots.

"Do you dye your hair?"

"What? Of course not."

"Yes, you do! I see gray!"

"Keep your voice down, would you?" Shooting her another glare, he wrestled the door open and shoved inside. He lowered her carefully to the couch before returning to shut the door and crossing his arms over his chest, his expression turning almost sulky. "Fine. Yes, I dye my hair. But if you tell anyone, I will paddle your ass so hard you won't even think about sitting for a week. Got it?"

"Yes, Daddy," she agreed with a giggle. "Any other secrets I should know about?"

"Sometimes when I'm working on the computer for too long, I need glasses. And I have high cholesterol."

"I bet you look hot with glasses. Like a sexy professor."

One corner of his mouth curved up in a smirk. "We could roleplay some time. Your ass would look gorgeous with a dozen or so pretty cane lines on it."

A cane? That sounded terrifying. But in a way that made her all hot and tingly again. "Sure."

"For now..." Trailing off, he uncrossed his arms and moved to the other side of the room where he opened a cabinet. Lottie sat up straighter, craning her neck to try and see what he was doing, but his body blocked most of the cabinet.

But when he turned back around holding not just the promised blanket but a bar of chocolate and a bottle of water, everything inside her simply melted. She couldn't remember the last time anybody had taken care of her. So she didn't argue when he tucked the blanket around her and handed her the chocolate and water with orders to not move until she'd finished both.

And she especially didn't argue when he plucked her up off the couch and settled her on his lap like he had after her last spanking. Seriously, if this was her reward for enduring a punishment, she could totally live with getting herself in a little bit of trouble from time to time.

Silence filled his office, broken only by the occasional rustling of the candy wrapper or the sound of her sipping from her water bottle. Under other circumstances, she would have found the silence awkward, even stifling. But wrapped up in a cozy blanket on her Daddy's lap, it just felt... nice. Comforting in a way she couldn't remember experiencing since her mom's death, when he'd been around all the time, taking care of her and her dad in the weeks that had followed.

Tears clogged in her throat, and she did her best to sniffle them away discreetly, but given how quiet it was in the room, he must have heard her.

"What's wrong, Lottie-bug?"

"Nothing," she lied, forcing herself to drink more water in the hopes of washing away the tears.

"Nothing, huh? Then why are you crying, little one?"

If she told him the truth, she had no doubt she would be blubbering all over him in thirty seconds flat. And since she'd rather die than let *that* happen, she drained her water and shoved the candy wrapper into the bottle before wriggling out of the blanket so she could straddle him. "The only thing that's wrong is the fact that I sold my virginity over a week ago and yet here I am, with my cherry still unpopped."

"Ah. I see." Strong, firm hands drifted up her thighs to cup her ass, and the welts from the flogger came roaring back to life at his touch. "And you want me to relieve you of this burden?"

"Yes, please."

"I'd love nothing more than to be your first, Charlotte. But I need something from you, before that happens."

"What's that?"

"The truth. About why you put yourself up for auction in the first place. Once you tell me that, I will happily fuck your sweet little pussy as often as you like."

15

DENIAL

LOTTIE

Dammit. He had to latch onto the one thing she couldn't tell him. "I already told you why. I needed the money."

"But you haven't told me what you needed the money for. That's all I want from you, Charlotte. The truth."

"And I already told you it's none of your business."

Annoyance pricked at her when he simply shrugged as if it didn't matter. "That's your choice, then."

Putting on her best pout, she deliberately ground her pussy against the front of his pants. "But Daddy, don't you want me?"

"That's a dangerous game to play with me, little

one." His hand came up to fist in her hair, pulling her head back as he nipped at her exposed neck. "I want you so much I'm risking everything to have you. Your mistake is thinking I can't enjoy your body without putting my cock in your sweet little pussy."

"Won't you get tired of my mouth?"

"Never," he said with a wicked chuckle. "And you have more than two holes."

As if to demonstrate, the hand not tangled in her hair drifted toward the cleft of her bottom, and she instinctively clenched. Which reminded her, very uncomfortably, of the plug still lodged firmly in her ass.

"And if you think I won't thoroughly claim every single inch of you even if I can't actually fuck you, then you would be very mistaken, little one. Now, do you have something to tell me?"

God, it was tempting. Not just because she did desperately want him to fuck her, but because she was getting tired of carrying the weight of her father's failures on her own shoulders. It would, she was certain, feel so fucking good to let him carry some of it for her, even if just for a little while.

But that wasn't fair to her father, or to her Daddy. So she kept her mouth shut, even though it killed her a little inside to do it.

"Guess you'll have to be satisfied with my mouth and my ass, then."

Disappointment flashed in his eyes, making her feel about two inches tall. "Have it your way then, little one." Releasing his hold on her hair, he moved her off him onto the couch. "Daddy needs to get some work done. You'll stay here until I'm ready to take you home. If you get hungry, I can order some food to be sent up to the office."

"But... aren't you going to..." Unable to force the words out, she gestured helplessly at her pussy, which was still aching from that scene downstairs.

Taking his seat behind his desk, Mr. Elliott raised an eyebrow. "I don't generally reward naughty girls with orgasms. But since you're rather new to all this, I can allow for some leniency. If you'd like to relieve yourself, you may."

"I'd much rather have you do the relieving, Daddy."

The corner of his mouth lifted in a smug smile. "I'm sure you would. But no."

"But—"

"Your options are your own fingers or no orgasm at all, Charlotte. Take it or leave it."

"Fine. I'll probably have more fun by myself, anyway." She already knew that was a damn lie, but she wasn't about to give him the benefit of knowing how much more she'd enjoy the orgasm he'd given her the other day.

"Then by all means, enjoy." That smug smile still in place, Mr. Elliott leaned back in his chair, his gaze locked on her.

"Like... now?"

"Now."

"Can I at least go to the bathroom or something?"

"No."

Damn him and his one-syllable answers. "Never mind. I'll just wait until I get home."

"Ah, thank you for reminding me we haven't gone over your rules yet." Looking far more chipper than the situation called for as far as she was concerned, he raised a hand and began counting off fingers. "One, your orgasms belong to me. If we are not together and you want to make yourself come, you will ask permission. When we are together, you'll learn to wait until Daddy gives you permission to come. Two," he continued, rolling over her outrage, "Lying is not tolerated. Period. Three, what Daddy says, goes. That means if I tell you to do something, you do it without arguing. Four, your health and safety are my utmost concern. If I find you risking either, you will be punished. Any questions?"

"So, what? I'm just expected to be your obedient little sex doll?"

"I'm sure it seems that way, especially to someone so new to the lifestyle." His expression softened, just a fraction. "I'm a demanding man, Charlotte. I will expect to have access to you at all times, unless you are working. If you don't think that's something you can handle, I'll understand if you don't want to continue our relationship after tonight."

"I didn't say that. But, not to sound crude, what's in it for me?"

Pushing out of his chair, he slowly prowled the office, closing the distance between them without breaking eye contact for even a second. "In exchange for your complete and total submission, you get... a Daddy."

"Okay, but what does that *mean*?"

"It means, little one"—he placed his hands on either side of her, caging her in against the back of the couch—"you get someone who will take care of you. I take pride in caring for and protecting my possessions, Charlotte. And you would be my most cherished possession. You will never want for anything. Your happiness and your needs will be the most important things in my life."

"It sorta sounds like your needs come first."

"No. My wants, my desires... yes. But all of that comes secondary to making sure you are properly cared for. Protected, at all costs. That, little one, is what's in it for you."

If she hadn't been desperately horny before, that little speech certainly would have done the job. "Oh."

"Say yes, Charlotte. Say yes, and let me give you everything you've ever dreamed of, and all the things you haven't even realized are possible."

"I'm not a doormat," she managed to say, though her voice trembled a bit on the words. "I won't let you walk all over me."

"And I would never expect you to. Submission doesn't make you weak, little one."

"I know that." Frankie was the strongest, smartest woman she knew, and she loved being a submissive. And there was that part of her, the part of her desperate to *know*, that was all but screaming at her to say yes. "All right. I'll give it a try."

"Good girl. Now, spread those pretty legs for Daddy and show me how you touch yourself when you think of me."

BRADEN

Returning to his desk instead of giving in and taking her right there on the couch when she was looking up at him with those wide, innocent eyes was the hardest fucking thing he'd ever done. But he intended to start as he meant to go on, and right now that meant sticking to his guns and not letting her pretty pout sway him.

So he forced himself to sit in his chair and watch as she spread her thighs, her fingers sliding with an agonizing slowness toward her pussy. The smell of her arousal filled the room, and he very nearly wiped at his mouth to ensure he wasn't drooling.

Her eyes drifted closed on a sigh as her fingers dipped between her bare lips. Transfixed, he watched as she pumped those perfectly manicured digits in and out of her pussy, until they glistened under the lights in his office.

"Good girl." Even to his own ears, his voice was rough with desire. "Play with your clit, baby. But slowly. You're not allowed to come yet."

Without opening her eyes, she arched up, her voice pitching up to a wine that had his cock hardening despite the fact he'd just come down her throat not half an hour earlier. "But Daddy, you said I could."

"I also said you would be learning to control your orgasms until Daddy gives you permission to come. We're going to start practicing tonight." Leaning back in his chair, he freed his cock from his pants and wrapped his hand around the hard length. "Play with your little clitty, Lottie-bug, but try not to come until you ask for permission."

Another pitiful whine as she circled her clit with the pad of her finger. Slowly, so slowly he wondered how she could stand it, she worked herself toward her climax.

Soon, his office was filled with the sounds of pleasure, her soft sighs and whimpers, and his occasional grunt or groan as he forced himself not to come until she'd finished.

"That's it, little one. Are you close?"

"*So* close, Daddy."

"Ask me to let you come."

A muscle in her jaw tightened, and his cock twitched as he watched her struggle to submit. This was his favorite part, even more than the impact play, the restraints, the feel of a woman gagging on his cock. Watching a strong woman give herself over to him, submit of her own free will...

It was fucking intoxicating.

"Ask me, Charlotte, or you'll spend the night in cuffs without being allowed to come at all."

That seemed to get through to her. Eyes screwed shut, she arched up again, her desperate cries ringing out in the enclosed space. "Please let me come, Daddy, please!"

"Five more seconds, baby. Can you hold out five more seconds?"

"I don't know!"

"Try for Daddy, little one. Five..." She whimpered again, her head thrashing back and forth against the back of the couch. "Four..."

"Daddy, please!"

"Almost, baby. Three... two..."

"I can't, I can't, Daddy *please*!"

"One. Good fucking girl. Come for Daddy. Now."

She screamed, and even from across the room he could see her body quake with the force of her orgasm. Watching her, he grabbed a tissue from his desk and covered his cock just as his own pleasure erupted.

For several long moments the only sound in the office was the sound of their ragged breaths. Until, finally, her eyes fluttered open and she smiled dreamily at him. "Thank you for letting me come, Daddy."

"You're very welcome, little one. Why don't you grab your blanket and come snuggle on Daddy's lap while he works?"

To his delight, she did exactly that. And maybe he wasn't nearly as productive as he might have been without her curled up on his lap, but he wouldn't have traded it for all the money in the world.

The only dark spot on the evening was the lingering knowledge that she was hiding something from him. But one way or another, he would find a way to get his little Lottie-bug to come clean. And then he would finally claim every last part of her for his own.

❧ 16 ☙

MAKE DADDY PROUD

BRADEN

Sunrise had a tendency to shine a light on things, not only physically but metaphorically as well. Last night, tucked away in the safety and privacy of his club, laying claim to Charlotte had seemed not only like a good idea, but the only possible outcome.

Now, in the harsh light of day, Braden was faced with the reality of his situation. Not that he regretted what he'd done in the slightest, but there was one very large fly in the ointment. A fly by the name of Emmett Duvall.

It was one thing to keep a singular incident a secret, like when he'd spanked her for entering that damn auction. But he couldn't and *wouldn't* hide an entire relationship from his best friend.

Which was how he found himself ringing the doorbell at the Duvall home well before lunchtime, growing more and more irritated as he waited for Abigail to open the door.

Just as he was pulling his phone from his pocket to give Emmett a call to see if he was even home, it swung open, revealing a delightfully disheveled Charlotte glaring daggers at him. Her eyes widened slightly when she recognized him. "Mr. Elliott?"

Stepping over the threshold, he nudged her to the side and closed the door behind them. The urge to kiss her was like an itch under his skin, but that was a risk he couldn't take until he'd spoken to Emmett. "Under the current circumstances, I think you should probably start calling me Braden, don't you?"

Her nose wrinkled. "I like Daddy better. Calling you Braden just feels wrong."

"I love hearing you call me Daddy, little one. But perhaps not in... polite company."

"I've never really cared what 'polite company' thinks of me."

He did, more than he should according to his brothers. And while he enjoyed letting her play the brat for him in private, he did have certain expecta-tions for how his partner behaved in public. "Charlotte."

There was just enough 'Daddy' in his tone to have a flush rising to her cheeks. "Fine. What are you doing here, *Braden?*"

"I came over to talk to your dad, but if my naughty girl needs her bottom warmed so she can remember how to speak to me, I'd be happy to make a detour to somewhere private, first."

"Sorry. The doorbell woke me up and I'm cranky when I don't get enough sleep."

"Where's Abigail? Does she have the day off?"

The flush on Charlotte's cheeks darkened as she jerked a shoulder. "How the fuck should I know? I don't keep track of her schedule."

Lack of sleep made for a very cranky Lottie-bug, indeed. Braden tucked that bit of knowledge away as he sent her a stern look. "That's two."

"Two what?"

"Strikes. We get to three and you'll be going back to bed with a very sore bottom."

"That's not fair!"

"It's very fair. I'm giving you the opportunity to correct your behavior on your own before I correct it for you. I won't always be so understanding, Charlotte."

As he had the night before, he watched her, captivated by the open struggle to submit stamped all over her stunning face. Until she finally sighed, her shoulders slumping and her bottom lip pushing out into a pout. "Sorry, Daddy."

"Good girl. Now, is your..." Referring to Emmet as her dad only served to highlight everything that was wrong with the situation they'd found themselves in. "Is Emmet home?"

"I think he's in his office. You know where it is."

Glancing around to ensure they weren't seen, Braden slid an arm around her waist and pulled her close. "Thank you, little one." He brushed an almost chaste kiss across her lips. "If you're a good girl the rest of the day, I'll have a surprise for you tonight."

At the mention of a surprise, her eyes lit up. "What kind of surprise?"

"I guess you'll have to be a good girl so you can see, now won't you?"

This time when she sighed it was filled with drama, and he couldn't help but laugh. Still pouting, but with her eyes now sparkling with mischief, she tilted her chin up, as if inviting him to come and taste. "I could be a *very* good girl for you if you wanted me to, Daddy."

"Are you going to tell me why you signed up for the auction?"

Irritation and, if he wasn't mistaken, a hint of sadness flickered across her face. "No."

"Then I'll have to settle for you being a good girl and not getting yourself into any trouble." Leaning down, he pressed another kiss to her sulky mouth. "Be good, Charlotte. I have plans for you tonight, and you'll enjoy them much more than you'd enjoy spending your evening with your nose in the corner and your bare bottom on display in my office while I work."

"You wouldn't!"

"I would. Ball is in your court, little one."

With another too-light kiss, he released her and headed toward Emmett's office, all the while pretending he didn't hear her calling him all manner of names under her breath as he walked away.

Little brat. He was so going to enjoy taming her.

For now, however, he had a very difficult conversation to have with someone he cared very deeply for. Standing outside Emmett's office, Braden dragged in a deep breath to steady himself, then gave a cursory knock before pushing open the door.

"Emmett? Are you in here?"

The door opened fully, and Braden was treated to the shocking sight of his closest friend sitting in front of his computer, his hair sticking up in a million different directions as he frantically clicked his mouse. Emmett glanced up from his screen, his smile distinctly forced. "Braden! I wasn't expecting you."

"Clearly." Stepping into the office, Braden closed the door behind him, concern sitting like a weight on his chest. "Emmett... is everything all right?"

"Of course. Just getting some things off my plate. No rest for the weary, am I right?"

Something was wrong. Not just 'grieving widower hiding himself away from everyone for two years' wrong, but *wrong*. Braden could feel it in his bones. "It's Saturday, Emmett."

"Is it?" Pausing his frantic clicking, Emmett blinked owlishly at the computer screen. "I didn't realize. Ah, well, you know how it is. Some things can't wait for normal business hours."

Before Nat's passing, Emmett had been a bit of a workaholic. So it really shouldn't have been worrisome to find him busy at work on a Saturday. But Braden knew for a fact he was little more than a figurehead at his company these days. The board kept him on, mostly because the Duvall name still brought in clients with deep pockets, but he was fairly certain Emmett hadn't actually worked a day since Nat's death.

Which begged the question... What *was* he doing? And why did he seem like he was hiding something?

"What are you working on?" Settling into one of the oversized visitor chairs on the other side of Emmett's desk, Braden kept his tone as casual as possible.

"Little bit of this, little bit of that. You know how it is."

"Emmett."

At the sound of his name, Emmett looked up again. Now that he was closer, Braden could see the hints of panic in his eyes, the tightness around his smile. "Braden."

"Is everything okay? You seem a bit... frazzled this morning."

"Everything's fine." Emmett's smile brightened, but it was almost too bright. "Just busy. You know how it is."

That was the third time in less than five minutes Emmett had used the phrase and Braden couldn't help but feel like he was being deliberately kept at bay. Concern for his friend's wellbeing overrode any desire Braden had to fill him in on his relationship with Charlotte. "Okay. Well. I suppose I'll let you get back to it."

"Sorry I'm not better company this morning." Emmett's expression shifted to a passable facsimile of an apologetic smile.

"My fault for surprising you. But we should have

dinner soon. Catch up a bit." Inspiration struck, and Braden flashed his friend a grin of his own. "Why don't you and Lottie come over Tuesday for dinner?"

Charlotte was off Tuesday night. It would also give Braden a few days to talk to her and let her know he planned to tell Emmett about their relationship.

And to see if she knew anything about what the hell was going on with her father.

❧

LOTTIE

Whoever designed her father's office doors deserved a fucking award for soundproofing. Even with her ear pressed to the wood, the most she could hear was the sound of their muffled voices and not any actual words.

It hadn't occurred to her until Mr. Elliott—*Braden* —had been in there for a few minutes that he might be telling her dad about them. So here she was, trying to listen through the door in case she needed to interrupt him before he did something stupid. But she couldn't hear a damn thing, and she didn't want to just bust in there if they were just talking about business or whatever other boring things men like them talked about behind closed doors.

She was so focused on what she didn't hear, however, that she completely neglected to take note of the sound of footsteps approaching the door until it was too late. At the last moment, she jerked away from the door. The sudden movement caused her to lose her balance, and she ended up sprawled on the floor just as the door opened, revealing her Daddy.

He glanced down at her, his eyebrow raising in that look she'd come to associate with being in Big Trouble, and she felt her bottom clench as if anticipating the spanking she was about to get.

When he pulled the door shut, she flashed him a bright smile. "Hi, Daddy."

"Eavesdropping, Lottie-bug?"

"Umm..."

"Bathroom. Now."

Scrambling to her feet, she hurried down the hall to the half bath, her stomach exploding with butterflies as she waited for him to join her. "I just wanted to know if you were telling him about us!"

"I was going to, but it didn't seem like the right time." There was an odd flatness to Braden's tone that had the hairs on the back of her neck standing up. "He said he was working."

"Really?" Joy and hope lit up inside her, so bright it was nearly painful. "That's great!"

"Yes." Braden's smile didn't quite reach his eyes,

but she was so excited by the prospect of her dad getting back to work she deliberately ignored it. "But we still have the issue of you eavesdropping to discuss."

"Okay, I know I shouldn't have, but *you* shouldn't have made the decision to tell him about us without talking to me first."

To her surprise, he paused as if considering her statement. "You're right. I shouldn't have. Are you all right with me telling him?"

Nerves churned in her stomach, making her feel vaguely nauseous. "I told you from the beginning I didn't want him to know about us. And you agreed."

"That was when it was a one-time thing. We can't keep sneaking around behind his back. It's not fair to him, and it's not fair to whatever this is between us."

"What if we tell him and then we break up? What's the point of putting him through all that stress and worry, potentially ruining your friendship, if it all amounts to nothing in the end?"

Braden's eyes darkened as he lifted his hands to cup her face. "Charlotte. Even if you decided tomorrow you don't want to be my little girl anymore, I can promise you even the short time I've had with you wouldn't amount to 'nothing'. This, what we have, matters to me. Too much to keep it a secret from a man who matters to both of us."

Jesus. How was she supposed to argue that? "I just don't want to hurt him."

"I know, little one. I can't guarantee it won't, but hopefully if we're honest with him upfront instead of sneaking around behind his back, it will help mitigate that hurt."

Meeting his piercing gaze, she let out a shaky breath. As much as she hated to admit it, Braden had a point. "All right. We can tell him."

"Good girl. We're having dinner together Tuesday night, the three of us. I was thinking we could tell him then, but if you'd rather I tell him beforehand, I will."

Her heart swelled with gratitude at being included instead of being told how it would go. "No, I think it's best if we tell him together. He's less likely to murder you if I'm there. I think."

"Fair enough," he said with a chuckle before sobering again. "I am sorry I didn't talk to you first."

"It's okay. I figure it cancels out the whole eavesdropping thing." But her stomach sank when he raised an eyebrow. "Doesn't it?"

"That's not how this relationship works, little one. You're still going to be punished for eavesdropping. Turn around and face the sink."

"But Daddy! That's not *fair*!"

"I never claimed to be fair. Turn around." When

she didn't move, everything about him, even his voice, seemed to harden. "Now, Charlotte."

Huffing out a breath, she turned and braced her hands on the vanity.

"Eyes on me."

She lifted her gaze to meet his in the mirror, and the intensity in his eyes knocked the breath clear from her lungs.

"Fortunately for you, we need to keep this quiet. Unfortunately for you, I am very practiced at giving naughty little girls the discipline they need, wherever and whenever the situation calls for it."

Sliding his fingers into the waistband of her leggings, Braden slowly pulled them down over her hips and her ass, exposing all of her most intimate parts to him. When she was bare to the tops of her thighs, he slipped a hand around her waist, down to where she was already embarrassingly wet for him.

Without breaking eye contact, he pressed a finger inside her, and Lottie had to fight back a whimper as need coiled in her belly.

"Naughty little girls who put their noses where they don't belong get punished," he murmured in her ear as he drew an arousal-slicked finger from her and circled her clit. Despite her best attempts at acting nonchalant, she couldn't stop the shiver that racked her body at his touch.

"But my nose did belong there! You were going to tell him about us!"

"Did you know that when you decided to eavesdrop?"

"No, but—"

"Stop. I've already conceded I should have spoken to you instead of making the call to tell your dad about us on my own. That was my screw up." He pressed harder against her clit, drawing a whimper from her lips. "But my mistakes don't excuse you from trying to listen in on a private conversation. You can officially consider yourself on orgasm restriction for the rest of the day. I will be calling you at random points throughout the day to give you instructions on how I want you to touch yourself. If you come without my permission, or if you lay a single finger on this pretty pussy of mine without my permission, I will ensure you do not sit comfortably once you join me at the club. Am I understood?"

"Yes, Daddy," she said as sweetly as she could manage when she knew damn well she was just saying what he wanted to hear. A spanking? That was nothing. She would gladly take a spanking in exchange for getting herself off after he left.

"I can see the wheels turning in your mind, little one. You're thinking you'll just go up to your room when I leave, take the edge off a bit. There's no way

Daddy will know, right? And even if I do figure it out, you can handle a little spanking."

Because his words did so accurately describe her thought process, she didn't bother to try and pretend otherwise. "Pretty much."

"You're right. But you're forgetting one very important detail."

"What's that?"

With his eyes still locked on hers, he leaned closer, his voice dropping to a gravelly whisper. "How much you want to make your Daddy proud."

Daddy's very proud of you. The memory of the night before, when she'd been on her knees with him smiling down at her, praising her for taking his cock down her throat slammed into her.

And she knew in that moment she would do whatever it took to see that look on his face again. To hear those words again.

Damn him.

"Maybe I don't care about that."

He chuckled at her bravado, his finger still doing deliciously tortuous things to her clit. "Keep telling yourself that, little one. We'll see who's right tonight. I'll call you in a bit."

She nearly wept when he pulled his hand away from her pussy, but she did her best to pretend it didn't affect her in the least. In the mirror, she watched as he lifted his finger to his lips and sucked himself clean of her juices.

"Be good, Lottie-bug. Make Daddy proud."

It was going to be a long fucking day.

LOTTIE

Braden Elliott was the most sadistic man she'd ever met. Granted, she hadn't met many sadists, but she couldn't imagine they held a candle to her Daddy.

By his second phone call of the day, when he'd made her tell him how close she was to coming as she'd touched herself on her bed, she was ready to risk a punishment and make herself come while he listened. But then he'd said those fucking words again. *Make Daddy proud.* And she'd chickened out at the last minute.

By the fourth phone call, she'd resorted to begging. She was pretty sure she'd made several promises she had no hope of keeping with regards to never being naughty again and giving him any and every sexual favor he could think of.

"Oh, little Lottie-bug," he'd said with a low, wicked sort of chuckle in her ear, "you have no idea what you're offering me, do you? Pinch your clit for me, baby, and tell me how it feels."

She'd obeyed, over and over again, hating and loving every second of it.

Needless to say, by the time the car he'd sent for her pulled up in front of the club, her entire body felt as though someone had rubbed sandpaper over every nerve. She was fairly certain it wouldn't take more than a stern look or a word from him to set her off. With each step, her panties brushed against her clit, and she had to grit her teeth against the scream that wanted to burst out of her.

Shane was at the front desk tonight, and he waved her up with an enthusiastic grin she did her best to return. But judging by the confused look on his face, she failed miserably. Which did nothing to improve her mood as she stomped up the stairs to Braden's office.

"I hope you know what an asshole you—oh." Stopping short as she stepped through the door she'd just dramatically shoved open, Lottie blinked at the couple sitting on Braden's couch. "Who the hell are you?"

The girl, all gorgeous curves and a pretty, girl-next-door sort of face, widened her eyes while the man next to her frowned so fiercely Lottie nearly slammed the door closed again to avoid his glare. He looked familiar, vaguely so, but she figured she would have remembered running into an absolute silver fox like him before.

"I'd like to ask you the same question."

"Stand down, Damian. This is Charlotte, my..." Pushing away from where he'd been leaned against his desk, Braden frowned. "It's complicated."

Complicated? Complicated was what people said when they were stuck in a relationship they didn't really want to be in. So much for all those sweet words he'd whispered in her ear that morning. Asshole.

Plastering on a bright smile, Lottie approached the couple with her hand out. "I'm his next-door neighbor. And the woman he's fucking."

"Charlotte!" Braden's scolding tone might have made her wince if she wasn't so pissed at him.

The woman beside Damian accepted the handshake with even wider eyes, which Lottie wouldn't have thought possible until she'd watched it happen. "Nice to meet you. I'm Emily."

"Lottie. I hope you don't mind me saying so, but gosh you're pretty. Is that your natural hair color?"

Emily raised her free hand to run it over her honey-colored locks. "Yes?"

"Seriously? I know women who pay hundreds for highlights like that. I might have to hate you just for that."

"*Charlotte!*"

Rolling her eyes at Braden's scolding tone, she let go of Emily's hand and turned to face him. "What? It's a compliment!"

"Apologize. Now."

"Oh, that's okay, Braden." Emily smiled. "She doesn't need to apologize."

Lottie flashed Emily another bright smile. "We're going to be such good friends."

An adorable pink flush crept across Emily's cheeks. "We are?"

"Definitely."

"Braden, what the hell is going on?" The grouchy-looking older man somehow managed to look even grouchier as he glared at Braden. "Who is this and why the hell are you letting her act like a spoiled brat?"

"Probably because I am one," Lottie supplied cheerfully. Tweaking Mr. Grouchy Pants was doing wonders for her mood, and she was almost able to forget about the painful ache between her thighs as she watched his silver beard twitch.

"Charlotte, please stop baiting my brother before you give him a coronary. I'm not sure Emily here will ever forgive us if we murder her fiancé."

"Fiancé?" Squealing, Lottie spun back to Emily and held out her hand. "Let me see the ring."

Her cheeks turning even pinker, Emily held her left hand up for inspection. Lottie gasped at the sight of the gorgeous cushion cut diamond, flanked on either side by sapphires on Emily's finger. "It's gorgeous. Mr. Grouchy Pants has good taste."

"All right. Now that you've met everyone, you can march your naughty bottom over to the corner for five minutes. Maybe a time out will remind you of your manners."

Letting go of Emily's hand, Lottie turned to glare at her asshole of a Daddy. "Maybe I would be able to remember my manners if *someone* hadn't been so mean to me all day."

Braden smiled, a flash of teeth that made the butterflies in her stomach jump. "You haven't seen mean yet, little one. Corner, now, before I decide you'd look much better wearing stripes from Daddy's belt across your ass."

The part of her that was pissed from being kept on edge all day wanted to fight with him. To push, just to see how far she could go before he followed through on his threat. Hell, that part of her almost *wanted* him to follow through. Maybe a good hard spanking would make her feel a little less antsy.

But there was something about being punished in front of his brother and Emily that just seemed humiliating. Even more so than when he'd plugged her and flogged her in front of the entire club. She just couldn't imagine sitting down to Thanksgiving dinner and having to look them in the eye, knowing they'd watched her get her bottom spanked like a naughty little girl.

"Fine. I'm going."

Tilting her nose in the air, Lottie turned on her heel and sashayed over to the corner Braden had pointed to.

"Dress up, panties down, Charlotte."

"What?" Though she'd meant for the question to sound as outraged as she felt, it came out as a shocked squeak that only added to the embarrassment of the situation. "No! I'm not doing that."

"Then Daddy will do it for you."

Air clogged in Lottie's lungs, and she could hardly breathe as he crowded her, trapping her between him and the corner. "This is what happens when my little girl decides to act out in front of company. You had no problem showing your ass a moment ago, so you can stand here with your bottom bare while you think about how I expect you to behave. Now, you can either bare yourself, or Daddy can do it for you. Which would you prefer?"

"Neither!"

"That isn't an option, Charlotte."

Before she could answer, he had her pinned against the wall, and he was working her panties down to her knees.

"Daddy, no!" Humiliation flooded her, making her stomach churn as tears filled her eyes. "I'll be good, I promise!"

"You can start by taking your punishment like a good girl," he said as he hiked her dress up to her hips. "Stand up straight and put your hands on your head."

Sniffling back tears in a desperate attempt to salvage at least something of her dignity, Lottie positioned herself as instructed.

"That's my good girl." Braden pressed a kiss to her shoulder. "It's only five minutes, baby. You can handle it. But if it gets to be too much, just use your safeword and I'll come get you."

Her safeword. Right. In the thrill of pushing his and his brother's buttons, she'd all but forgotten she could stop all of this if she really wanted to.

But she had been kinda rude. And she'd definitely been a brat. So, even though she sorta thought she might die of embarrassment standing there in the corner, she didn't actually want to use her safeword.

"I'll be okay, Daddy."

"Good. Five minutes, and then Daddy has a surprise for you."

It was silly and childish, but the promise of a surprise perked her up considerably. "Yes, Daddy."

⚜

BRADEN

Pulling his phone from his pocket, Braden set a timer for five minutes. And though he wanted nothing more than to pull Charlotte into his arms and tell her it was all forgiven, he forced himself to turn away and walk back to his desk.

"All right, where were we?"

"Uh, we were at the part where you tell me why a girl half your age is calling you Daddy and standing in your office half-naked?" Damian's brows lifted so high they practically disappeared into his hairline. "What the hell is going on, Braden?"

"You remember the auction."

Laying his hand over Emily's, Damian nodded, his expression turning grim. Emily was how they'd learned about the auction in the first place, after

Damian had unknowingly bought her virginity in a previous auction. "How could I forget?"

"Charlotte was in the last one. Killian O'Rourke bought her."

"Killian?" Damian frowned. "That seems... out of character."

Braden jerked a shoulder. "Yeah, well, like a lot of people he got duped into thinking it was all above board. But when he showed up here with my next-door neighbor's daughter..."

"Wait. That's Emmett Duvall's little girl?" Letting out a low whistle, Damian shook his head. "Dangerous ground, baby brother."

"You would know, wouldn't you?"

Considering Emily was not only best friends with Damian's daughter, but her father had once upon a time been Damian's best friend, Damian really didn't have any room to talk. Which he obviously knew, judging by the way his scowl deepened. "That's why I'm telling you it's a bad fucking idea, Braden."

"So marrying me is a bad idea?"

Emily's soft question pulled their attention straight to her. Sitting stiffly, she glared at both of them with the fiercest expression Braden could ever remember seeing on her face.

"Ah, Sunshine. You know that's not what I meant."

"That's sure what it sounded like. If it's a bad idea for Braden, then it's a bad idea for you. Unless you're a great big hypocrite."

"Careful, Sunshine." But despite the slight censure in his words, Damian sighed. "You're right, though. I shouldn't judge. It's just... shit like this can get messy. We got lucky that Katrina is mostly okay with it, and, well, nobody gives a shit about Don's opinion anyway."

"If it gets messy, I'll figure out a way to clean it up. But Charlotte is mine, and I don't have to justify our relationship to you." The alarm on his phone chose that moment to ring, and Braden hit the button to turn it off. "If you'll excuse us, Charlotte and I have some things to discuss. I reserved a VIP booth for us. Have Ivy show you up and we'll join you in a bit."

"All right." Rising from the couch, Damian held his hand out to help Emily up. "I hope you know what you're doing, Braden."

"I do." At least, he was fairly certain he knew what he was doing. There was still the potential for this to all blow up in their faces, but he was trying to be optimistic. For once.

He waited for the door to close behind Damian and Emily before calling for Charlotte. "Come here, Lottie-bug. Corner time is over."

If he was being honest, he wasn't exactly sure how

he expected Charlotte to act after her timeout. But whatever he might have thought, he certainly wasn't prepared for her to turn away from the corner and drop to her knees, hunger in her eyes as she crawled across the floor to him.

When she stopped in front of him, she rose up, her gaze still locked on his as she reached for his belt buckle. "I know I was naughty, Daddy, but I'd really, really like to suck your cock now. May I? Please?"

Well, how the hell was he supposed to turn down an offer like that?

DOES IT HURT?

LOTTIE

S he'd just been about to risk a meeting with her Daddy's belt by turning around and telling Damian Elliott exactly where he could stick his opinions on her relationship with his brother when Braden had stepped in and said exactly the right thing. Hearing Braden tell Damian that she was *his*, well, it had her feeling some kind of way.

A way that made her want to show him exactly how much she appreciated him.

"Hmm." Braden's expression turned playfully stern. "You were a very naughty girl, Charlotte. Do you think you learned your lesson?"

"Yes, Daddy. I'm sorry I was so rude to…" Mr.

Damian? Just Damian? What the fuck was she supposed to call him? "Our guests."

"Then yes, you may take Daddy's cock down your pretty throat if you want."

All but salivating for him, she pulled his cock free from his pants and immediately took him into her mouth as deep as she could manage. Using all the things she'd learned from the first blow job she'd given him, she licked and sucked and gagged around him.

"Fuck, baby. Your mouth feels so good on Daddy's cock. Are you going to be a good girl and swallow all of me?"

Since her mouth was stuffed full of his dick, she could only nod her agreement. A moment later, his cock swelled, and the hot, salty taste of him filled her mouth.

As promised, she swallowed every drop, and then licked him clean until he gently pulled her away from his cock.

Cupping her face, he smiled down at her. "Such a good little girl when you want to be, aren't you?"

"Yes, Daddy."

"Stand up and take your clothes off. Daddy has a surprise for you."

She'd forgotten about her surprise! Rocking back on her heels, she rose as gracefully as she could manage to her feet and began stripping off her clothes as Braden tucked himself back into his pants and made his way over to his desk.

When he returned, she was just unhooking her bra as he held up what looked like a long, slender jewelry box.

"For me?" she asked, excitement bubbling up inside her. "But, why did I have to get undressed for a necklace?"

"You'll see. Open it."

Curiosity mingled with excitement as she opened the box. There, nestled on the black velvet, were multiple gold chains, and three gold clips of some kind. "What is it?"

"These"—picking up two of the clips, he lifted them from the box, allowing the third clip to dangle from a much longer chain between them— "are clamps. Any guesses where they go?"

She was really starting to hate guessing games. "I suppose it's too much to hope they might be for my ears or some equally innocuous body part."

"You'd suppose right. Play with your breasts for me, Charlotte. Make those pretty nipples nice and hard."

Lifting her hands to her breasts, she cupped each one, rolling her nipples between her fingers. "Is it going to hurt?"

"A little. But don't worry, we won't leave them on for too long."

Her relief at his words was short lived as he stepped closer and raised one gold clip to her nipple. "Of course, they'll hurt a lot more coming off, but that's half the fun."

"I think we have different definitions of 'fun', Braden."

Heat flashed in his eyes. "Keep it up, little girl. I can keep you on edge all night if that's what it takes to teach you some manners."

If she hadn't already been so fucking desperate for an orgasm, she might have tested that threat. But as it was, she wasn't about to push him any further than she already had. "Sorry, Daddy."

"Good girl. Move your fingers, little one."

With more than a little reluctance, she dropped her hands. She watched, equal parts fascinated and terrified as the first clamp closed around her nipple.

"Oh, fuck! Take it off, please, Daddy, it hurts!"

"Shh, baby. Just give it a second. Breathe through the pain."

Inhaling sharply, she did as she was told, and the pain ebbed a bit with each breath.

"Better?" he asked with the barest hint of a smile.

"Yes. Still hurts, though."

"It will probably feel uncomfortable until they come off."

"And then it'll hurt a whole fucking lot?"

"Yes." He clamped the other nipple, and she clenched her teeth against the fresh wave of pain. "But if you're a good girl, you'll be coming so hard when I take them off you'll barely notice the pain."

"I doubt even you can make me come that hard, Daddy."

"Challenge accepted." Chuckling, he ran his fingers down the longer chain, which tugged slightly at the chains attached to her nipples, making them ache all over again. "Spread your legs, little one."

"Oh, hell no. You're not putting that on my... you're not putting that down there."

"This one won't hurt, I promise."

Since he'd never actually lied to her before, she didn't see any reason not to trust him, so she stepped wider, exposing her most sensitive parts to him.

Braden cupped her pussy with his hand, and she swore she almost came just from the heat of his skin against her clit. And when he pressed a finger inside her, she almost wept with pleasure.

"Daddy... please," she whispered, rocking her hips in a desperate attempt for relief.

"Stay still," he scolded mildly as his fingers spread her lips, further exposing her clit. "If you hadn't been so naughty earlier, I would have let you come this morning. And then you wouldn't be quite such a needy little girl, now would you?"

"N-no, Daddy."

"Keep that in mind while you're wearing your jewelry. And if you can keep a civil tongue in your head while we visit with my brother and Emily, you'll be allowed to come when your bottom is stuffed with Daddy's cock."

Shock had Lottie's mouth falling open. "You're going to... *there?*"

"I absolutely am." Determination shone in his eyes. "Unless you'd like to tell me the truth about why you signed up for the auction. Then I'd gladly fuck your sweet little pussy instead."

"You're not being fair."

"I've been exceedingly fair, I think." The third clip closed around her swollen clit. As promised, it didn't hurt, but the pressure made her already agitated state even more so as the clamp squeezed her poor tortured little bud. "I told you my expecta-tions. You chose to defy me. And naughty little girls who defy their Daddies do not get rewarded."

There was no point in arguing. He'd made up his mind, and she couldn't tell him. Not without exposing her father's most shameful secrets. "Fine."

"One last thing before we leave. Go bend over my

desk so I can plug your bottom and get you ready for Daddy's cock."

Moving stiffly, she crossed the room to his desk, lowering her torso so that her arms rested on top of the papers scattered across his desk and her bottom was offered up for his pleasure. Every step made the clamps tug at her various parts, making her throb with pain and pleasure in equal parts.

"Good girl. You remember how to take a plug?"

"Yes, Daddy."

It wasn't quite as hard as the first time, though she still struggled to relax and allow it in. And, if she wasn't mistaken, it was a hell of a lot larger than the last one he'd used, so it burned more going in than she remembered.

When it was finally seated, he helped her to stand and pressed a kiss to her lips. "Come on, Lottie-bug. Let's go have a drink and then Daddy has a room reserved for you to lose at least one virginity tonight."

LOTTIE

She should hate him. That was the one thought that kept running through her mind over and over as they made their way past the other tables to the VIP booth where Damian and Emily were snuggled up together.

But the admiring glances she got from various patrons of all genders helped to soothe out her ruffled feathers. Maybe it made her vain, but nothing improved her mood like knowing that people were watching her. Admiring her.

Wanting her.

So by the time they settled into the booth with their guests, she was feeling much more chipper than she had been when they'd left his office, even though the walk hadn't been very long and all her naughty bits were still throbbing in their confines.

Her good mood was bolstered even more by the way Emily's eyes nearly fell out of her head. And, she was petty enough to admit, by the deepening of Damian's scowl.

"We can't stay long," Braden said, wrapping an arm around her shoulder and pulling her close. "Charlotte and I have an appointment in the princess room in a few minutes."

"The princess room?" Lottie asked, excitement buzzing along her skin once more. "That sounds like fun."

Braden and Damian shared a smug look that sent her stomach churning. "I think you'll enjoy it, Lottie-bug. I certainly will."

"That sounds ominous."

"Anyway." Damian's no-nonsense tone had Lottie rolling her eyes, which Braden either didn't notice or chose to ignore. "We need to talk about the auction."

That was absolutely the last thing she wanted to do, but one look at the Elliott brothers' stern faces told her she wasn't getting out of it. "Fine," she snapped, crossing her arms and immediately regretting the decision when the move tugged painfully at her clamps. "What do you want to know?"

"We know how Emily learned about the auction. How did you hear about it?"

"If I tell you, will the person who told me be in trouble?"

"As long as they aren't actually involved in the auction there won't be any trouble, little one. Who is it?"

As much as she didn't want to rat Frankie out, she wasn't about to earn herself another punishment. And Braden had said she wouldn't be in trouble, so maybe Frankie would forgive her if Braden decided to question her. "My friend Frankie. Francesca Legare. She's—"

"I know Frankie," Braden said with a sigh. "And I've already spoken with her. She found out from some of my employees, so that's another dead end."

"Is there anything else you can think of, Charlotte?" Damian asked, his expression turning earnest. "Anything at all that might help us figure out who's running the auction?"

"No, I'm sorry. I didn't even realize it wasn't Braden running it until he confronted me and Master O."

Damian snorted. "Is he still going by that ridiculous nickname?"

"Yes." Braden's single-syllable response was clipped, piquing Lottie's interest.

"What ridiculous nickname? I thought it was just because his last name starts with an 'O'."

Pulling Lottie even closer, Braden pressed a kiss to her hair. "And as far as you'll ever know, that's exactly the reason why."

"But Damian just said—"

"Okay, I'm sorry, I have to interrupt." The words seemed to explode out of Emily, who was in the process of turning roughly the same shade of red as a tomato. "But I am dying to know. Doesn't that hurt?"

She gestured wildly in Lottie's direction and Lottie glanced down at the gold chains decorating her nipples. "Not as much as they did when he first put them on. Mostly I'm just really fucking horny. But I think that's because of the one he put on my clit."

"On your *what?*"

"My clit. Wanna see?"

At Damian's exasperated glare, Braden laughed. "And I believe that's our cue to go. Emily, Damian, enjoy your evening. We'll see you around."

Braden nudged her out of the booth and Lottie smirked up at him as he looped an arm around her waist. "Was it something I said?"

"Not at all, little one. But I have far better things in store for you tonight than corrupting my brother's fiancé."

"Oh. Then by all means. Lead the way."

19

THE WRONG VIRGINITY

BRADEN

He was practically vibrating with excitement by the time he opened the door to the princess room. Even more so when Charlotte gasped and hurried inside, her expression filled with awe as she turned in place to study the spacious space from every angle.

Not that he could blame her. He had, if he did say so himself, outdone himself with this room especially. Every room at BDE had its own carefully selected theme, but this was one of his favorites.

Everything was done in shades of rose and gold, with hints of silver here and there. Floggers with thick leather falls in deep pink with gold handles were hung along the walls. Two armoires filled with dozens of other implements flanked the giant bed along the far wall. The bed itself was piled high with plush blankets and pillows, and the deceptively comfortable-looking headboard was framed with thick drapes in those same shades of pink and gold.

"There are even thrones!" Squealing with delight, Charlotte raced toward the two 'thrones' in the middle of the room.

The first one she approached looked more like a traditional throne, with leather that matched the floggers along the wall and metal in a darker, burnished gold. Other than the gaping hole in the middle of the seat, one might confuse it with an actual throne.

"That one isn't for you, little one," he said with a chuckle as she ran her hands along the supple leather.

"But it's so pretty."

"It is. But that's a throne for a queen." Resting his hands on her shoulders, he turned her to the other throne. "This one is for naughty little princesses."

The second throne was clearly meant to be knelt on instead of sat on, with two knee pads in a pale pink. White metal rose up high, with multiple rings attached to the sides and the top.

He had plans for those rings.

"Oh." Charlotte's response was breathless, and he couldn't help but laugh.

"Up you go, your highness."

Taking her hand, he helped her up onto the throne, kneeling with her legs spread slightly and her bottom pushed out enough for him to have access.

"Don't you look so pretty, your highness, seated on your throne. Waiting for your prince to come… rescue you."

A delicate shiver wracked her body. "Thank you, Daddy."

Crossing the room to one of the armoires, he opened the chest and pulled out a set of leather cuffs that had been painted a gorgeous gold.

When he turned back, Charlotte was watching him, with the guarded curiosity of a submissive who wasn't sure exactly what her Dominant had planned for her. Or if she would enjoy it.

That expression was a fucking aphrodisiac for a sadist like him.

"Arms up, princess."

LOTTIE

Heart hammering against her ribcage, she raised her arms up and gripped the top of her throne. Braden wrapped one wrist in leather, then attached the chain to the top ring of the throne before repeating the process on the other side. By the time he was done, her arms were stretched up above her head, but with her weight resting on her knees, it wasn't painful or really even super uncomfortable.

She had a feeling it wouldn't stay that way for long.

A feeling that was confirmed when he gripped the top of the plug in her bottom. "Last chance to change my mind, princess. Tell me the truth, and I'll take the virginity you really want to lose tonight."

She wanted to. Why couldn't he see how badly she wanted to tell him? "I can't. I'm sorry, but I can't."

"Pity."

The plug was pulled from her, stretching her wide again, and she whimpered at the bite and burn of pain. Behind her, she could hear him moving around, but she couldn't quite tell what he was doing.

Then he was behind her again, the heat of his naked body all but slamming into her as the head of his cock pressed against her bottom hole.

"Ready, princess?"

As much as she wanted him to fuck her the right way, she was so hungry for him she would take whatever she could get. "Yes, Daddy."

"That's my good little girl." His cock pressed into

her at the same time his hand came up to wrap around her throat, forcing her head back. "Goddamn, baby. You feel so fucking good on Daddy's cock. How does it feel?"

With his hand around her throat, she couldn't breathe as deeply as she wanted to, and the limited oxygen made her head swim in the most delicious way. "Full. So full."

His chuckle rumbled in her ear. "And I'm not even halfway in yet."

Oh, she was so screwed.

Pulling back, he rocked inside her, short shallow thrusts that sent ripples of pain and pleasure up her spine. And still she wanted more.

"Daddy, please."

"Yes, my princess?"

"More," she rasped out. "More. Please, Daddy, I need more."

This time when he rocked forward, he pressed deeper, filling her. "As you wish, princess."

It took a few more of those rocking strokes, but then he was buried inside her, his cock splitting her open, filling her up.

"Do you remember what I told you, baby?"

"N-no, Daddy."

The hand around her throat tightened, cutting off even more of her air as his other hand slid down her front toward her clit. "I told you if you were a good girl, you'd get to come with your bottom stuffed full of Daddy's cock. And you've been a *very* good girl."

Pleasure, brain-scrambling, molten-hot pleasure flooded her system as he pulled the clamp from her. And when he pressed his fingers against her clit, she screamed as the most intense orgasm she'd ever experienced slammed into her.

A scream tore from her throat, a wordless cry of need and desire as he forced more and more of that unimaginable pleasure on her.

Then he was moving again, his cock slowly sliding from her, pushing back in as he fucked her ass with slow, sure strokes.

"I love watching you come for me, baby. Ready to do it again?"

She sobbed as his hand left her throat, to the chains still attached to her nipples, while his other hand continued to play with her pussy. The pleasure from her clit had already morphed into pain. There was no possible way she could take another orgasm like the one she'd just had. "I can't, I can't. Daddy, please."

"Oh, little one. It's so cute that you think you have a choice."

As he spoke, he pressed harder against her clit, pleasure and pain melding together so completely she lost track of where one ended and the other began. And all the while, he fucked her ass, adding layers and layers to the sensations overwhelming her body.

Just as the pain in her pussy gave way to pure pleasure, he tugged at the chains, sending a jolt of agony through her breasts and straight to her clit. She cried out again, begged again, though she'd long since lost track of exactly what she was begging for.

"Are you going to be a good girl and come for me again, princess Charlotte?"

"I don't... I can't... I don't know." Her words were broken up by heaving, sobbing breaths. "Daddy. Daddy, please."

"Daddy's so fucking proud of how well you're taking his cock in your tight little ass, princess. You can give me one more, baby. I know you can. Make Daddy *proud*."

In perfect timing with that final word, he yanked the clamps from her nipples. Pain, white hot and piercing, flooded her system, bringing with it a tidal wave of pleasure.

Drowning. She was drowning in him. The world around her went black, and the wave was a roar in her ears that blocked out every other sound.

Gradually, the roar receded, and she was dimly aware of her Daddy's voice, soft and coaxing just like his hands as they caressed her aching body.

"My beautiful princess," he whispered in her ear, his voice hoarse with desire. "You were born for this, baby. Born for my cock. Born to take me, just like this. Only me. Say it, Charlotte. Say you belong to me. Only me."

"Only... only you," she managed to gasp out. "I belong to you, Daddy. Only you."

"Good girl. That's my good fucking girl. I'm going to fill you up now, and you're going to spend the rest of the night walking around the club with your ass full of Daddy's cum. Ready, princess?"

"Yes, Daddy," she said with a dreamy sigh, her head falling back against him as he pressed a kiss to the side of her neck.

With a groan, he slammed into her one final time, his cock swelling inside her bottom and filling it with the warmth of his pleasure. Inside that most private, shameful part of her, his cock twitched and spasmed until finally, at long last, he was finished.

It was like watching someone else as he slid free from her, then pushed the plug back into her ass. She winced when he freed her arms, and he murmured words of comfort to her as he scooped her up and carried her to the impossibly plush bed.

His hands on her were almost more than she could bear as he stroked her, cuddled her. But she couldn't stand the thought of being apart from him for even a second, so she ignored the slight discomfort and burrowed into him, wishing she could somehow get closer even though the logical part of her knew the only way to actually get any closer would be to climb inside his skin.

"That was fucking perfect, Lottie-bug," he said once their systems had a chance to settle. "How are you feeling?"

"Wrecked," she replied with a weak laugh. "Kind of like you just reached inside me and scrambled up my insides. But in a good way."

"I'll take that as a compliment." He pressed a kiss to her forehead. "We have the room for another hour if you'd like a nap."

Already, her eyes were drifting close. "A nap sounds lovely."

She was almost asleep when she heard him, his voice low as though he was trying to avoid waking her.

"Goddammit. I think I'm in love with you, Charlotte Duvall. What the hell am I going to tell your father?"

In that moment, she didn't give a flying fuck what they told her father. Her Daddy loved her, and that was all that mattered.

20

PASS THE SALT, DADDY

BRADEN

He'd never been so nervous for a dinner in his life.

Even when he'd proposed to his first wife, at the most expensive restaurant he could afford at the time, he'd been so sure of her answer he hadn't really been nervous at all.

Because, he was forced to admit, he'd been more or less in control of that situation. He and Laura had discussed marriage extensively, and they'd even gone ring browsing together so he'd had a fairly good idea of what she might like. Barring some unforeseen circumstances, it had been pretty much a done deal before he'd even gotten down on one knee.

Tonight, however... tonight was a completely

different story. Every scenario he ran through his head had a wildly different outcome. And while some outcomes seemed more plausible than others, he still had absolutely zero control over what happened.

And he fucking hated it.

But his momma hadn't raised the type of man who ran when things got hard. So, he put on his big boy pants—and the nicest suit he owned that wasn't a literal tuxedo—and greeted his closest friend at the door for the sole purpose of telling him he was in love with his daughter.

"Emmett. Charlotte. Come in." Stepping aside, he ushered them in. "Dinner's just about ready."

"Something smells delicious." Emmett rubbed his hands together and breathed deeply. "Oh my. Is that beef Wellington I smell?"

"It is. I know it's your favorite and I haven't had it in a while." It couldn't, he'd figured, hurt to butter Emmett up a bit before dropping the bombshell of a lifetime on his head.

"Excellent. Shall we?"

"Make yourself at home."

From behind her father, Charlotte smiled, her eyes dancing with mischief. She waited until Emmett disappeared around the corner on his way to the dining room to close the distance between herself and Braden, her head tilted back as if inviting a kiss. "So, what's the plan, Daddy?"

"I'm not sure," he confessed, giving in to the urge to run his fingers down her bare arms.

"And I bet that's killing you," she said with a throaty laugh.

"It is. I don't particularly enjoy situations where I'm unsure of the outcome."

"Poor Daddy." Reaching between them, she cupped his groin and squeezed. "Maybe we should go find an empty room where I can help you... relieve some stress."

"And ruin your makeup before dinner? I don't think so, little one."

"Why would..." Her eyes went wide with understanding as he pressed the pad of his thumb to her bottom lip, pulling it down and forcing her mouth open.

"As much as I would enjoy using your mouth for stress relief right now, having you show up to dinner looking deliciously rumpled and used isn't exactly how I planned on telling your father about us. So you'll have to wait until after dinner for me to wreck you."

Feeling somewhat bolstered by her uneven breaths and the soft whimper that escaped when he stole a kiss, he nudged her gently toward the dining room.

No matter what happened tonight, at least he had something to look forward to when it was all said and done.

❧

LOTTIE

She couldn't remember the last time she'd seen her father this happy. Certainly not since her mother's diagnosis. Watching him with Braden, laughing and drinking and sharing stories from their past was like watching him come alive again.

Granted, it was a little weird listening to him share stories about her as a child. Weirder, still, when Braden would laugh along and add his own memories to the mix. But if it made her father happy, she was willing to let herself be embarrassed for an evening.

That didn't mean she couldn't have some fun at their expense.

Slipping off one of her heels, she reached her foot out toward Braden, who happened to be seated directly across from her. When her toes slid up over his dress pants, his gaze flicked over to her. And even though it was only for a split second, there was a wealth of warning in that look.

She'd never been very good at heeding warnings, as the story her father was currently telling about how she and Frankie had nearly burned the Legare's house down with the chemistry kit Frankie had gotten one year for Christmas clearly confirmed. So she simply slid her foot higher and higher, up his calf to his knee.

In a move so smooth she wouldn't have noticed it if she hadn't been watching him so intently, he reached under the table and grabbed her foot. Lottie tried to pull away, but he had a firm grip on her and she didn't want to alert her father that anything was amiss by yanking too hard.

Braden held her foot hostage all the way up until her dad excused himself to the bathroom as the soup was exchanged for the main course. When they were alone, Braden gave her foot a hard tug, and she slid down in her chair with a yelp.

"If you're looking to get your bottom spanked tonight, you're well on your way, Charlotte Ann."

Pushing herself back up in her chair, she glared at him. "I didn't even do anything!"

"You're being a tease, and you know it. Now, if I let go of your foot, are you going to be a good girl?"

"Yes, Daddy."

"That's my girl." With one more squeeze of her foot, he released her just as her dad returned to the dining room.

"So, Braden," he said as he settled back into the seat beside Lottie. "Have you been seeing anyone lately?"

Lottie had to bite the inside of her cheek from laughing when Braden, who had the bad luck of taking a sip of water at exactly the same time Emmett asked that question, inhaled too sharply and nearly choked on his drink.

"Ah..." Braden cleared his throat and set his glass down, where it wouldn't be a threat to his wellbeing. "You know who I haven't talked to in ages? Mandy Andersen. After Victor went missing she stopped coming around as much. I tried to get her to join the club a while back, but she wouldn't come without Victor. I think she's still convinced he's coming home."

Dammit. Was he really going to chicken out on her, after he'd given her that lecture about not sneaking around her dad's back?

Annoyed by that possibility, she sent him a dark look that he pointedly ignored. Which only made her even more irritated as she drained what was left in her wine glass and poured another. Now it was her turn to ignore *his* disapproving frown as she filled her glass up almost to the rim.

To Lottie's left, her dad shook his head somberly. "Poor thing. It's almost worse, I think, not knowing. At least with Nat we had some sense of closure."

Danger, danger, danger! If her dad got to talking about her mom, the whole evening was destined to go downhill. And after watching him come alive over the past hour, she was damned if she'd let him withdraw into himself again.

She needed something, anything to divert his attention. Even better if it forced Braden to come clean about their relationship like he'd been so fucking gung-ho about doing just a few days ago. Racking her brain, she took another bite of beef wellington and glanced around the table, desperate for inspiration.

And inspiration she found.

"Daddy," she said sweetly, making sure her desperation didn't come through in her tone. "Will you pass the salt, please?"

"Of course, honey."

"Sure thing, Lottie-bug."

As she'd hoped, both men reached for the salt shaker in the middle of the table at exactly the same time. And froze with their fingers less than an inch apart.

The look of sheer terror on Braden's face had her slapping a hand over her mouth to smother the laugh that threatened to escape. If she laughed at him now, she had no doubt she'd be in for the spanking of a lifetime. But the alcohol and the sheer absurdity of the situation was making it increasingly difficult to hold back her mirth.

"Ah... my mistake." Braden's smile was distinctly forced, and if she wasn't mistaken, he was looking a little green around the gills as he pulled his hand back. "I'm just so used to having Aria around..."

"That makes sense." Though her father's voice was completely calm, there was a tone to it that had the hair on the back of Lottie's neck standing on end. "Other than the fact that you clearly said my daughter's name."

Braden's face paled even further as he held his hands up in a time-honored gesture of surrender. "Look, Emmett, I can explain—"

Her dad's chair toppled over as he leapt to his feet, startling a shriek out of Lottie. "Explain what, Braden? That you put your filthy hands on my sweet little Lottie?" A vein in his neck popped out as he leaned over the table, invading Braden's space. "How long have you been waiting? Watching?"

All of a sudden, the color drained from her dad's

face as he spun around to face her. "Oh, god. Lottie. Did he... How old were you...?"

"No, no, no, it wasn't like that, Dad, I swear." Desperate to ease her fears, she laid her hands on his arm and squeezed reassuringly. "It wasn't even Braden's fault."

Wrong thing to say, judging by how the color came rushing violently back into her father's cheeks. "Not his fault? That's exactly what abusers want you to think!"

"Emmett, please sit down so we can talk about this." In contrast to her father's increasingly shrill voice, Braden's was calm, soothing, and Lottie found herself wanting to crawl into his lap to let him cuddle her.

But she was legitimately worried doing so might give her father a coronary.

This was not the fun little prank she'd hoped it would be.

"I will not sit down. I can't even fucking look at you, Braden. How could you? She is my *child*. My everything."

"She's my everything, too," Braden replied quietly. "I swear to you, Emmett, I never meant for this to happen."

"You really expect me to believe that?"

Fuck, fuck, fuck. This was spiraling out of control

so fast. "He's telling the truth, Dad. He was trying to protect me."

"Protect you? With his dick?"

Heat flooded her cheeks at her father's crude words. "Stop that. It's not... you don't know the whole story."

"I know my supposed *best friend* apparently fucked my daughter. You think I don't know what kind of club he runs? What it means for you to call him Daddy?"

"I really, really don't want to think about that," Lottie mumbled.

"That makes two of us." Eyes blazing with fury, her dad turned back to Braden, who was watching the scene unfold with a carefully blank expression. "We're fucking done, Braden. I don't want you anywhere near me or my daughter ever again. Come one, Lottie, we're going home."

"Dad, no. I need you to *listen*."

"There's nothing he can say that will change my mind."

"I did it for you!"

The words burst out of her, tiny little winged demons born of desperation. Braden and her father both froze in place and turned nearly identical confused expressions her way.

"You... slept with my best friend... for me?" Her

dad's voice was so full of pain, it threatened to shatter her heart. "I don't understand."

Oh, god. She'd never intended to tell him what she'd done. Even if she'd eventually caved to Braden's pressure and told him why she'd put herself up for auction, she would have made him promise not to let her father know.

But it looked like that was no longer an option.

"I... I... I..." Air. She needed air, but she couldn't seem to get it into her lungs.

"Charlotte. Explain. Now."

Surprisingly, the whip crack of her Daddy's voice seemed to break down the walls holding back her words, and they came pouring out of her in a rush. "I was at brunch with the girls, and it was my turn to pay but my credit cards kept getting declined, so I came home and I snuck on your computer to see what the problem was and I'm sorry, I know I'm not supposed to but I was sure it was just a glitch or something. But then I saw your accounts, and the gambling, and I didn't know what to do, and then I found out about this auction and I just..." Feeling as helpless and alone as she had that day, she held out her hands. "I didn't know what to do."

"Gambling?"

"Auction?"

Their questions clashed in the air around her, and

once again she couldn't breathe. Suddenly, the thought of actually explaining everything was more than she could bear. "I'm sorry. I'm so sorry. I can't... I'm sorry."

Half-blinded by tears, she shoved her chair back and raced for the front door, ignoring the voices calling her name. By some miracle, she made it all the way to her room without anyone catching her.

Yanking her phone from her pocket, she swiped at her eyes as she pressed buttons with trembling fingers.

"Frankie? Oh, thank god. I need somewhere to lay low for a bit. Does your dad still have that cabin?"

21

SHOW ME YOURS, I'LL SHOW YOU MINE

BRADEN

What the hell had just happened?

Sitting in his dining room, with one empty chair half-haphazardly shoved away from the table and his best friend still standing over him like some avenging God, Braden was, for once in his life, at a complete loss for what to do next.

He wanted to go after Charlotte, to hold her and comfort her and tell her everything would be okay. Before finally taking the virginity she'd been all but begging him to take.

But as much as she might need him, he had a feeling that if he left now, the damage to his and Emmett's relationship would be irreversible. And in the long run, that would be far more painful for Charlotte than crying alone in her room for a bit.

"Gambling?"

He winced internally. It wasn't what he'd meant to say, but apparently it was what his brain had latched onto.

Grimacing, Emmett slid back down into his chair. "I have it under control."

"Obviously not, if your daughter felt like she had to auction off her virginity to save your ass." Shit. That definitely wasn't how he'd meant to break that particular news. Hell, he'd never meant to tell Emmett that at all. But his nerves were scraped raw, and his filter had apparently been turned off by the absolute shit show the night had turned into.

All the color seemed to drain out of Emmett's face. "Her... you... what the *fuck* is going on, Braden?"

"I think this conversation calls for something stronger than wine." Rising from his chair, Braden made his way over to the small liquor cabinet at the far end of the room and poured them each a healthy shot of bourbon. Back at the table, he returned to his seat and slid one of the glasses over to Emmett. He wasn't quite convinced that if he got within arm's reach Emmett wouldn't still deck him.

Not that he could say he wouldn't deserve it. But he wasn't really in the mood for a fist to the face.

"To answer your main question, no, I haven't. Not yet. But I will, because I'm in love with her, Emmett. I know that's a hard fucking pill to swallow, I do, but I am. I meant it when I said she's my everything. I've never loved another woman the way I love your daughter, and I plan to do everything in my power to make her happy as long as she'll have me."

"Even Laura?" Emmett asked, his brows raising.

"Yes." Laura had been his high school sweetheart. And while he'd loved her, the way only an eighteen-year-old boy could love the girl he was determined to marry, they'd never been quite right for each other. Laura had enjoyed a bit of kinky play in the bedroom from time to time, but she'd balked at submitting to him outside of that. It had taken them far too long to realize they could never be what the other truly needed.

But Charlotte... not only had she eagerly accepted his dominance, she'd blossomed under it in ways Laura never had. Where Laura had told him he was controlling and domineering, Charlotte gleefully pushed his buttons and then took her punishment like the good girl she was beneath the sass and sarcasm.

Lifting the tumbler to his lips, Emmett drained half the glass in a single swallow. "I can't give you my blessing, Braden. That's my little girl, and you're literally old enough to be her father. You watched her grow up, for fuck's sake."

"I know. I'm not asking for your blessing, but I'd settle for... acceptance, I suppose. Anything less than open hostility. But for now, I assume you'd like to know exactly how all of this went down."

"From the sound of it, you bought her at an auction, like a fucking cow."

"I wouldn't let her hear you comparing her to cattle," Braden said with a humorless laugh. "But no, I did not pay for her. Well, I suppose I did, but after the fact. Killian O'Rourke bought her, originally."

What color had returned to Emmett's face immediately disappeared again. "You let a fucking mob boss take my daughter's virginity?"

"No. Luckily for all of us, Killian brought her to the club. When I saw them together, I dragged them both to my office and told him she was off-limits to him."

"I suppose you think I owe you for that."

"Never. You would have done the same if it was Aria." Perhaps not for the same reasons, exactly, but Braden liked to think he would have stepped in even if he hadn't already been developing feelings for Charlotte. "But I made Killian a deal. I paid him back what he'd bid on Charlotte, she got to keep the money, and she came to work for me."

"Lottie's been working at your club? For how long?"

"A little over a week. I've been trying to get her to tell me why she put herself up for auction, but she's a stubborn little thing."

"Gets that from her mama." A ghost of a smile graced Emmett's face. "Once Nat made up her mind she was or wasn't going to do something, even paddling her ass wouldn't get her to change her mind." As if suddenly realizing exactly how Braden had been attempting to extract information from his daughter, Emmett pulled a face. "That's a rabbit hole I'd rather not fall down."

"Can't say I blame you." Braden took a deep swallow of his bourbon. "All right. I showed you mine, you show me yours. How bad is it, Emmett? Really."

"Bad. I've known it was bad for a while, but I didn't realize just how fucked we were until the other day, when you came to visit. I think Lottie must have been on my computer, because when I logged in that morning some of the accounts were still up and I was finally forced to acknowledge how bad things had really gotten. It's not 'we're going to lose everything and be homeless' bad but bad enough. And I haven't the first fucking clue how to dig myself out of the hole I've dug for us."

"First things first, no more gambling, and no more drinking. I'm serious, Emmett. Whatever plan you make is just going to unravel if you keep pissing away your money like that."

"I know. I do," he insisted when Braden raised a brow. "I've already closed all of my accounts. Just wish I knew what the fuck to do next."

"What you're going to do next is accept some help." That part was non-negotiable as far as Braden was concerned. Emmett could hate him all he wanted, but he wasn't going to sit idly by as people he cared about struggled unnecessarily when he was more than capable of helping. "The money Charlotte received from the auction is going to be invested. I'll call my guy in the morning and have him talk her through all of that. She deserves to know her future is secure, regardless of what either of us do. And then you and I are going to sit down and go through your accounts one by one and make a plan. I assume you have assets that can be liquidated?"

"Some. Not as many as I would like, but enough, I think, to plug the dam a bit."

"Then that's what we'll do." Draining the rest of his whiskey, Braden set the glass down and stood, feeling lighter than he had in weeks. "Come on. We should go check on Charlotte. Poor thing is probably locked in her room thinking the worst."

Emmett polished off his drink as well, and they made their way toward the front door together in what Braden assumed to be a companionable silence.

"Braden?"

"Yeah?"

He turned as they reached the front door, and pain exploded across his right cheek. Stumbling backward into the wall, Braden lifted a hand to his face and rubbed at the spot where Emmett's fist had connected. "Jesus. You've got one hell of a right hook."

"Good. That's for whatever the hell it is you've been doing with my little girl behind my back. But I'll mess up a lot more than just your pretty face if you break her heart. Understood?"

"Understood."

"Good."

They made it over to Emmet's house without any more violence and were greeted by almost complete silence when they stepped inside. Braden was reminded of the times he'd come to visit recently and been surprised by the lack of staff in his friend's home. But Emmett had obviously already been trying to plug those holes in the dam he'd been talking about even before Charlotte had realized what was going on.

Thinking about his little girl taking on that kind

of burden made him want to strangle Emmett a bit. If he didn't get his act together soon, that might still be on the table. For now, he was willing to give his friend the benefit of the doubt and do whatever it took to make things better for him, and for Charlotte.

"She must be up in her room," Emmett said as they made their way toward the stairs.

But even as they started the climb, alarm bells rang in the back of Braden's mind. He couldn't put his finger on it, but something just felt... off. The house was too quiet, even if Charlotte had locked herself away in her room.

"Lottie?" Standing outside her room, Emmett leaned into the door, listening for her response. "Open up honey, it's Dad..." He trailed off and grimaced. "It's Dad. Open the door honey, Braden and I just want to talk to you."

"Is it locked?"

Emmett tested the knob. "No."

"Open it. Just do it, Emmett," he snapped when Emmett shook his head.

Frowning, Emmett turned the knob and pushed the door open. Braden stepped in behind him, his suspicions confirmed as he scanned the room. His stomach sank, fear and worry churning in his gut.

"Son of a bitch. She's gone."

LOTTIE

"So, yeah. Now Braden knows the real reason I put myself up for auction and my dad knows I sold myself to pay off his debts." Groaning loudly, Lottie grabbed a throw pillow and pressed it against her face, as if hiding herself physically could make the problem go away.

"Well, that's good."

Yanking the pillow from her face, she glared at Frankie, who was curled up in the armchair beside the couch Lottie had thrown herself onto when she'd arrived at the cabin. "Good? How is any of this *good*?"

"No more secrets. Your dad knows about you and Braden, and you can finally get your cherry popped." Frankie scowled. "I can't believe he held out on you like that. The bastard."

The moment Lottie had stepped foot in the cabin, she'd broken down and told Frankie every dirty little detail of her short-lived relationship with Braden Elliott. Frankie had, in a very un-Frankie fashion, listened silently throughout the entire sordid story.

"Weren't you listening? I ruined their friendship, Frankie. They're never going to forgive me."

"Well, I think that might be a little dramatic. Your dad loves you and it sounds like your Daddy does, too." Wrinkling her nose, Frankie shook her head. "Okay, yeah, I hear how weird that is, now."

"Fine. Maybe they'll forgive me. But how the hell am I supposed to look my dad in the eye after this? He's never going to look at me the same way again."

"Honey, I hate to break it to you, but that's pretty much any dad after he discovers his precious baby girl has done the deed. He'll get over it."

"Yeah, but most dads don't also have to come to terms with their daughters whoring themselves out."

The look Frankie sent her was the very definition of withering. "Okay, first of all, not a fan of that phrasing. Second of all, if he has a problem with it, then he needs to look in a mirror. You never would have done the auction if he hadn't pissed away all your money."

"I'm not sure he'll see it that way."

"We won't give him a choice."

Love and gratitude welled in Lottie's chest. And her eyes. Blinking back tears, she sent Frankie a watery smile. "I love you."

"Love you, too. Are you going to call them and let them know where you are?"

"I don't think I can face them yet."

"And you have the nerve to call Portia the drama

queen." Giggling, Frankie just managed to duck and avoid the pillow Lottie threw at her. "At least text them and let them know you're safe. Trust me, if you let Braden worry about you while you're tucked safely away in a luxurious cabin, you will never sit comfortably again."

"Ugh. I hate that you're probably right."

"I'm definitely right. Text him, and I'll go grab us a bottle of wine so you can go over all the filthy, filthy details of your night in the princess room. I have *questions*."

Laughter helped to break up some of the tension in Lottie's chest as she pulled her phone from her pocket and tapped out messages to Braden and her dad. Then she turned the phone off and pushed all thoughts of what a horrible daughter and girlfriend she was out of her mind as Frankie handed her a glass of wine larger than her head.

22

FOUND, SAFE AND SOUNDLY SPANKED

BRADEN

I'm with a friend and I'm safe. I'm so
sorry. I'll be home soon.

Nearly twenty-four hours after Charlotte's disappearing act, Braden was all but pulling his hair out as he reread her one and only text for what felt like the millionth time. Her phone was either dead or deliberately turned off, so every phone call he made went straight to voicemail. And now even that was full, mostly with increasingly more threatening messages from him.

The last one he'd been able to leave had promised her the spanking of a lifetime if she didn't call him back in the next hour.

That had been nearly two hours ago.

A knock on his door had Braden pausing his path across the office floor, his head jerking up as hope beat painfully at his chest. But it wasn't his Lottie-bug on the other side. It was Desmond, with his partner Bastian following closely behind, the former with an amused smile tugging at his lips, while the latter at least had the decency to look concerned.

"Still no word?" Bastian asked.

"No. Emmett even tried her friends, all of whom either genuinely don't know anything or who are being frustratingly tight-lipped about the whole thing."

"We did some digging. As much as we could without an open investigation." When Braden opened his mouth, Desmond just rolled his eyes. "For the tenth time, Braden, we can't open a missing persons case on an adult who hasn't even been gone for a full twenty-four hours and who has already told you she's safe."

"Damian would," Braden mumbled.

"Because Damian has absolutely zero regard for law and order." There was a snap to Desmond's voice that had Bastian sighing and shaking his head.

"There's probably some truth to that." And because there was, Braden couldn't help wondering if he'd called the wrong brother. Not that Damian had the connections his twin did, but at least he'd be willing to *do* something. "I'm just going out of my fucking mind here, Des. I hate not knowing where she is, who she's with, if she's okay. I just want my little girl back, so I can blister her ass for making me worry and then tie her to my bed for the rest of her life so she can never pull something like this again."

"For our own sanity, we're going to assume you mean that last part figuratively," Bastian said dryly. "As for the spanking, I can't say I blame you there. But maybe that should wait until you've given her a chance to explain why she took off."

"Bastian, if you're going to bring logic into my nervous breakdown, I'm going to have to insist you leave."

A smile curved Bastian's lips as he shrugged. "I'm nothing if not logical, my friend. And you know I'm right."

"Yeah, yeah. I know. But the only thing keeping me halfway sane right now is envisioning exactly how she's going to look over my knee when I finally find her."

"Fair enough."

The phone Braden hadn't let go of for more than a few seconds at a time since last night buzzed in his hand. Staring down at the unknown number, he hit the button to answer it, his heart pounding as a dozen different scenarios ran through his mind. "Hello? Lottie, is that you?"

"Sorry to disappoint you, Master Braden," an amused voice answered. It sounded familiar, but Braden couldn't quite place where he'd heard it before. "This is Frankie. Lottie's friend?"

"Yes. I remember. Holden Prescott's little girl," he added, more for the notes Desmond was furiously tapping out on his phone than anything.

"Former," Frankie replied, her tone bland as if her apparent break-up hadn't affected her in the least. "But yes. Look, I'm breaking literally every girl code rule here, but Lottie isn't listening to reason. Before I tell you where she is, though, I need to know what your intentions are with my friend."

Braden held up a finger to halt Desmond's note-taking. "Do you mean before or after I blister her ass for disappearing on me without a word?"

There was a beat of silence before Frankie's throaty laughter came through the speaker. "After. And I meant more long-term."

"I want whatever she's willing to give me. I love her, Frankie. And I'm damn well not letting her out of my sight again for a very long time after this stunt."

Another long pause. "All right. She's going to kill me for this, but... My father has a cabin a couple hours outside of Charleston. I'm about to go let Lottie know that I need to leave for a bit. Oh, and I have her keys, so she will be stuck here if someone wanted to come paddle some fucking sense into her ass."

"Frankie, you just bought yourself a lifetime membership to Club BDE, on me. Text me the address. I'm on my way."

❧

LOTTIE

Hiding out in Frankie's cabin had been a lot more fun with Frankie here. And she couldn't even find her car keys so she could go into town and ease her woes with some retail therapy.

She'd probably be less bored out of her mind if she turned her phone back on. But she had a feeling if she did that, she'd be bombarded with messages from Braden and her dad, demanding to know where she was, blah blah blah.

Or, worse yet, she'd turn her phone back on and there would be *no* messages because they'd both decided she wasn't worth the trouble she'd brought to their friendship. When she'd expressed that concern earlier in the day, Frankie had simply stared at her with an 'are you fucking kidding me' sort of expression before disappearing into her bedroom for nearly an hour. After which she'd emerged freshly showered and dressed, announced that she was going into town for supplies, and that by the time she got back she expected Lottie to have pulled her head out of her ass and called Braden.

That had been over two hours ago, and Lottie still hadn't gotten the nerve to even turn her phone back on.

Sorry Frankie.

The sound of tires on gravel and footsteps on the front steps had Lottie bolting upright on the couch like an eager puppy waiting for its master to return home. "Jesus, Frankie, what kind of supplies did you —you're not Frankie."

"I certainly am not." His expression almost eerily calm, Braden closed the door behind him. All of a sudden, the spacious cabin was far too small. His presence seemed to fill up the room, and Lottie froze in place, watching him as he approached the couch.

Unbuttoning one shirt sleeve, he carefully rolled it to his elbow as he advanced. She just barely caught herself before she licked her lips at the sight of his muscular forearm being exposed inch by inch, the thick veins flexing as he finished tucking the sleeve into place. "You have about ten seconds to convince me why I shouldn't spank that naughty little bottom of yours until you can't sit comfortably for a week."

"I, um..." All the reasons she'd given Frankie for fleeing suddenly seemed silly and childish. "Because you're just so happy to find me, safe and sound, you've decided you're not mad anymore?"

"I am very happy to have found you. But I've had about three hours to get over my relief at knowing where you are, so unfortunately for you, that's not going to save you."

Climbing down from the couch, she backed away, carefully keeping herself out of reach. "Can't we talk about this, first?"

"Sure." Despite his agreement, he didn't so much as pause his advancement. "You can start by telling me why you disappeared, turned your phone off, and left me wondering where the hell you were."

"I was upset."

"That makes two of us."

The backs of Lottie's legs hit something hard, making her stumble. Braden lunged for her, hauling her against him, and her breath caught in her chest at the furious, determined look in his eyes.

"Naughty girl," he murmured, a moment before

he dragged her back to the couch and sat, pulling her uncaremoniously down over his knees.

"Daddy, no!"

Grabbing the hand she threw behind her in a vain attempt to protect her bottom, he pinned her wrist to the small of her back as he wrestled her leggings down to her knees.

Pain radiated across her backside as his hand smacked against her bare skin over and over. Holy shit, had he been holding back this whole time? She didn't remember her other spankings hurting nearly this much.

"You do not run from me." His words were punctuated by sharp, stinging slaps that had her drumming her feet against the couch cushions. "If you're upset about something, you can cry, you can yell, you can even tell me you need some time to yourself. But you will not run from me ever again, Charlotte Ann, or I can promise you that this spanking will seem like nothing more than a few love taps by the time I'm finished with you. Am I making myself perfectly clear, little girl?"

"Yes, Daddy! I'm sorry, I'm sorry! I won't do it again!"

"Good."

To her immense relief, the spanking stopped, and his hand came to rest on her bottom, rubbing and squeezing the heated flesh. Sniffling quietly, she turned her head to look up at him. "I really am sorry. For everything."

"I know you are, Lottie-bug. But we're not finished."

"We're not?"

"Nope. You're going to stay right here while we talk about what happened at dinner last night, and then you're going to bend over that armchair and present your bottom for Daddy's belt."

"Shit."

"That about sums it up. Let's start with the elephant in the room. Why didn't you tell me how much trouble you and your father were in?"

"I didn't want to embarrass him."

Sighing heavily, Braden gave her bottom another squeeze, this time hard enough to make her yelp at the flash of pain. "You have such a big heart, Lottie-bug. But from now on, you will come to me when you're in trouble or when you need something. Even if it involves your father."

"But—"

"No. There are zero exceptions to this rule. And if I find out you've broken it, you will find yourself right back here, over Daddy's knee getting your bottom soundly spanked."

"That's not fair! It wasn't my secret to share. And frankly, it was none of your business."

"You made it my business the second you involved my club. Anything that happens there is my business, full stop. But more importantly, *you* are my business. Protecting you, providing for you is my business and has been since the moment you agree to be my little girl. Understood?"

"Ugh, have you always been this bossy?"

"When it matters, yes. And you matter, Charlotte."

Dammit. How did he always know exactly the right thing to say to break down her defenses? "Fine. I will come to you *if* it doesn't involve someone else's personal business."

A flurry of spanks landed, reigniting the pain in her bottom and making her squeal and squirm over his lap.

"Do you really think you're in a position to negotiate with me right now, little girl?"

"No, Daddy, but—"

"Stop. I'm not asking you to share other peoples' business with me *unless* it involves you. Keep all the secrets you want, but if you put yourself in danger or break any of our other rules because you were trying to keep someone else's secret, I promise you it will end badly for you every single time."

She supposed she couldn't really argue with that logic. "Fine."

"Good girl. Now, let's talk about why you ran away from me last night, instead of talking to me and your father like a big girl."

Something about the phrase 'big girl' instead of 'adult' made her feel very much like a naughty child, which she assumed was his intent. "Do we have to?"

"Yes."

Groaning, she did her best to bury her face in the couch cushion. "Don't wanna."

Fingers tangled in her hair, gently forcing her face to turn to the side again. "Then maybe you need another spanking to loosen your tongue."

"Daddy, no," she whined, wiggling against his hold even though she knew she wasn't going anywhere.

"Then talk. Why did you leave, baby? And why did you turn off your phone? I was so worried about you."

Fuck. He had to play *that* card. "I'm sorry. I didn't mean to worry you. Actually, no, that's a lie." Closing her eyes, she breathed deep and forced herself to be honest for once. "I think on some level, I wanted you to worry because I wanted to know you still cared about me after I ruined your friendship with my dad. I know that's awful and petty and I deserve whatever punishment you think I've earned, but there it is. I dropped a nuke on the only real friendship my dad has left and I was terrified you'd both hate me for it."

"Baby. Come here."

Choking back a sob, she scrambled to curl up in his lap, letting herself be rocked gently in his arms. "I'm sorry. I'm so sorry, I know I ruined everything and I'm just so fucking sorry."

"Look at me, Charlotte." Braden nudged her away, just enough for him to cup her cheek, his dark eye boring into hers. "You didn't ruin anything. For starters, my actions were my own. I take full responsibility for them, just as I expect you to take responsibility for your own. Secondly, your dad and I have... an understanding. It's probably going to take us a while to get back to normal, but you haven't ruined anything. And even if Emmett had decided he never wanted to speak to me or see me again, I wouldn't hate you. I could never hate you, Charlotte Duvall."

"R-really?"

"Baby, I'm so fucking in love with you, I can't think straight."

"That's really good, because I'm pretty sure I'm in love with you, too."

"Thank god." Closing his eyes, Braden pressed his forehead to hers, and the intimacy of that simple touch was somehow even deeper than anything they'd done before. "You're still getting that strapping I promised you, little girl."

"But you just told me you loved me! You can't spank me!"

"Actually, I can't think of a better way to drive home exactly how much I love you. Over the chair, Charlotte."

23

YOU'RE NOT ALONE ANYMORE

BRADEN

"But Daddy," Charlotte whined, her bottom lip puffing out in an adorable pout.

It took every bit of willpower he had not to grin at her. Fixing a stern expression on his face, Braden tapped her hip with his hand. "If I have to tell you a second time, you'll be taking Daddy's cock in your bottom again, instead of your needy little pussy."

That got her moving. Wide-eyed with a mix of shock and hunger, she hopped up from his lap and naughty girl shuffled her way over to the armchair.

Rising to his feet, Braden reached for the buckle of his belt, silently berating himself for not coming more prepared to deal with his little brat. But he'd been so focused on getting to her he'd basically just hopped in his car and headed for the hills—literally.

"Bottom up over the armrest, baby. Keep your arms on the cushion and out of the way." With the leather looped over and the buckle gripped in his fist, he tapped the belt against her bare skin. "Do you know why you're getting Daddy's belt across your naughty bottom, Charlotte?"

"Because I kept secrets and almost ruined your relationship with my dad and I'm basically just a shitty human being."

It wasn't a question, but a statement of fact that nearly broke his heart. "First of all, you are not at all a shitty human being and if I catch you talking about my little girl like that again you'll be tasting soap for a week. Understood?"

"Yeah."

He snapped the belt across the middle of her thighs, making her cry out, her legs kicking up in the air. "How do you respond to me when you're being punished, Charlotte?"

"I meant 'Yes, Daddy'! Ow, fuck that hurt."

"Now for the real reason you're here, Charlotte." Crouching down in front of the chair, he waited for her head to turn, for those beautiful blue eyes to meet his. "I'm not going to punish you for keeping your father's secret. I understand why you did it, and

I can understand why you felt you couldn't tell me. What I am punishing you for is running away instead of talking to me. I know you haven't had anyone to lean on in a long time, baby, but that's all over now. I expect you to come to me, even if you think I'm going to be angry with you, so we can talk through whatever you're worried about."

He reached out to brush a lock of hair from her face. "You're not alone in this, Lottie-bug. Daddy's here now, and you don't have to carry it all alone any longer. Understood?"

Tears shimmered on her lashes even as her lips curved up in a small smile. "Yes, Daddy. I understand."

"Good girl." Pushing to his feet, he positioned himself beside the chair and raised the belt high.

LOTTIE

The snap of leather across her bare skin tore another cry from Lottie's lips, but she didn't care. Even as the sting settled into her flesh, all she could think about were Braden's words.

You're not alone. Daddy's here now.

With every stroke of the belt across her ass, the

pain seemed to burn away bits and pieces of the burden she'd been carrying ever since she'd uncovered her father's problem.

Before that, really. Ever since her mom's diagnosis, she'd watched her father withdraw, become a shell of his former self. And she'd tried to bury the pain under shopping sprees and brunches with the girls. But it had always been there, growing heavier and heavier as she'd watched her father practically wither away before her very eyes.

There was relief in knowing she didn't have to face any of that alone anymore. In knowing her Daddy would be there to help her, to guide her.

And yeah, to punish her when she was naughty.

"Ow! Daddy, that hurts!" The belt had caught the sensitive curve under her ass, jolting her out of her thoughts and into the present.

"Good. Maybe it will help you remember this lesson for a long time. Because from now on, refusing to talk to your Daddy will land you right back here and I do not want to repeat this lesson any time soon, little one."

"You won't, Daddy, I promise!"

"Two more, baby. Can you take two more for Daddy?"

Sniffling back tears, she nodded, her fingers digging into the soft cushion beneath her.

"That's my girl. Now, what are you going to do the next time you're worried or scared or upset?"

"T-talk to you, D-Daddy."

"Good girl." A soft *whoosh* met her ears a moment before the leather cracked across the most sensitive part of her ass again, making her cry out as her tears dripped onto the chair.

"No more secrets. No more hiding things from me. Agreed?"

"Yes, Daddy."

One final time, the belt whipped across her bottom and she collapsed against the chair, her tears coming hot and fast. The last little bits of the burden she'd carried for so long dissolved as her Daddy lifted her from the chair, scooping her up into his arms.

"Which bedroom is yours, Lottie-bug?"

Unable to speak through her tears, she pointed to the bedroom on the left side of the hallway.

She was dimly aware of him shouldering open the door and carefully lowering her to the bed before joining her. And then she was wrapped around him, soaking his shirt with years of frustration and worry.

"Shhh, baby. Everything is alright. Daddy's got you."

All the things she'd kept to herself since her mother's illness welled up inside her, but she was crying too hard to actually get the words out. Until, at long last, the tears slowly dried up, leaving her feeling lighter than she had in years.

"Thank you," she said with a sigh, her eyes drifting closed as she snuggled closer to him.

"You're welcome, little one. Do you want to talk about it? That seemed like a lot more than just tears from a spanking."

"I'm not sure how I feel about you being able to read my mind," she grumbled.

"Daddy superpowers."

Braden's teasing tone made her giggle and she forced her eyes open to look up into his. "I don't even really know where to start. I... honestly, I don't think I even knew how alone I felt until you told me I didn't have to carry it all anymore. My dad, he hasn't been okay in a long time, and I think I was so sure that if I could keep anybody from noticing he'd just get better."

"You both went through something incredibly traumatic, little one. It makes sense you'd both be struggling. I'm sorry I didn't step in sooner."

"And done what? Forced him to go to therapy? Taken over our finances? There's nothing you could have done, Braden."

"I would have figured something out, if I'd been paying closer attention."

While part of her had no doubt that he would

have done exactly that, it also wasn't his burden to bear. "I don't blame you. Not even a little bit, I promise. If anything, I blame…" She trailed off, shame heating her cheeks. "Never mind. It's nobody's fault."

Cupping her cheek in his hand, Braden brushed at a stray tear with the pad of his thumb. "It's okay to say you blame him. Even if, to an extent, he couldn't help how he handled your mother's death, he still let you down. He was your father, and you should have been able to lean on him, and he wasn't there for you. It's okay to be angry about that. You can recognize his pain while honoring your own."

"Doesn't that make me a shitty person, being mad at him after everything he lost? Mom was the love of his life. Losing her just about destroyed him. It's not fair to be mad at him for that."

"It wasn't fair for you to have to take on the burden of worrying about him because he couldn't or wouldn't care for himself." He hesitated, looking uncharacteristically unsure of himself. "I think therapy would probably be a good idea for both of you. I won't push it on you, but I will pay for it if you decide it's something you want to do."

"I'll think about it." She already had a therapist, like any good little rich girl, and she'd been thinking about making an appointment with her for a while. But she always found a reason to keep putting it off.

"That's my girl. And if we have to, we'll gang up on Emmett and bully him into going, as well."

"Thank you, Daddy."

Still cupping her cheek, he leaned in to press a kiss to her forehead. Love for him swelled in her chest, and for a moment she couldn't even draw a breath.

"That's what Daddies do, little one. You've had a long couple of days. Why don't you take a nap and we can talk more when you wake up."

"Oh, but... you said we could... you know." She wiggled her eyebrows suggestively, making him laugh.

"And that's why you need a nap. You're going to need plenty of energy for what I have planned for you later, little one."

"Well how the hell am I supposed to go to sleep after you said that?"

"I have faith in you. Because you're a good girl who wants to make Daddy proud, isn't that right?"

Goddammit. There was that phrase again. "Yes, Daddy," she said with a sigh.

He kissed her again, then rolled out of bed and tucked her in. And despite her protests, she was asleep before he left the bedroom.

BRADEN

Closing the door behind him, Braden pulled his phone from his pocket and made a call. "Frankie? It's Braden Elliott. Are you still in town?" He paused, listening to her response, and grinned. "Excellent. I need you to pick me up a few things."

24

AN UNEXPECTED QUESTION

LOTTIE

She woke groggy and disoriented, blinking owlishly at her surroundings as she tried to remember where she was. Then she rolled onto her back, her sore bottom pressing into the mattress, and it all came flooding back.

Dinner. Her dad finding out about her and Braden. Spilling her guts about why she'd really put herself up for auction. Fleeing into the mountains with Frankie and—

Bolting upright in bed, Lottie narrowed her eyes as the realization hit. "That little traitor!"

The bedroom door opened, and Braden stepped inside, his lips tilting up in an amused smile. "Who's a traitor?"

"Frankie! I just realized she must have called you and told you where I was. That bitch."

"You owe Frankie a thank you, little girl."

"How do you figure?"

"Because." Crossing the room to the bed with slow, deliberate steps, he placed his hands on either side of her, caging her in, his dark eyes glittering in the waning sunlight. "If I had to find you myself, or worse, wait for you to come home, you wouldn't have gotten off nearly as easily as you did today."

"Um, my ass *still* hurts. I don't call that getting off easy."

"Well, you did. I can prove it when we get home, if you like."

There was just enough of a hint of danger beneath his words to have her rethinking her position. "No, thanks. I believe you."

"Good girl. Since you're up, I'm going to run you a bath. You can soak as long as you like; dinner won't be ready for a bit yet."

"Dinner?" Her stomach chose that moment to growl, giving her away. "You made dinner?"

"Something like that. What scent do you want in your bath?"

"Anything with peppermint." She grinned when he raised an eyebrow in surprise. "It's supposed to boost your energy levels. You did say I was going to need plenty of energy for tonight."

"And I stand by that. I'll see what's in the package Frankie picked up for us."

"Is Frankie here?"

"No. She picked up some supplies I asked for and headed back to Charleston. But she said the cabin doesn't have any renters for another week so we can stay a couple days if we want."

"That would be amazing."

"Agreed." Leaning in, he brushed a kiss across her lips. "Let me go run that bath for you, little one."

"Okay, Daddy."

She managed to wait until he'd disappeared into the bathroom to silently throw her hands in the air and do a little celebration dance on the bed. It was finally happening! She was finally going to lose her v-card!

It was about fucking time.

By the time he returned to the bedroom, wiping his hands dry on a small towel, she'd gotten herself back under control. "No peppermint, but there was a bath salt mixture just labeled 'Energy' so I scooped some of that in there for you. I think it has orange in it."

"Thank you, Daddy."

"You're welcome, Lottie-bug. Go enjoy your bath,

I'll come get you when dinner's ready if you don't join me first."

Stripping out of her clothes as he closed the bedroom door behind him, she made her to the bathroom. First things first, she stood with her back to the mirror, twisting around to try and see the evidence of her spanking. There were two lingering welts, right across her sit-spots, but other than that all evidence of her punishment had faded, save a bit of soreness.

"Well, that's just rude," she mumbled to herself as she slid into the blissfully hot water filling the giant tub. It seemed completely unfair that as much as the spanking had hurt, she had nothing to show for it. What would it take, she wondered, to leave marks that stayed longer than a couple of hours?

She'd have to ask Braden. Maybe once things were a bit more settled and she was fairly certain she could go more than a day or two without getting her ass spanked.

Letting her mind drift to the possibilities of what her Daddy could have planned for her, she drifted in the tub until the water cooled around her. With more than a little reluctance, she rinsed off and grabbed the towel he'd left hanging by the tub for her, wrapping it around her body as she walked back into the bedroom.

Apparently Braden had been a busy bee while she'd been soaking in the tub. Unlit candles were scattered around the room, and a white dress was laid out on the bed. There were no accompanying panties, but that seemed par for the course with Braden, so she shimmied her way into the dress and reveled in the sinful luxury of silk against her bare skin.

Since she'd been in a rush the night before, she only had the bare essentials with her, but she made do. It was enough to put on a light coat of makeup and pin her hair up before stepping out of the bedroom.

She found Braden in the kitchen, looking adorably domestic as he bent and pulled what looked to be two baked potatoes from the oven.

"Smells delicious."

Placing the pan on top of the stove, he turned—and froze in place, his eyes all but bulging out of his head at the sight of her. "Looks delicious," he returned, a wicked smile curving his lips. "Red or white wine?"

"Red, please."

While he poured a glass for each of them, she took in the candles in the middle of the table, the white linen of the napkins, and her heart tripped in her chest. "What's all this for?"

"You," he replied simply, handing her a glass.

Lifting his own as if in a toast, he brushed his fingers across her cheek, and even just that simple touch had her body trembling with need. "After everything, I thought you deserved a little romance."

"If I'd known you'd be this romantic, I would have asked you to take my virginity a long time ago," she teased, clinking her glass against his.

"I'm usually not. This romantic," he added when she tilted her head in question. "But I don't just want to be your first, Charlotte. I want to be your only. And that kind of commitment deserves a little... more."

"Jesus." Swallowing a large gulp of wine, she willed her racing heart to slow. "You always know exactly what to say, don't you?"

"No." Despite her teasing, his tone and expression remained serious. "Half the time I speak, I end up with my foot in my mouth, especially when it comes to relationships. I'm not an easy man to get along with. I'm controlling and demanding, and I work too much. At times, I'll expect more of you than you think you can give, especially where your submission is concerned. But I promise you if you agree to be mine, your happiness will be the most important thing to me."

"I already agreed to all this, Braden."

"Yes. But I want more. Marry me, Charlotte."

Literally nothing he could have said would have shocked her more than that particular question. It wasn't even a question, more of a demand. A politely worded, romantic-as-fuck demand, but a demand none the less.

Which, she supposed, was also par for the course.

"You can't be serious."

"Completely. I've never been one to wait around for something I wanted. And I want you. Forever."

"Braden, I... I don't know what to say. We haven't even had sex yet."

A smug smile tugged at the corner of his mouth. "Do you have doubts about my ability to satisfy you in that regard?"

"No. But I never thought I'd marry the first man I slept with, either."

"Plans change."

That they did. She'd also never thought she'd sell her virginity to the highest bidder, either, and look how that had turned out.

Marrying Braden was an easy choice, on the surface. She'd literally be able to live next door to her dad, and Braden had more than enough money to keep her in the lifestyle she'd grown up in.

And if she married him, that's exactly what everyone would think. That she was marrying him for his money. The thought left a sour taste in her mouth. "I don't need you to rescue me, Braden."

"I never said you did."

"Then why do you want to marry me?"

"Because I'm in love with you." When she simply stared at him, he sighed. "Because you're stubborn, and mouthy, and you have the biggest heart of anyone I know. Because you were willing to put yourself in a dangerous position just to save your father's reputation. Because I want to spend the rest of my life spanking that gorgeous ass of yours when you're naughty, and making you come so hard you see stars when you've been a good girl. Because your laughter instantly makes my world brighter, and I can't imagine going a single day without seeing you smile."

Tears pooled on her lashes and once again she was left feeling like she couldn't breathe with the love for him crowding her chest. "Those are a lot of really great reasons."

Setting his glass on the table, he knelt down on one knee in front of her, taking her free hand in his. "Marry me, Charlotte Duvall."

Everything in her was screaming to say yes, but she held back. "I want children."

"I'm still young," he said with a grin. "And spry. But we should probably get started on that pretty soon."

"Okay." Love, terror, and a dozen other emotions burst out of her on a nervous laugh. "Oh, god. Okay. Yes. Yes, I'll marry you."

With a whoop of joy, he jumped to his feet and hauled her up out her chair, spinning her around the kitchen in a very clumsy sort of waltz.

"Braden, the wine!"

"Better not spill it, Lottie-bug, or I'll have to spank you."

It was tempting to dump it on him, just to see where the spanking led. But she'd been waiting long enough, dammit, and she had better plans for the evening.

So she put her wine down and looped her arms around his neck, rising up on her toes so their lips were just a whisper apart. "Daddy?"

"Yes, little one?"

"Will you please, for the love of god, fuck me now?"

"As you wish, my princess."

BRADEN

For the second time that day, he carried her to the bedroom. Only this time, she wasn't sobbing her heart out, for which he was eternally grateful. Unlike earlier, now she was beaming up at him, excitement and desire slowly turning the blue of her eyes sapphire.

"I was going to light the candles," he said as he lowered her to the bed.

"I don't care about candles. I just want you inside me."

"Impatient little brat." Chuckling softly, he pressed a kiss to her collarbone. "You're going to have to wait a bit longer, little one. I want to taste you properly, first."

"Daddy," she whined, tugging at his shirt. "Please. I need you."

"I love the way you whine when you're feeling needy. But you're going to need to put those hands on the headboard and keep them there if you want to be allowed to come tonight."

"You're mean." With a pretty pout, she raised her arms over her head and pressed them against the cushioned headboard.

"So mean," he agreed with another low laugh. "So mean, I'm going to eat this sweet little pussy of yours until you cream all over my face before I fuck you."

"Oh." Her breath hitched as her pupils dilated even further. "I guess that's okay."

"Good girl. Remember to keep your hands right where they are."

He took his time, trailing light kisses down her chest, over her stomach, down to her covered mound. There was a wet spot on the silk already, and he grinned as he pushed it up to her hips. And nearly had to wipe the drool from his chin at the sight of her perfect pink lips, glistening with arousal.

Hooking his arms around her legs, he settled between her legs. And feasted.

"Oh, god. Daddy!" Charlotte's hips bucked beneath him as he tortured her with tongue and teeth, licking and sucking her swollen little bud.

She tasted of sin and innocence all at once, and he didn't think he'd ever tire of the taste.

Legs trembling, she writhed beneath him, and when he slid two fingers inside her, stretching her, she sobbed out his name. "Daddy. Daddy, please."

Taking pity on her, he curled his fingers up, pressing against that spot inside her designed to drive her wild at the same time he pulled her clit between his lips and sucked. Hard.

Hard enough to have her hips arching up from the bed, her screams echoing around the room as he sucked and stroked and teased every last ounce of pleasure from her beautiful body.

When she finally collapsed onto the bed again,

her ragged breaths and soft whimpers filling his ears, he sat up and smiled when he saw her palms still pressed flat against the headboard. "Such a good girl," he murmured, kissing her so she could taste herself on his lips. "Daddy's so proud of you, baby. Ready for more?"

"I'm ready for everything, Daddy."

25

THE RIGHT VIRGINITY

LOTTIE

Floating. She was floating on a gentle sea of pleasure. Well, it was gentle now, though it had been anything but when he'd been using that wicked tongue of his on her.

But now it had stilled, and she was floating, barely aware of his cock pressing against her entrance. Until he rocked forward, stretching and filling her in a way she'd never experienced before.

"Oh!" Gasping, she arched up, her fingers digging into the fabric of the headboard. "Daddy!"

"Look at me, Charlotte."

Forcing her gaze to his, she watched his eyes darken with pleasure as he pushed somehow even deeper into her. "That's my good girl. Does it hurt?"

"No, Daddy."

"Good. It might in a second, so hold onto me, baby."

Her arms ached a bit from the effort to hold them in place, but she didn't mind. Every sensation, be it pain or pleasure, was a gift from her Daddy, and it all only served to enhance her pleasure.

Wrapping her arms around him, she slid one hand into his silky hair, clinging to him as he rocked forward again. Now there was a pinch of pain, but it disappeared almost as quickly as it came.

"Almost there, baby," he murmured, brushing a kiss over her lips. "Ready?"

"So ready."

With that, he thrust forward again. Another flash of pain, this one more biting than the one before, making her tense slightly as he sank completely into her.

She whimpered as he rained kisses over her face in between apologies and assurances it would feel better soon.

Little by little, the pain faded, and she was able to relax again. "Okay. I'm okay."

"You're better than okay, little one. You're fucking fantastic. I'm not going to last very much longer."

Laughing, she flexed her hips experimentally, her

laugher fading to a gasp as pleasure flooded her. "I'll take that as a compliment."

"It is. I want to feel you come on my cock, but I'm not sure I'll make it."

"Next time, then," she assured him as he moved inside her.

"And every time after that, for as long as I live."

It was a promise, a vow as meaningful as any they would say on their wedding day as far as she was concerned. "Yes, Daddy."

Words faded, giving way to gasps of pleasure, to the sound of their bodies moving together as one for the first time. It was a different kind of pleasure, being filled so completely by him, and one she intended to indulge in as often as humanly possible.

And when he filled her for the last time, the warmth of him spreading deep into her womb, she knew that even if he hadn't asked her to marry him, there never would have been anyone else for her.

Her father's best friend had officially ruined her for any other man.

LOTTIE

"How are you feeling, little one?"

Snuggled into his chest, enjoying the post-coital glow, Lottie grinned. "Pretty fucking amazing, actually."

His chest rumbled with laughter. "Was it everything you wanted?"

"More. So much more. I can't wait to tell the girls."

But the mention of her friends instantly dampened her mood. Even if she was marrying Braden, now that she'd stepped back and taken a hard look at her spending habits, she couldn't see herself going back to her old ways. Would her friends still want to be her friends if she couldn't jet off on some luxury holiday whenever someone got a wild hair? Or if she couldn't splurge on brunch for everyone once a month?

"Hey." Placing his finger beneath her chin, Braden nudged her head up, concern filling his eyes. "What's wrong?"

"How do you *do* that?" she mumbled, deliberately avoiding the question.

"Daddy instincts. As soon as you mentioned your friends, you tensed up. What's going on?"

"Nothing. I'm just being weird."

"Charlotte."

"You know, if you're going to call me Charlotte when I'm in trouble you should probably start calling me Lottie when I'm not in trouble. Otherwise, the full name loses its impact."

"First of all, you're not in trouble. Second of all... well, you might have a point, Lottie-bug."

"Feels like I'm in trouble."

"You're going to be if you don't tell Daddy what's going on. No more secrets, remember?"

"It's not really a secret, per se. I'm pretty sure I'm creating problems where there aren't any."

"What kind of problems?"

"Ugggh." Groaning, she pushed up in bed, wrapping her arms around her knees and pulling them to her chest. "You're not going to let this go, are you?"

"It's adorable that you even thought that was an option."

"Fine. I'm being a whiny little brat because I'm worried my friends won't like me anymore. Happy?"

"Thank you for telling me." Gentle hands tugged her back down to the bed and pulled her back into his chest. "Why do you think they won't want to be your friends anymore?"

"Our whole friendship revolves around shopping and expensive vacations."

"Do you think I won't let you do those things anymore?"

"That never even occurred to me, honestly." Though she supposed it should have. It seemed a very 'Daddy' thing to do, giving her a budget, controlling her spending.

"Then what's the problem? I don't mind you going on the occasional trip, though you will definitely have a shopping budget," he added with a chuckle, echoing her own thoughts so closely it was almost eerie.

Odd how that thought would have sent her reeling even just a few weeks ago, and now it almost felt comforting to know she wouldn't have to be in charge of all that. She could trust her Daddy to tell her how much she was allowed to spend. There was freedom in that, she realized, in letting someone else bear those mental burdens. A freedom she'd always taken for granted, and that she now promised herself she never would again.

"It just doesn't appeal to me the way it did before. Like, I never really thought about how much I was spending, because the money was just *there*. But now, after knowing how close we are to losing everything, the thought of spending that kind of money again makes me a little sick to my stomach."

"Ah. That makes sense." His hand stroked down her back, comforting and arousing all at the same time. "But do you really think Frankie, for instance, would love you any less just because you chose not to go on a trip or to spend less money?"

"Well, no. But Frankie's different." As soon as the words left her mouth, Lottie wrinkled her nose. "That's not fair. She is different, mostly because she's so much fucking smarter than all of us put together. Eva and Portia... I don't know, honestly. I want to think they'd stick around, but I've seen money troubles break up plenty of friendships in our circles."

"Why don't you get together with them when we get back to Charleston and talk things out? Brunch is on me."

"No. You already spent nearly half a million dollars on me, no way in hell are you giving me more money."

"Is that what you think?"

Before she could even formulate a reply, she was on her back, her arms pinned over her head as his free hand moved up her body to cup her breast. She arched up with a cry when his fingers closed tightly around her nipple.

"Ow, ow, ow! Daddy, let go!"

"Are you listening to me, little girl?"

"Yes! Ow, fuck that hurts."

His fingers tightened even further, bringing tears to her eyes as she writhed beneath him. "If I want to spend my money on my little girl, I absolutely will. Do you understand me, Charlotte?"

"But—Goddammit, Braden, that hurts!"

"There's no negotiation here, little one. Like I told you from the beginning, I take very good care of my things and you are my most prized possession. And if taking care of you right now means paying for brunch so you can have an important conversation with your friends, then that's what I'm going to do. Now, be a good girl and say 'Yes, Daddy'."

"Yes, Daddy," she parroted, adding in a deliberately dramatic sniffle as he released her breast.

"Good girl." Lowering his head, he pulled the nipple he'd just finished torturing into his mouth, soothing the ache with his tongue. Once she was squirming and whimpering beneath him for a completely different reason, he moved to the opposite breast, teasing and tormenting her until she was begging him to take her again.

Which he did, and he kept his promise about making sure she got to come all over Daddy's cock. Over and over again, until her voice was hoarse from screaming and her body ached from being so beautifully, thoroughly used.

BRADEN

"I don't wanna."

Forcing himself not to laugh at how adorably put out she looked, Braden folded his arms and stared down at her. "You can either do it now, or you can do it sitting on a sore bottom. The choice is yours."

"That doesn't sound like much of a choice," she grumbled, her pouty lip puffing out even further.

"Maybe not. But I bet a spanking would improve your mood. Come here."

"Daddy, no!" Squealing with faux terror, she jumped up from the couch and danced out of reach. "I'll call him, I'll call him!"

"Use video."

"Bossy britches." Despite her grumbling, she had a smile on her face as she held the phone up and waited for her father to answer.

"Hi, pumpkin. I was hoping you'd call."

Tears welled in Lottie's eyes, breaking Braden's heart. "I didn't know if you'd wanna talk to me. Do you hate me?"

"Oh, honey. I could never ever hate you. I love you more than anything in this whole entire world."

"I love you, too, Dad. I'm sorry I didn't tell you about me and Braden."

"I'm sorry I didn't tell you about the gambling.

And I'm so fucking sorry you felt like you had to..." Emmett trailed off, then cleared his throat. "To do what you did to rescue my sorry ass."

"Will you go to therapy with me?" The question seemed to burst out of Lottie's mouth, like she couldn't hold the words back any longer. And Braden couldn't have been more fucking proud of her than he was in that moment.

"I don't know..."

"Please? You don't have to go with me, but I want you to go. Actually, no, I need you to go, Dad. Not just for the gambling, but for everything. I need you to get better, because I don't know what I'd do if I lost you, too."

There was a long, strained silence, and Braden was just about to step in when Emmett's sigh came through the speaker. "All right. I'll go. Just for you, pumpkin."

"Thanks, Dad."

They spoke a while longer, with Braden keeping an eye on his little girl off camera. But she seemed lighter, happier by the time she hung up the phone and settled herself on Braden's lap.

"Thank you for making me call him."

"Of course, Lottie-bug. Feel better?"

"Much. I'm still kind of mad at him, I think, but not as much as I was. Therapy will help."

"I think so, too. And I'm so proud of you for bringing it up all on your own."

"Yeah?" Eyes sparkling, she shifted so she was straddling him on the couch. "I bet I can make you even more proud, Daddy."

"Oh, yeah?"

"Yeah."

And she absolutely did.

LOTTIE

Three days after losing her virginity, she was back at the restaurant where it had all started. Only this time, she had Braden's credit card tucked away in her wallet and a very sore bottom to sit on. Apparently arguing with Daddy once he'd made up his mind about something was a surefire way to get her ass lit up with her own hairbrush.

Good to know.

"Lottie!" Eva practically squealed her name when she came rushing into the restaurant, her blonde hair pulled up high in a ponytail. "I feel like I haven't seen you in ages. I've missed you!"

Tears blurred Lottie's vision as she stood to accept her friend's hug. "I've missed you, too."

"Portia will be here in a sec. She spotted this to-die-for bag a couple stores down and she said it couldn't wait. But I couldn't wait to see you." Laying her hand over Lottie's, Eva squeezed, concern filling her dark eyes. "I've been meaning to call you and check on you, life just got... well." The corners of her mouth tightened. "Life got in the way, I suppose."

"Tell me about it."

But before either of them could say anything further, Portia came hurrying in, her cheeks flushed with excitement, though whether it was the excitement of seeing her friend or of snagging a great sale, Lottie wasn't sure. "Lottie! I'm so happy to see you! You've been so quiet lately. Is everything okay?"

That little bit of concern was all it took to break her. Looking from one of her closest friends to the other, Lottie opened her mouth—and promptly burst into tears.

"Oh my god. What did you two say to her?" Frankie's voice cut through the sound of Lottie's sobbing. "Come here, Lottie baby. What's wrong?"

But she was crying too hard to do more than shake her head.

"We didn't do anything, swear to god!" Portia's voice had pitched up to almost a panicked squeak. "I just asked her if everything was okay because we hadn't heard from her in a while."

"Same," Eva said. "What's going on, Frankie?"

"It's a long story, and it's not mine to tell." Someone pressed a wad of tissues into Lottie's hand as Frankie gently rocked her. "Lottie, honey, people are starting to stare. Gonna need you to take a deep breath for me, okay?"

Dragging in a deep, if shaky, breath, Lottie dabbed at her face with the tissues. "Sorry. I'm sorry. I just—I really fucking love you guys."

"We love you, too." With a smile that was as much confusion as affection, Portia patted Lottie's hand. "What's going on?"

"Okay." Lottie dragged in two more deep breaths and forced a smile. "Okay. Like Frankie said, it's a really long story and it would be super helpful if you guys could just listen and let me get through the whole thing, okay?"

"Yeah, sure."

"Of course."

And to their credit, they didn't interrupt, not even once, as Lottie took them through the whole sordid ordeal. Through uncovering her father's debts, to Frankie telling her about the auction—which did earn Frankie a shocked gasp and a glare from Portia— to having her virginity purchased by a mob boss and then basically sold again to Braden, to her and Braden's growing relationship, and finally to her father finding out and Braden chasing her into the mountains to propose.

"So, yeah. It's been... a lot. I'm sorry I didn't tell you guys sooner, I guess I was just embarrassed."

Eva frowned. "Why would you be embarrassed? You aren't the one who gambled away your fortune."

"I know. But a part of me was worried you guys wouldn't want to be my friends anymore if I wasn't, you know, as rich as you, anymore."

"Wow, you have a really shitty opinion of us," Portia said, her baby-blue eyes snapping with anger. "You really think we'd dump you when you needed us the most?"

"No. I don't know. It's just, we've spent our whole lives going on these extravagant vacations and shopping and having brunch. I didn't think you'd want me around if I couldn't do those things anymore."

"You know, it really sucks to have the rest of the world think we're shallow and vapid. I never expected one of my best friends to see me that way." Hurt echoed in Portia's words and to Lottie's surprise tears shimmered on her lashes. "I thought we knew each other better than that."

Lottie winced. "You're right. And I'm sorry."

"We forgive you." Eva shot Portia a dark look when Portia opened her mouth to protest. "I wish you'd come to us, but we understand how upset and stressed you must have been. Don't we, Portia?"

Although she didn't look at all like she was ready to forgive, Portia nodded stiffly.

"I really am sorry. I think I let my own insecurities get in the way and I projected that onto you guys, and I shouldn't have. I'll do better."

Waving a hand as if to brush all the hurt and upset aside, Eva leaned in, her eyes sparkling. "Now that we've got all the messy stuff out of the way, you have to tell us. How's the sex?"

Portia groaned, but Lottie couldn't help but grin. Finally, it was her turn to share all the delicious, dirty details of her sex life. "Fucking *spectacular*."

And as she shared all the details of the things she'd done with her Daddy—well, a slightly less scandalous version, anyway—even Portia seemed to be hanging on every single word.

Maybe everything would work out in the end after all.

26

PROPERTY OF DADDY

BRADEN

Braden glanced up as his office door opened and Lottie poked her head inside. "Busy?"

"Never too busy for you, little one. Come in." He watched as she stepped in and closed the door behind her. The uneasiness that had been in her eyes before she'd left for brunch had disappeared from her eyes, and he was relieved to see her looking like the happy, carefree girl he'd always known. "How was brunch with the girls?"

"Excellent. I think Portia's still a little pissed at me, but I can't really blame her. I'd be pretty annoyed if any of them assumed I'd drop them as a friend just because their financial situation changed a bit."

"She'll come around, I'm sure."

"She will." Mischief crept into her smile and danced in her eyes. "Frankie won't give her a choice."

"I still haven't decided if Frankie is a good influence or a terrible one."

"Yes," Lottie answered, tossing her head back and laughing. "The answer is yes."

"Mmhmm." Snaking out a hand, he pulled her down onto his lap so he could nibble at her neck as she giggled. "And what kind of influence was she today?"

"Umm, well…"

The hesitant tone, as well as the way she was squirming on his lap sent his Daddy radar pinging wildly. Lifting his head, he pinned her with a stern look. "Well, what, little girl?"

"I should probably just show you."

She slid from his lap before he could tighten his hold, but it was clear his little girl was up to something, so he let her go.

Standing in the middle of his office, she reached behind her to unzip her dress, letting the straps slide down her arms before she wiggled the rest of it down her body to pool at her feet.

"Holy fucking hell. You look…" At a loss for words, he crooked a finger, indicating she should come to him.

"You like?" Beaming the way only a woman who knew she had a man in her thrall could, she posed, showing off her outfit.

If it could be called that. Pink lace and white leather crisscrossed over her torso, cupping her breasts, and framing her bare mound. Attached to the leather and lace around her hips were four leather straps holding up thigh-high white stockings. The look was completed by a pair of perfectly white heels with infamous red bottoms.

She looked like innocence, deliberately wrapped up in the most tempting package imaginable.

"I haven't even shown you the best part." With a high-pitched giggle, she turned around and bent over.

And right there on her ass was a tattoo stating *Property of Daddy* with a giant pink bow.

"You got a tattoo?"

"Just a temporary one. I thought it would be fun for tonight, since we're telling your family about our engagement."

Tilting his head to the side, he studied the tattoo, his cock pressing painfully against his pants. "One of our members owns a tattoo shop. How would you feel about making it permanent?"

Straightening, she turned and straddled him. "Sure. On one condition. You have to get one, too. Maybe one that just says 'Daddy' to match mine."

"Done."

A knock on the door interrupted him just as he was leaning in to kiss her, and Braden swore under his breath. "Goddammit. Whoever it is can wait. Go away," he called, praying the interloper would listen.

But his prayers went unanswered. Killian opened the door, striding inside as though he owned the place, his eyes widening slightly as he took in the scene in front of him. "Well. Isn't this a cozy sight."

"What part of 'Go away' don't you understand, Killian?"

"Killian!" Hopping off Braden's lap, Lottie squealed with delight and raced over to the other man, throwing her arms around his neck in an embrace that had Braden's eyes narrowing. "It's so good to see you again."

"You too, sweetheart. But, ah, I'm not looking to die tonight so perhaps you should let me go before your Daddy decides it's necessary to try and feed me to the alligators. Not that I'd let him," he added in a loud whisper, with a wink that had Lottie giggling.

Twisting her neck around, Lottie glared over her shoulder at Braden. "Daddy, be nice."

"This *is* me being nice, little girl. But unless you want your bottom paddled in front of Master Killian, I suggest you let go. Right now."

She turned around fully now, but looped her arm through Killian's, temper sparking in her eyes. "So, what, I'm not allowed to have friends?"

"I'm not going to argue with you, Charlotte." Mostly because he knew he was being irrational, but it didn't stop him from not wanting another man's hands on his fiancée. Especially when that man was Killian O'Rourke.

"You're being ridiculous, Braden."

Rising from his chair, he crossed the room, those dark parts of his soul positively cheering when her eyes widened with fear. Capturing her chin between his fingers, he tilted her head back. "What does that tattoo on your ass say, little one?"

"That was just a joke."

"What does it say?"

"Property of Daddy," she said with a sigh and a roll of her eyes.

"Which is exactly what you are. Especially when we are in the club. And since you obviously need a reminder of that, you can go put your nose in the corner with your pretty tattoo on display while Master Killian and I talk."

"But Daddy!"

Out of patience with the situation, he pulled her away from Killian and marched her over to the corner with one hand wrapped around her arm while he swatted her ass with the other. By the time they reached the corner, her bottom was a nice pretty pink, which highlighted the tattoo beautifully.

Oh, yeah, they definitely needed to make that permanent.

"Stay here until I call for you. Feet apart, hands on your head."

"Yes, Daddy," she replied sulkily.

"Good girl." He pressed a kiss to her hair before turning and making his way back to a very amused-looking Killian.

"You're going to have your hands full with that one."

"I wouldn't have it any other way. Did you need to talk to me about something?"

As if flipping a switch, Killian immediately sobered. "It's about your auctioneer. Whoever he is, he's not just good with computers, he's a goddamned genius. Every time my men get close to him, he changes things up. It's going to take us longer than I expected to pinpoint him."

"Dammit. Meanwhile, he's setting up another virgin auction right under our noses. I was hoping we'd have it shut down before the next one."

"I know. I'm sorry, I wish it was better news."

"Me too. Fucking hell. You don't have a lead on him at all?"

"No. Though, given how thoroughly they've woven their operation in with the club, I'm inclined to believe it's someone who works here."

Braden's blood ran cold. "Not just a member?"

"Not a chance. Unless you've outsourced some of your computer operations to someone within the club."

"No. Everything pretty much goes through Martin and his team." Braden ran his hands through his hair, fury and helplessness twisting his stomach into knots. "Fuck. Somehow that's worse than it just being a member."

"I've already done a deep dive on Martin and he's clean as a whistle. If it's alright with you, I'll bring him in on this, see if he has any idea who on his team could manage to do all this and stay under the radar."

It was a relief to know there was someone on his payroll he could trust, at least. "Whatever you need."

"I'll get on it immediately, then." Killian turned to leave, then hesitated, looking back over his shoulder with a smirk. "And don't be too hard on her, Braden. I am rather difficult to resist, after all."

"Go away, Killian."

The door closed, cutting off Killian's laughter, and Braden turned to the corner where his naughty little girl was standing exactly as he'd instructed her to, with her hands laced behind her head and her feet shoulder width apart. God, he didn't think he'd ever get tired of that sight.

"Come here, Charlotte." He deliberately made his voice more stern than he was actually feeling. Now that she was nowhere near Killian, the possessive jealousy gripping him had faded and he could see the amusement in the situation.

But the fact remained that whether she'd agreed with him or not, he'd given her an instruction and she had disobeyed.

Naughty little girl.

Lottie turned, a pout on her lips and a hint of anticipation in her eyes. "Yes, Daddy?"

"What are you supposed to do when Daddy tells you to do something, little one?"

"I'm supposed to do what you tell me to, but—"

"No." He raised a hand, cutting her off. "There are no 'buts' in this situation, other than yours, which is going to be nice and red by the time I'm done with you. At home, I'm willing to grant you a bit more leeway, but when we are in the club or in a scene, you either obey or you are punished. It doesn't matter if you think I'm being absolutely ridiculous; you still obey."

The corners of her mouth lifted. "So you admit you were being ridiculous."

"I admit that Killian O'Rourke makes me feel a bit more... territorial than usual. Especially when it comes to you."

"I suppose that's fair. He's loaded and gorgeous, but with that hint of danger, you know? Super sexy."

"And completely off-limits to you, little girl."

"Completely off-limits?" She tilted her head, tapping a finger on her lips as if giving the situation serious consideration. "But what if he gets seated in my section when I'm waiting tables?"

"Charlotte..."

"I'm just saying! You can't keep me hidden away from everyone you find threatening to your manhood."

"Enough." Twining his fingers in her hair, he forced her to her knees. And not even that wiped the smile from her face. "Open your mouth."

Luckily for her, she obeyed immediately, parting her lips wide as he freed his cock from his slacks. "If you can't listen without being a smartass, then I'll just have to keep your mouth occupied."

She started to roll her eyes, and he thrust forward, the tip of his cock hitting the back of her throat and making her gag. Pleasure shot through him at the feel of her throat constricting around him, and he held there for a moment before pulling back and giving her a chance to breathe.

"Eyes on me, Charlotte."

Watery eyes met his and he smiled down at her. "Good girl. Now, as I was saying. Whether you think a request is ridiculous or not doesn't change a damn thing. As long as what I'm asking of you doesn't put your safety at risk or violate your hard limits, I expect you to obey. When you don't, you'll be punished. It's that simple. Understood?"

Because he wanted an actual answer, he pulled free of her mouth and used his hold on her hair to force her head back even further. "Yes, Daddy," she replied, her voice raspy from the throat-fucking she'd just endured.

"Much better, little one." Softening a bit, he cupped her face with his other hand. "For what it's worth, I'm aware my response to Killian is borderline irrational. I'll try to work on it, but I'm not making any promises."

"I suppose that's fair. And I'll do my best to avoid making you unnecessarily jealous."

"Thank you. And the next time you're in trouble, are you going to get sassy with me?"

Mischief sparkled in her pale eyes. "Probably."

"We'll see about that."

He filled her mouth again, not bothering to be

gentle. It was, after all, a punishment, and even though he wasn't upset with her, he was determined to teach her to hold back on the sass when she was already in trouble. Getting her to stop talking back altogether was a lost cause, but he'd settle for a modicum of respect when she'd been naughty.

By the time he poured himself down her throat, her makeup was a mess. Lipstick was smeared halfway across her cheek and her mascara had begun to run. Pulling out of her mouth, he brushed his thumb in a circle around her mouth, deliberately smearing her lipstick even further

"Still feeling sassy?"

"Not so much, Daddy."

"That's my good girl. You did such a good job taking Daddy's cock down your throat. Daddy's very proud of you, baby."

As always, her eyes lit up at his praise. "Thank you, Daddy."

"Up you go. Our guests are probably waiting on us."

"Just a second. I need to go fix my makeup."

"Absolutely not." With his hand still tangled in her hair, he helped her to her feet, forcing her head back so he could claim her lips in a hard, punishing kiss. "I want the whole club to see what a filthy mess I've made of my little girl."

Eyes darkening with need, she swallowed hard. "Yes, Daddy."

"Good girl. And if you're very good, I'll make sure the rest of your makeup gets properly ruined when I'm done paddling your ass later."

"I can't wait."

27

I OWN YOU, CHARLOTTE DUVALL (REPRISE)

LOTTIE

She tried not to be self-conscious of the fact that her makeup was probably completely ruined. At the very least, she was positive her lipstick hadn't survived the very thorough face-fucking her Daddy had just given her.

"Stop fussing or I'll tie your hands behind your back."

"I can't help it! I feel weird."

"Well, you look beautiful. So leave it alone."

Dammit. He made it so hard to be mad at him when he said things like that. "Yes, Daddy."

"Good girl."

Luckily, they made it to the VIP booth he'd reserved for his brothers and their plus ones not too much later. And if any of them noticed how messed up her makeup was, nobody said a thing.

"All right, what's the big news?" Desmond—she was pretty sure he was Desmond and not Damian, since he was sitting with a gorgeous man instead of Emily—asked, his voice hard and a tad annoyed sounding.

The man beside him, Bastian, if she remembered Braden's rundown of who was who in his family correctly, laid a hand on Desmond's thigh and squeezed. It reminded her of the way Braden touched her when she was pushing her luck.

Interesting.

Sliding his arm around her waist, Braden pulled her closer and pressed a kiss to her temple before grinning at his family. "Lottie and I are getting married."

"Oh my gosh!" With a happy squeal, Emily vaulted from her seat and threw her arms around Lottie's neck. "We can wedding plan together! Have you gotten a dress yet? I haven't, and I don't really even know where to go." Pulling away, Emily's expression dimmed. "Sorry, I shouldn't make assumptions. You probably want to go dress shopping with your mom."

A lump formed in Lottie's throat. "I..."

The arm around her waist tightened. "Lottie's

mom passed away a few years ago. I'm sure she'd love to go dress shopping with you, honey."

"Oh, god." Eyes widening, Emily pressed her hands to her cheeks. "I'm so sorry. I didn't know."

Gratitude and love filled her as she leaned into Braden. "It's okay. And yes, I'd love to go shopping together. As long as you don't mind my friends coming along. Portia will murder me if I leave her out of the dress-selection process."

"That sounds like a lot of fun, actually. My bestie —Damian's daughter—is on the other side of the country, and I don't really have a lot of other girl-friends."

"It's a date, then."

Emily returned to her spot beside Damian, who immediately gathered her close and pressed a kiss to her hair, and Braden took a seat on the bench oppo-site the snuggling couple, pulling Lottie down with him.

"Congratulations," Damian said, and to Lottie's surprise it sounded like he actually meant it.

"Yes, congratulations." Beside Braden, Desmond's partner was smiling indulgently at them. He reminded her of a kind uncle, not that she'd ever had an uncle, kind or otherwise.

Which begged the question...

"So I've been wondering..." Turning to Braden,

she pointed at him. "If you're my Daddy, and they're your brothers"—she waved her finger between Damian and Desmond—"does that make them my uncles?"

Emily dissolved into giggles. "I had the exact same thought! Uncle Braden and Uncle Desmond!"

"And Uncle Damian!"

"Absolutely not." Damian leveled a glare at both of them, but it only stopped Emily's laughter for a moment before she snorted and lost the battle again.

"Aw, what's the matter, Uncle Damian?" Lottie teased. "Don't you like your name?"

"Braden. Get your brat under control before I do it for you."

Instead of scolding her, Braden leaned over and whispered something in her ear that had her grinning ever wider. "Oh, I'm sorry, Uncle *Blake*. I didn't realize I was using the wrong name."

Damian sent a glare in Braden's direction that had her Daddy bursting into loud, nearly howling laughter. "Jesus Christ, Braden, you're an even bigger brat than she is."

Emily smacked Damian's chest, earning her a glittering look. "Daddy, don't be mean to Uncle Braden."

"Careful, Sunshine. Just because I can't spank the sass out of Charlotte doesn't mean you have the same immunity."

To Lottie's never-ending delight, Emily didn't drop her gaze submissively like Lottie half expected. She glanced over at Lottie, as if looking for support, which Lottie immediately gave in the form of an enthusiastic nod. Emily then looked back at her Daddy—and stuck out her tongue.

"Oh, you're going to pay for that, Sunshine. If you'll excuse us, apparently my naughty girl needs a lesson about disrespecting her Daddy."

"Uncle Damian, don't be such a—"

A hand slapped over her mouth, cutting her off. "If you finish that sentence, little girl, I absolutely will let Uncle Damian spank your ass. You can be a brat, but I draw the line at you being disrespectful."

When he pulled his hand away, she pouted up at him. "How did you know I was going to say something rude?"

"I can't think of any way that sentence would have ended that *wouldn't* have been rude."

"Oh. You have a point." She gave Damian a sheepish smile. "Sorry, Uncle Damian."

"The 'uncle' thing is *not* going to stick. But thank you for apologizing." His expression softening considerably, Damian smiled at Braden. "I can't believe you're getting married again. Just let me know what you need best-man wise, I'll take care of it."

"Who said you're going to be the best man?" Desmond asked with a scowl.

"Because I'm Braden's favorite. Clearly."

Fascinated, Lottie watched the argument devolve into what were clearly old, practiced insults between the twins. Beside her, Braden simply looked resigned, as if he'd watched some version of this argument play out so many times he'd lost the desire to even try and stop it.

"Desmond. Enough." Authority rang out clearly in Bastian's voice, halting the argument in its tracks. "Thank you. Now, has anyone thought to ask *Braden* who he'd like as his best man?"

"Actually, I was thinking of asking you, Bastian."

"Me?" Bastian's face lit up with surprise and joy. It was kind of adorable, actually, watching someone as tough-looking as him get all giddy over being asked to be in a wedding. "I'd love to."

"To quote our favorite candy-corn-obsessed submissive, 'Dis sum bullshit'," Desmond said, and if Lottie wasn't entirely wrong, it almost looked like he was pouting.

"Yeah, well, maybe if you two weren't constantly fighting I'd let you both be my best men. But you'll have to be happy with groomsmen roles. And if you keep it up, I'll bump you down to ushers and make you babysit Aunt Dolly."

Her 'uncles' visibly cringed. "Who's Aunt Dolly?" Lottie asked.

"Our mother's aunt." Braden smirked. "She's about a hundred years old, and an absolute terror. You'll love her."

"I can't wait."

Damian rolled his eyes. "Well, since I'm not needed here, I'm going to take Emily down to the pit. See you all in a bit, if you're sticking around."

"Actually, if you all don't mind, Lottie and I have an appointment downstairs and I'd like for you all to join us. At least for the first part."

Curious, Lottie tilted her head, studying him. She knew she still had a punishment coming for defying him back in his office, but she wasn't sure why he'd be inviting their wedding party to come watch. "What are you up to?"

"You'll see in a minute. Come."

BRADEN

Nerves danced up and down his spine as he led Lottie down to the pit. Logically, he knew it was ridiculous. She'd already agreed to marry him. There was no reason for her to turn down the collar he had tucked in his pocket. But his heart was still pounding in his chest, even more so than it had been when he'd popped the question back at the cabin.

Beside him, Lottie was all but radiating nervous energy, albeit for an entirely different reason. As far as she knew, she was going to get her bottom spanked and maybe get fucked in public for the first time, which she'd been adorably excited about the night before when they'd discussed having a scene to celebrate their engagement with the club members.

The collar was a surprise, and one he hoped she'd enjoy. Sliding his hand into his pocket, he ran his fingers over the supple pink leather, which helped to calm his nerves somewhat.

Down in the pit, he helped her up onto the platform where she'd gotten her very first flogging from him. His play bag was already there, and Lottie bounced excitedly on her toes. "Where do you want me?"

"On your knees." The command came out harsher than he'd intended, and judging by the way she cocked her eyebrow at him, Lottie hadn't missed the change in tone.

But she sank gracefully to her knees without argument, for which he was grateful. Any other time, he'd happily force her, then punish her defiance, but tonight he wanted to savor her submission.

"Good girl. Eyes up, Charlotte. Daddy has something for you."

She raised her head to look up at him, love shining in her eyes. And with that simple look, all his nerves disappeared.

Lottie was his. The collar was just a symbol of what they already had, a way of showing the world his claim on the stunning woman at his feet.

"I love you, Lottie-bug."

"I love you, too." Lifting her hand to cup her mouth, she asked in a loud whisper, "But why are you acting so weird?"

A ripple of laughter went through the crowd, and he couldn't help but join in. Reaching back into his pocket, he pulled out the collar and held it up for her, and their audience, to see.

"Is that for me?" she asked, her eyes widening with surprise and wonder.

"Yes. A symbol of my love and my protection. Do you accept it?"

"Duh. Put it on me already!"

Another wave of laughter, even louder this time, ran through the crowd, though he saw some of the stricter Doms in the group giving her a hard stare. No doubt they were worrying about what kind of influence she was going to be on the other submissives in the club.

He was wondering the same himself. And he couldn't wait to find out.

Lowering himself onto one knee, just as he had when he'd proposed, he slid the collar around her throat and buckled it. "I own you, Charlotte Duvall," he said more quietly, for her ears only.

Eyes wide, she brushed her fingers over the leather, down to the gold heart tag. "What does the tag say?"

"Good girl on that side." Grinning, he flipped the tag over. "Brat on this side. It seemed fitting."

"I suppose it is."

"Ready for your spanking, baby?"

She pouted prettily, batting her lashes at him. "I don't suppose we could skip that part and go straight to you fucking me in front of all these nice people."

"Not a chance. Up you go."

With an exaggerated sigh, she rocked back on her heels and rose to her feet with a grace he knew many subs would envy. Pride filled him as he led her to the spanking bench he'd had placed in the middle of the platform. He helped her onto the bench, her bottom presented beautifully for his discipline with her all but folded in half, her calves and arms strapped to the leather rests.

"Comfortable?"

"Yes, Daddy."

"Good. Stay there, I'll be right back."

The dark look she shot him clearly said she didn't find his joke as funny as he did. "Right. Like I could go anywhere if I wanted to."

Chuckling at her obvious annoyance, he crossed the platform to his play bag and knelt to pull out what he needed for their scene. It wasn't overly complex, but sometimes the best scenes were the simplest. With his items in hand, he carried them back to the bench and placed the small leather paddle he'd chosen on her back.

"What's that?" she asked, craning her neck to try and see.

"If I told you, it would ruin the surprise."

"Maybe I don't like surprises."

"That just makes it even more fun for me."

"Uncle Damian is right. You are an even bigger brat than me."

"Do you really think it's a good idea to call your Daddy names when you're tied to a bench about to get your ass spanked?"

"No, Daddy. Sorry."

There wasn't an ounce of actual apology in her sulky tone, but it was good enough, especially since he wasn't actually upset with her. "Thank you, Lottie-bug. Now, let's talk about what it means to be a good girl and follow Daddy's instructions."

28

LOOPHOLES AND HAPPILY EVER AFTER

LOTTIE

She'd expected him to start spanking after that dire pronouncement, but instead she felt the cool trickle of lube on her exposed bottom hole, and her face nearly burst into flames. This wasn't at all what she'd expected, and so she hadn't braced herself for the humiliation of having her ass fucked with an audience. "Daddy..."

"Yes, little one?"

"I thought you said you were going to, you know. The *right* way tonight."

"I am." Something cold and hard pressed against her hole, and she had to fight the urge to squirm. "But I never said I wouldn't fill your bottom hole, first."

"Stupid loopholes."

Whatever it was in her ass was larger than the plugs he'd used before, but not quite as large as his cock. And unlike the plugs, it never seemed to get smaller, even as he worked it deeper and deeper into her bottom. So it burned, the whole way in, with no relief. Worse than the burn, though, was the way the pain made her clit throb with need and her pussy clench emptily, as if it was jealous of how full her ass was.

It was horrible, and humiliating, and absolutely wonderful.

"Daddy, it hurts," she whined, her breaths turning to soft pants as she struggled to submit. She wanted to be a good girl, to take whatever he'd chosen to give her, but her body and mind were fighting him every inch of the way.

"I'm sure it does," he said with a low chuckle. "This is what happens to naughty little girls who don't listen to their Daddies."

Between the pain and the humiliation, she had zero energy to put into filtering her response as her temper flared. "You were being ridiculous!"

There was a pretty blonde standing in front of her, watching the scene unfold with eyes that went suddenly wide. Even without that visual cue, Lottie would have known it was the wrong thing to say.

"I'm sorry, Daddy, I didn't mean it!"

Too little, too late.

Whatever had been sitting on her back disappeared, and a moment later her entire right cheek exploded with pain. The punishment was repeated on her left cheek, then her right again, over and over until she was squirming and whimpering on the bench. Not just from the pain, but from the need building between her thighs. A need which wasn't helped in the least by him slowly fucking her ass with whatever it was he had put in there.

By the time he was done paddling her, fire had spread across her bottom, inside and out, her pussy was soaked to the point she was worried about the mess she must be leaving on the bench, and she was feeling very, very sorry for being such a brat.

"What do you do when Daddy gives you an order, Charlotte?" Daddy's voice was hard, making her feel even more sorry than she already was.

"O-obey," she said with a quiet sniffle.

"And what do you do when Daddy gives you an order you think is ridiculous?"

"Obey!" she repeated, this time crying out her response as he plunged the hard column even deeper inside her.

"Who owns you, Charlotte?" Another flurry of

swats landed across her ass, reigniting the pain and sending little jolts of pleasure straight to her clit.

"You do, Daddy!"

"That's right. Every single inch of this gorgeous fucking body belongs to me. And if I have to claim every single one of your sweet little holes every day to remind you of that, then I will. Do you understand me, Charlotte?"

"Yes, Daddy, I'm sorry, I'm sorry!"

The spanking stopped, leaving her breathless and on the verge of tears as the thick head of his cock pressed into her pussy. With her bottom full, she felt her muscles stretch more than usual and panic wrapped around her chest.

"Daddy, stop! You're too big!"

His laughter reached her ears at the same time he pushed forward just a little more. "Thank you for the compliment, baby, but I promise I'll fit. I just need to go a little slower than usual. Can you be a good girl and relax for me?"

"I-I don't know."

"I think you can. Don't you want to make Daddy proud, little one?"

As if he'd flipped a switch, those words instantly had some of the tension leaching from her muscles. She let out a shuddering breath as he thrust forward a bit, stretching her until she was impossibly full. It was so reminiscent of the night he'd finally popped her cherry, she couldn't help but feel like she was losing her virginity all over again.

In his club. In front of dozens of witnesses.

God, that was fucking hot.

"That's my good girl. Just a little more, baby. You're so fucking wet for me, Lottie. Did you enjoy getting your naughty bottom spanked in front of all our friends? Maybe I'll make sure all your punishments are in public since you seem to enjoy them so much."

She wanted to deny it, but how could she when her pussy clenched greedily around him at just the thought of everyone watching her get spanked and fucked and whatever else it was he might have planned for her on a regular basis? There was, she was slightly ashamed to admit, a part of her that loved the attention. That loved being on display, that loved knowing all eyes were on her, for whatever reason.

"Fuck, you're so tight with that glass cock in your ass. If I could stand the thought of another man touching you, I'd share you with someone new every night. And you'd let me, wouldn't you, baby, because you're Daddy's good fucking girl. Aren't you, Charlotte?"

Was that even a question? Whatever he asked of her, she would give. "Yes, Daddy."

"But I won't, because I'm the only man who will ever get to feel this sweet pussy or your tight little asshole on my cock. For as long as I live, Charlotte, you are *mine*."

His words, the friction of her clit rubbing against the bench with every hard, slow stroke, it was all too much. Pleasure exploded inside her, hot waves of it rushing through her veins. A scream tore from her throat as it ripped through her, shredding her into a million tiny pieces from the inside out.

As if from a distance, she was vaguely aware of her Daddy's own roar of release, of his cock swelling and twitching inside her. Of more words of praise showering down on her as he caressed her sweat-soaked skin.

And then he was in front of her, crouching down so they were eye-level, his lips curved up in that approving smile she'd come to crave more than the air she breathed. "Did I do a good job, Daddy?"

"Oh, baby. You were fucking fantastic. Daddy's so proud of you."

"Thank you, Daddy."

"Let's get you down from that bench and get some food in your tummy, little one."

"Mmm. Okay, Daddy."

BRADEN

With Charlotte on his lap, wrapped up in the blanket he'd brought from his office, he scooped some brie onto a cracker and lifted it to her lips. "Open, baby."

Still looking somewhat shell-shocked from their scene, she obediently parted her lips so he could pop the cracker into her mouth. "Oh, man. That's delicious."

"Is it?" He repeated the process for himself, nearly moaning as the flavors exploded on his tongue. "God-damn, that is delicious."

After feeding her a few more crackers in silence, he pressed a kiss to her forehead. "How are you feeling, Lottie-bug?"

"Sore. But a really, really good kind of sore," she added with a lopsided grin.

"What about here?" He tapped her chest. "You've had a rough couple of weeks, and there's been some big changes the past few days. Are you feeling okay about everything?"

"Yes." At her too-quick answer, he raised an eyebrow, which only earned him a roll of her eyes in response. "I really am. All my life I've done things because it was what everyone else expected of me. Being with you is the first thing I think I've ever really done for myself, and I feel happier about agreeing to marry you than I've ever felt about anything else in my life. You can stop worrying about me."

"Sorry, little one. It's in my job description to worry about you."

"Fair enough," she replied with a giggle. "But try to stop worrying that I'm going to suddenly change my mind and leave you. Okay?"

He hadn't even realized he'd been worrying about that until she'd put it into words. "Who's the mind reader now?"

"Oooh, maybe it's rubbing off on me." Beneath the blanket, she rubbed her hands together, her eyes shining with glee. "That could come in handy."

"I'm sure it will. Just as my ability to read your mind will come in handy when you're plotting something naughty. So just remember that."

"Spoilsport."

"I know. I'm such a grumpy old man."

"Nah, that honor is reserved for your brothers."

"That's true." Leaning in, he captured her lips with his own, inwardly crowing when she instantly melted into him. There was, in his opinion, nothing more satisfying than the submission of a strong woman. His Lottie-bug had proven she could face even the most impossible situations with her head held high.

She didn't need him to save her. She was more than capable of rescuing herself when push came to shove. Which made her surrender all the sweeter, in the end.

The only dark spot on their happily ever after was the auction. They were no closer to finding the person running things than they had been when Lottie had put herself up for auction.

But they'd find him. Or her. It was impossible to hide that kind of activity—or the kind of money it brought in—forever. One way or another, he and his brothers would find the person responsible for taking advantage of women like Emily and Lottie and however many dozens of other vulnerable, innocent young girls.

And when they found whoever was behind the auction, the Elliott brothers would damn well make sure they paid for what they'd done.

The End

EPILOGUE
NOBODY ARGUES LIKE FAMILY

DESMOND

Hoping to get some answers, Desmond followed Damian, his twin, into their younger brother Braden's, office. Aside from Damian's darker hair and full-sleeve tattoos, he and Damian were identical with brown eyes and neatly trimmed beards. As usual, Braden was clean-shaven and wearing one of his customary suits.

The suit was probably apropos, considering Braden managed Club BDE. Desmond and Damian were silent partners.

"So, let me get this straight." Damian sat in one of the matching club chairs across from Braden while Desmond took the other. "Delia told you she got an email about the auctions from you?"

"And she thought you set up the auctions instead of giving her and Ivy raises?" Desmond asked.

"That's what she said." Braden scowled and pushed the printed email toward his brothers. "The email went to everyone except the three of us, and it's not in my sent folder. My IT guy, Martin, says the email header was spoofed and routed through a virtual private network."

The Club BDE gossip tree was too well-fertilized to let the auctions die, making it that much harder to put a stop to them.

"Meaning, we can't track it." Desmond studied the email, then passed it to Damian. "Where is Martin anyway?"

"Sick as a dog with some upper respiratory thing, so he's not much use for tracing it." Grimacing, Braden added, "Not that he found anything to begin with, even though I hired him to help prevent this kind of shit from happening. Now, everyone believes the auctions are legitimate because they thought I was sanctioning them."

"And then you made a deal with Killian O'Rourke for information." Desmond rubbed his face and gave his idiot brothers an ugly glare. "It was bad enough for Blake to vouch for his membership. I have no idea what you were thinking when you made a deal with a mob boss. It's like you both were trying to trash the decade Bastian and I spent trying to put him in prison."

Calling each other by their first names was a childish game. Desmond knew it, and so did Damian, but neither one of them wanted to be the first to stop. Hell, Desmond couldn't even remember when it started.

"Did you ever think you might not have found anything on Killian because there isn't anything to find, *Bryce?*" Damian snapped.

"No, *Blake.* I never once thought that," Desmond retorted. "He's as dirty as your hands are after a day in your garage."

"Enough." Braden slapped his desk and glared at his brothers. "Yes, I was pissed at Damien for recommending Killian without telling me who he was, but that's on me for not vetting him as thoroughly as I should have. I hired Martin to close that hole in our onboarding procedure. Nobody, no matter who recommends them, gets a membership, guest pass, or employment without a full background check."

"But—"

Braden lifted a hand to cut Desmond off. "Regardless of our personal feelings, Killian doesn't bring his business into the club, and he's an excellent, safe dominant who has never caused a moment's trouble."

"That doesn't mean he won't in the future," Desmond muttered. "For all we know, he's the one running the auctions."

"Killian wouldn't do that," Damian replied. "Well, he might, but he wouldn't hide it behind Club BDE."

Desmond forced his fists to unclench before he punched Damian in the face. "And you know that because you're such good friends with a mob boss, and completely forgot your fucking twin is a cop?"

"I said that's enough. We have bigger issues on our plate," Braden snapped. "Aside from that, Killian got closer to finding the little asshole running the auctions than anyone else, and he's still pissed about coming up empty."

"Fine," Desmond muttered, giving Damian a poisonous sneer. "We'll agree to disagree."

Instead of replying, Damian rolled his eyes and flipped him off.

"Good." Braden stuffed the printed email into his desk drawer. "Moving on. Damian, before Martin got sick, I had him rush the background check on Rio Jimenez. He came up clean, so I'll make him a formal job offer later today."

"Wasn't he the guy who took down Don Graham after Emily maced him?" Desmond asked.

"Yeah. Rio is my neighbor. He's a stand-up guy." Damian cleared his throat, then added, "And he has no criminal record or dealings with criminals. If he takes the job, he'll be working as a security guard."

After a moment's hesitation, Desmond nodded. "Good. We could use another guard or two. I'll go through my contacts and see if we can scare up one more."

"Thank you, Desmond." Braden rested his elbows on his desk and folded his hands. "At least whoever is running the auctions is paying the participants quickly. The money is put into escrow, and tax forms are going out. It's exactly as I'd have done if I was actually hosting the auctions."

"Do we know the company sending the tax forms?" Damian asked.

Braden cursed under his breath and rolled his eyes. "You get three guesses, and the first two don't count."

"Club BDE's accountant?" Desmond asked, tightening his fingers on the arms of his chair. "Are you fucking serious?"

"Serious as the stroke you look like you're about to have," Braden replied.

"Son of a bitch." Damian got to his feet and paced the office. "When I get my hands on that little fucker..."

They nodded in agreement as Braden went to the sideboard and poured three glasses of scotch.

"Whoever is doing this has intimate knowledge of how the club is run," Desmond said after accepting his glass. "Presumably, if they're sending out tax forms, they're also familiar with our accountant. Have you checked with them?"

"Yes, but the information went to them in those spoofed emails," Braden replied.

"It has to be an employee." Damian sipped his drink and nodded approvingly. "But which one? Aside from Martin, who has computer skills like that?"

A lot of money was changing hands, and even though the auctions weren't technically illegal, nobody liked not knowing where it was going. Although most of it went to the people being auctioned, twenty-five percent was being siphoned into someone's pocket.

"Good question," Desmond said. "Since Club BDE isn't paying the participants, I think the tax forms would be evidence of fraud, but I know we'd all prefer to fix this ourselves. I just wish we could find one lead. That's all it would take."

"We'll get it." Braden rose to his feet. "I promise we'll find whoever is running the auctions and make them sorry they ever fucked with the Elliott brothers."

Meet the rest of the Cherry Popping Daddies! Check out Emily (By Golden Angel) and Titania (By Raisa Greywood)

ABOUT STELLA MOORE

Sassy heroines? Check. Strict, dominant heroes? Check. Pages and pages of spice, kink, and happily ever afters? Oh, yeah. Triple check.

Stella Moore is a *USA Today* Bestselling author of irresistibly sassy romances with a little something for everyone. From everyday heroes to men who rule the criminal underworld, Stella just straight up loves a good love story. Especially if it involves a naughty heroine going over someone's knee a time or two. You'll also find lovers of all shapes, sizes, and ethnicities in Stella's books because she believes everyone deserves their own happily ever after.

Can't get enough of Stella? Stalk her all the places, and sign up for her newsletter to snag a free short story!

https://www.stellamooreromance.com/links

facebook.com/authorstellam

bookbub.com/authors/stella-moore

x.com/authorstellam

instagram.com/authorstellam

tiktok.com/@stellamooreromance

Cherry Popping Daddies (Multi Author Series)

Emily (By Golden Angel)

Lottie (By Stella Moore)

Titania (By Raisa Greywood)

Lost River Littles

Taylor's Unexpected Daddy (Freebie Prequel!)

Carly's Second Chance Daddy

Noelle's Christmas Daddy

Ginny's Baby Daddy

Charm City Daddies

Daddy's Arms

Daddy's Laws

Daddy's Mercy

Black Light (Multi Author Series)

Black Light: Worthy

Black Light: Roulette Finale

Rawhide Ranch (Multi Author Series)

Hayleigh's Little Halloween

A Mischievous Little Mardis Gras

Judging Julia

A Little Double Wedding

A Little Christmas Caper

Dangerous Obsessions Series

Daddy's Vengeance

Daddy's Claim

Masters of the Zodiac (Multi Author Series)

Libra

The Rinaldi Family Duet

Daddy's Captive

Daddy's Little Spy